Lukas, I don't think we should be seen walking together. People will talk."

"People are already talking." He stepped forward, getting into her space. "People are talking a lot. Actually, I don't think they want to stop talking about you and me and the mill and the fire. From what I hear, and I don't hear much, we seem to be the favorite topic of conversation around most every coffeepot in Charm."

"See—"

"In fact, I think the only people not talking about you and me are you and me. Therefore, it's time to change things."

Part of her agreed with him, but she was learning that what she wanted didn't always matter. "Lukas, my family won't be happy."

"I don't care," he said quietly. "I don't care about how they react. I care about what you think and how you feel."

By Shelley Shepard Gray

Sisters of the Heart Series
HIDDEN • WANTED • FORGIVEN • GRACE

Seasons of Sugarcreek Series
WINTER'S AWAKENING • SPRING'S RENEWAL
AUTUMN'S PROMISE • CHRISTMAS IN SUGARCREEK

Families of Honor Series
THE CAREGIVER • THE PROTECTOR
THE SURVIVOR • A CHRISTMAS FOR KATIE (novella)

The Secrets of Crittenden County Series
MISSING • THE SEARCH • FOUND • PEACE

The Days of Redemption Series
DAYBREAK • RAY OF LIGHT • EVENTIDE • SNOWFALL

Return to Sugarcreek Series
HOPEFUL • THANKFUL • JOYFUL

Amish Brides of Pinecraft Series
THE PROMISE OF PALM GROVE • THE PROPOSAL AT SIESTA KEY
A WEDDING AT THE ORANGE BLOSSOM INN
A WISH ON GARDENIA STREET (novella)
A CHRISTMAS BRIDE IN PINECRAFT

The Charmed Amish Life Series
A SON'S VOW • A DAUGHTER'S DREAM
A SISTER'S WISH • AN AMISH FAMILY CHRISTMAS

The Amish of Hart County Series
HER SECRET • HIS GUILT

---

a son's vow

THE CHARMED AMISH LIFE

Shelley Shepard Gray

AVON

INSPIRE

An Imprint of HarperCollinsPublishers

Excerpt from *A Daughter's Dream* copyright © 2016 by Shelley Shepard Gray.

First Avon Inspire mass market printing: August 2017
First Avon Inspire paperback printing: January 2016

Print Edition ISBN: 978-0-06-274326-8
Digital Edition ISBN: 978-0-06-233780-1

Cover photograph and design by Laura Klynstra
Illustrated map copyright © by Laura Hartman Maestro

17 18 19 20   QGM   10 9 8 7 6 5 4 3 2 1

To my brother and sister, Gary and Kelley.
I'm blessed.

The author is grateful for being allowed to reprint
the White Chocolate Cranberry Blondies recipe from
Country Blessings Cookbook *by Clara Coblentz.*
The Shrock's Homestead
9943 Copperhead Rd. N.W.
Sugarcreek, OH 44681

If you forgive those who sin against you,
your heavenly Father will forgive you.

MATTHEW 6:14

Reach up as far as you can. God will reach
the rest of the way.

AMISH PROVERB

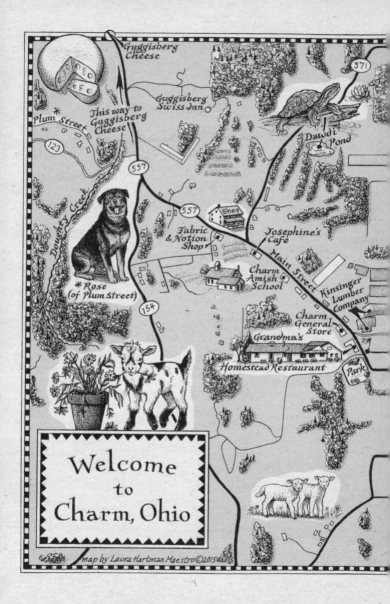

Guggisberg
Cheese

This way to
Guggisberg
Cheese

Guggisberg
Swiss Inn

Plum Street

123

557

Doughty Creek

557

Shop

Fabric
& Notion
Shop

557

154

Rose
(of Plum Street)

Dawdi
Pond

371

Josephine's
Cafe

Main Street

Charm
Amish
School

Kinsinger
Lumber
Company

Charm
General
Store

Grandma's

Homestead Restaurant

Park

Welcome
to
Charm, Ohio

map by Laura Hartman Maestro ©2015

371

369

157

157

369

the Kinsinger
Home

Oscar

Simon's
House

159

Charm Public
School

Bank

70

U.S. Post
Office

70

Darla's
Farm

Walnut Creek

557

600

159

* Many of these locations are real, but like Princess the goat
and Oscar the bulldog, Shelley imagined a few, too.

a son's vow

Chapter 1

March 20

It was another picture-perfect day in Charm.

The sky was pale blue, quietly complementing the acres of vibrant green farmland as far as the eye could see. Spring lambs had arrived. They were frolicking in the fields, their eager bleats echoing through the valley. The morning air was not too chilly or too damp. Instead, a hint of warmth teased, bringing with it as much hope as the crocus buds that peeked through the dark dirt of the numerous clay pots decorating cleanly swept front porches.

It was the type of morning that encouraged a person to go out walking, to smile. The type of day that reminded one and all that God was present and did, indeed, bestow gifts.

In short, it was the type of day that used to give Darletta Kurtz hope. A day like this should have made her happy, revitalized her. It should have made her want to pull out a pencil and one of her many notebooks and record the images she saw and list activities she wanted to do.

It was the kind of day she used to love and maybe, just maybe, take for granted.

But now, as she rested her elbows on the worn wooden countertop that had no doubt supported generations of postal workers before her, Darla could only silently acknowledge that another day had come. It was sure to feel as endless as the one before it, and would no doubt be exactly like the rest of the week.

It was another day to get through. A way to pass ten hours of expected productivity before she could retreat to her bedroom and collapse on her bed. Only then would she feel any sense of peace. Because only then would she be able to wait for oblivion. She'd close her eyes, fall into a peaceful slumber, and, hopefully, forget her reality for eight hours.

It had been ninety-nine days since her father died. Tomorrow would bring the one hundredth. It was a benchmark she'd never intended to look forward to. Wearily, she wondered if anyone else in Charm was anticipating the milestone as well.

Undoubtedly some were.

After all, her father hadn't been the only man to die in the December fire at Kinsinger Lumber Mill. No, he was one of five. And though it wasn't as if she'd ever forget that fact, there were many in Charm who took care to remind her constantly.

Just then, Mary Troyer pushed open the door to the post office. Darla braced herself.

"You have a lot of nerve, Darletta Kurtz, getting a job here," Mary said as she slapped a ten-dollar bill on the counter. "It's bad enough that your family stayed in town. Most folks would have left in shame after what your father did. Yet, here you are, thriving."

Each word hurt, as Mary no doubt intended for them to. Darla thought she would have been used to the verbal abuse by now, but it still felt as jarring as it had the first time. Mary's son Bryan had died in the same accident as Darla's father, and she took every opportunity to make sure everyone in town was aware of her pain.

Just as she had two days before, Darla did her best to keep her voice even and her expression impassive. "What is it you'll be needing today, Mary?"

Mary's cheeks puffed up before replying. "One book of stamps. The flags."

Quickly she gave Mary the stamps and her change, taking care to set the money on the counter so their fingers wouldn't have to touch. "Here you go." Then—though she would have rather said something, anything else—she added the words she'd heard her boss say dozens of times: "*Danke* for coming in."

Mary narrowed her eyes. "*That* is all you're gonna say?"

It was obvious that Mary was itching for a fight. But no way was Darla going to give it to her. She'd learned at least a couple of things in the ninety-nine days since the accident at the mill.

And even though she might be wishing Mary to perdition in her darkest moments, she knew it was always best to turn the other cheek. "There's nothing to say. Your mind is made up to be angry with me."

"My 'mind' has nothing to do with the facts. Everyone in Charm knows that your father caused the fire at the mill. That fire killed my Bryan, Clyde Fisher, Paul Beachy, and Stephen Kinsinger."

Standing as straight as her five-foot-two-inch frame allowed her to do, Darla added quietly, "You forgot John Kurtz, Mary. My father died, too, you know."

"All of us are struggling with our losses. Struggling to make ends meet with our men gone. But here you are almost every morning, standing behind this counter with a smile on your face."

Though Mary wasn't the first person to say such a thing to her—she wasn't even the *twenty*-first—Darla still didn't understand why she should bear the weight of her father's guilt.

Especially since it had been proven that it hadn't been just her father's negligence that had started the fire in the Dumpster. A variety of circumstances had taken place, which, when combined, had created a powerful explosion.

A rag, dampened by a flammable liquid, had been tossed into a Dumpster filled with wood scraps and hot metal that had been left heating over the course of the day. In no time at all, the rag had burst into flames, igniting the pine kindling. Before anyone was truly aware of the fire, the Dumpster had exploded, causing the nearby wood stacks in the back warehouse to catch fire, too. Though the emergency sprinklers had come on and the fire department and ambulances had been called, five people had died and scores of others had been injured.

Without a doubt, it had been the worst disaster to ever occur at Kinsinger Lumber Mill, and everyone who'd been there was marked by the terrible tragedy.

After the accident, fire marshals had investigated and declared that it had been caused by a series of unlikely events: a rare sunny day in December, hot metal in the Dumpster, and a pile of pine that someone had discarded instead of turning into wood shavings—all set ablaze by one rag.

No single person was to blame.

Furthermore, when Stephen Kinsinger's son Lukas had taken over the mill, he'd publicly forgiven her father. However, the speech had done little to change the general feeling of anger and hurt that pervaded their village. It seemed that everyone needed a scapegoat. And her father had given them one.

Now, because John Kurtz was no longer walking God's earth, more than a couple of people had transferred their pain and anger onto Darla and the rest of her family.

And after ninety-nine days of it, she'd had her fill.

Which was why, even though her words would likely fall on deaf ears, she stood up a little straighter and glared. "I'm merely doing my job, Mary."

Mary's blue eyes flashed with anger. "And what do you have to say about Aaron? He is still at the mill."

Clenching her hands, Darla fought to remain calm. Her relationship with Aaron was both confusing and difficult. "I canna speak for my *bruder*," she said quietly.

"Everyone says he is becoming a problem. Men have heard him fault the mill for your father's poor judgment."

"Any problem Aaron might have at work is between him and his managers," she said as the door opened and several more customers entered. "Now, do you need anything else?" she asked, anxious to get to work.

"I do not. You know I only came in here to give you a piece of my mind."

"And you've done that, Mary," one of the men who'd just entered called out.

Finally looking away from Mary, Darla saw Lukas Kinsinger. She knew him well. Very well. Until recently, they'd been close friends. Now? She wasn't quite sure what they were.

Mary turned to face him. "Lukas!" she exclaimed in a sickly sweet voice. "I didn't hear you come in."

"That seems to be obvious. I've been here long enough to learn that you've been berating Darla yet again," Lukas Kinsinger replied. "I must say that I'm shocked."

Mary stepped toward Lukas, who was standing with his arms folded over his chest. "Shocked?"

"I knew Bryan well, Mary. He would have been

mighty upset to hear his *mamm* speaking so viciously to a woman who has never done one thing against you."

Darla blinked, suddenly feeling on the verge of tears. It was good that at least part of their friendship remained intact.

"Do not speak to me of my Bryan," Mary said. "He knew I was proud of him. He was a perfect man."

"Forgiveness is a virtue," Lukas said. "You should try it. It's helped me with my grief."

"I'll forgive when I feel that justice has been served," Mary retorted. But when Lukas said nothing, merely stared at her coolly, she darted outside.

With Lukas's gaze now centered on her, Darla smiled.

She was about to speak when the front door opened again. Lukas stood against the wall patiently while she helped two customers who had been waiting behind Mary and the newcomer. When the room was at last empty but for the two of them, she walked around the counter.

"Lukas."

"Hello, Darla." His light blue-gray eyes remained serious though his lips curved into the slightest of smiles. "How are you today?"

"I am well, *danke*," she lied. There was no way

she was going to tell him just how difficult she was finding her life to be at the moment. He didn't need her burdens, especially since he, also, was mourning the loss of his father. That had to be mighty hard, given that he'd already lost his *mamm* years ago. "What are you doing here?"

"Rebecca told me you got this job here two weeks ago. I wanted to see how it was going."

Well, that sure came out of the blue. Her new job wasn't worth him taking note of. At least, she didn't think it was. "I am learning a lot," she said, trying to dwell on the positive. "It's a blessing, I think."

His eyes narrowed as he stepped closer. The thick-soled work boots he wore made him tower above her more than he usually did. "It didn't sound like this job was a blessing when I walked in the door. Mary said some pretty harsh things. Does that happen a lot?"

"Does Mary come in to give me grief? *Jah.*"

"I'm sorry about that. I'll talk to her for you."

He was now standing close enough for her to see that he had nicked his neck while shaving that morning. "*Danke*, but I'd rather you didn't, Lukas. Mary's anger with me isn't your problem."

"I think it is. She's upset about the mill accident. Since I now run the mill, she'll listen to me."

Darla had no doubt that Mary would listen to

Lukas. But then where would that leave Darla? She would still be seen as weak and helpless and that wouldn't do. "Mary is upset and grieving. Sooner or later she'll let go of her anger." Well, she hoped so.

Lukas tilted his head to one side, studying her. "What about you? Are you still grieving and upset?"

She didn't know how to answer that. They'd once been good friends—best friends. She should be able to converse with him easily. But ever since the accident, it felt like there was too much between them to ever speak easily again.

Lukas knew how close she'd been to her father. He'd meant the world to her. Surely, then, Lukas had to know how difficult life was now that her father's reputation was tainted. Couldn't he imagine how hard it was for her just to get through each day?

The accident that had killed both their fathers and three other men had created a chasm in their relationship that seemed impossible to bridge. Her brother Aaron was upset that pretty much everyone—even Lukas's brother Levi—considered their father the main cause of the accident.

Then, of course, there was the latest disaster: Darla's mother, after grieving and living in denial for weeks, had left their family almost two months ago. Now Darla and her six siblings hadn't just lost their father—they'd lost both parents.

But there was no way she was going to share her sob story in the middle of her workday.

"I'm doing about as well as can be expected," she murmured, thinking of their preacher's last visit. He'd prayed with her and spoken of forgiveness. She hoped one day soon that his advice would ease her heart. Seeing as how no other customers had come in, she forced herself to continue their stilted conversation. Sooner or later things between them would ease . . . if they both tried their best. "And you, Lukas? How are you today?"

"Pretty *gut* this morning."

"Truly? What happened?"

The smile that had been playing on his lips transformed into a full grin. "The lambs are out."

"I heard them this morning. The Millers have a lively bunch this year." She almost smiled back at him. Darla remembered how, even as a little boy, Lukas had loved the arrival of the spring lambs. Her *daed* used to ask him over just so Lukas could hold a newborn lamb from time to time.

Once he'd even spent the night at their house just so he could help her *daed* with the newborn lambs at daybreak. She'd been twelve to his thirteen and after seeing him dressed in only an old T-shirt and plaid pajama bottoms, she'd blushed for hours. Ack, but she'd had such a crush on him!

And just last year, she'd teased Lukas, saying that it was a shame that they no longer raised sheep because she would have enjoyed the sight of him holding a day-old lamb like it was the most precious thing on earth.

He stuffed his hands in his back pockets. "We should stop by the Millers' soon. You know they won't mind us visiting the lambs."

Just like they used to do.

Darla looked at the door longingly, wishing another customer would enter, and Lukas would move on instead of forcing her to remember how close they used to be. And how differently they were now treated by everyone else. Without a doubt, Lukas would be welcomed with a pleased smile at the Millers' farm. As for an appearance by her? She had a feeling she would be barely tolerated.

Knowing that made her sad. But since there was literally nothing she could do to change the town's perception of her, she forced herself to act uninterested. "I don't have time to visit lambs. With my new job, I am pretty busy, you know. Now, how may I help you?"

"Shouldn't I be asking you that?" he asked as he stepped a little closer.

His softly spoken question, laced with just the slightest bit of affection, made her flinch. She raised her guard. If she didn't keep herself firmly in check she was liable to weaken and say something she would regret.

"Lukas, if you don't need anything, I need to get back to work. I have a lot to do."

"I understand," he said quietly. "Fine. Give me a sheet of stamps."

She moved around the counter, thankful to have a barrier between them. Feeling as if she were helping a random customer instead of someone she'd known for most of her life, Darla placed the four choices on the counter. "Which design?"

He looked frustrated. "It don't matter," he said with obvious impatience.

Why hadn't she simply handed him his stamps and taken his money like she had with Mary? He would be gone by now.

Lukas leaned forward slightly, bringing with him the faint scent of oranges. Lukas had always been exceptionally fond of oranges. He lifted his eyes to meet her gaze. "You choose. What do you think I should purchase?"

Again, it felt as if he was asking her things she

didn't know the answer to. Feeling awkward, she glanced at the four choices. One showed hearts, another had a rose design—this year's wedding stamp. The third featured birds, and the final offering was the American flag.

"I . . . I don't know which one you want."

"I bet you do." His voice turned teasing. Almost as if they were friends again. "Come on, tell me the truth, Darla. Don't ya try to match the designs to the person buying them? I would."

He was standing too close. She could smell the soap on his skin, feel the warm knot of interest that always formed in her belly whenever he was near.

She tamped it down and kept her voice polite and crisp.

"They're simply stamps, Lukas. Just something to put on one's bills."

He stood up straight again, giving her space. "I suppose you're right." Staring at her intently, he added, "Some things just don't matter like they used to, do they?"

Nothing did, but she didn't dare go down that path. Some evenings it took everything she had to simply walk in her front door, bracing herself for Aaron's anger and her parents' absence. "That will be nine dollars and eighty cents."

He handed her a ten-dollar bill. "So, which ones did you decide to give me?"

She couldn't play his game. It was simply too painful. She missed him, missed their friendship. But, try as she might, she couldn't figure out how to move beyond the hurt. Unable to look at him directly in the eye, she pushed forward the birds. "Enjoy your day."

A muscle jumped in his cheek. "Darla, what time do you get off today?"

"Four. Why?"

"I'd like to walk you home."

Spending thirty minutes by his side was a bad idea. "*Nee.*"

"Come on," he coaxed. "We could talk. Catch up."

"Lukas, you came in here for stamps. Now you have them."

"I don't care about stamps." He frowned at the sheet before him. "Plus, you know how much I hate birds."

Against her will, some of the ice around her heart melted. "You are a man of superlatives. You always either love or hate things."

Looking relieved that she was no longer glaring at him, he said, "If you don't want me walking you home, how about I stop by tonight?"

Part of her hoped he would come over, but she

was sure it would only open up another can of worms. "You canna do that."

After shooting her a contemplative look, he fussed with the page of stamps resting on the counter. Far more hesitantly, he said, "You know, Darla, I thought it might do us both some good if we spent some time together. You know, like we used to do. It might help our families start to heal, too."

She thought of her brothers and sisters. Thought of how stunned they would be to see Lukas, and how angry Aaron would be if he imagined Darla was renewing their friendship again.

"I don't think you coming over is a good idea."

A muscle in his cheek twitched. "I've told you— and everyone else—time and again. Our family doesn't blame John for the accident."

She knew that wasn't exactly true. "Even Levi?" His brother had made no secret of his suspicions.

He brushed the lock of hair that had fallen across his brow away impatiently. "You know his temper. Levi is looking for someone to blame."

She did know his temper. And though she wasn't afraid he'd actually hurt her, she was pretty sure his words would be just as painful. "He ain't looking for someone, Lukas. He's found someone."

Something flashed in those beguiling silver eyes of his, something that looked suspiciously like a combination of agreement and embarrassment. Neither made her feel any better.

"I'm sure he doesn't really think your father *meant* to do anything wrong," he said at last.

That was the crux of it, wasn't it? Her father *had* caused the fire. But her family, especially her brother Aaron, wondered if some standard safety practices had been ignored.

Aaron thought that the Kinsingers had been negligent in making sure the warehouse was kept clean and clear of debris. He wondered if, perhaps, they hadn't been monitoring what was being thrown out into the Dumpsters. He said that the workers hadn't been thoroughly trained about the dangers of the stain and paint thinner, but Darla thought this was a bit much. Their father had been a careful and hard worker at the mill for decades. Whatever had happened hadn't been because he'd needed proper training from Lukas Kinsinger.

"I am so glad you, personally, aren't blaming my father," she said sarcastically. "Don't you think we ever wonder how everyone in the mill is so sure that it was *my daed* who caused the accident?"

He drew back, standing tall and strong, staring down at her from his six-foot height. "What are you saying, Darla? That someone else tossed the rag into the Dumpster?"

"Of course not."

"Then what are you saying?"

Why was he asking her that? All the optimism she'd been feeling vanished. "Why couldn't he be only partially responsible? The Dumpster was too close to the building. And someone had discarded pine scraps inside it instead of following proper procedure."

"You have no idea what you are talking about."

"All I'm saying is that maybe—just maybe—my father wasn't the *only* man responsible for five people's deaths."

"I've practically grown up in that mill," he stated, his voice now as cold as his glare. "I run it now. That isn't how things work there. We take care of the buildings and the men and the machinery. Everyone who works there is considered family."

"My *daed* loved that mill, too. He wouldn't have done anything foolhardy without reason."

The skin around Lukas's lips turned white. "You know, I came over here because I missed you. These last few weeks have been hard, really hard, for me."

"For me, too." Though, truly, "hard" didn't begin to describe how devastated she was.

"I had hoped that we could move on. You and I have been friends for years. For most of our lives."

"I haven't forgotten. But we can't erase what has happened. We simply can't be friends now."

He grabbed hold of the stamps and stuffed them in his jacket pocket, no doubt wrinkling them. "It was a mistake to come in here today. It was a mistake to feel sorry for you."

So he hadn't wanted to see her as a friend . . . he felt sorry for her.

Undoubtedly, he was thinking of his family's reputation. The Kinsinger family was everything to a lot of people in Charm. They not only paid hundreds of people's salaries but they had also somehow become models for proper behavior.

Now Darla knew that Lukas had come to find her because he'd wanted to do the right thing so the biddies sitting in the back of the church could whisper to each other how wonderful he was. Not only was he taking care of his family and the lumberyard, but he was good enough to reach out to the daughter of the man who'd caused so much pain and suffering.

Her heart was breaking, but she had to stay tough. If she didn't, they were both going to say more hurtful words to each other and she didn't know if she could handle that. It was hard enough coming to terms with the fact that she and Lukas couldn't ever be close friends again. "Next time you need stamps, you should probably send in someone else."

The look he gave her was so cold, it could have frozen her to the spot.

When the door closed behind him with the faint jingling of bells, Darla closed her eyes and tried to erase the pain. But just like the glory of the day's sunrise, it was unstoppable. There were some things that were simply destined to happen, no matter what.

Chapter 2

T hat girl. That, that . . . *woman*!

As he strode down Main Street toward the Kinsinger Lumber Mill's main office, Lukas felt like throwing his hat on the ground and stomping on it. And then turning right back around, yanking open the glass door of the post office, and marching in to tell Darla Kurtz exactly what he thought of her snide suspicions.

While he was at it, he would go ahead and tell her exactly what he thought about her standing on the other side of that worn counter and shoving an awful sheet of bird stamps at him without so much as a smile.

And then, well, he would tell her how much he

missed her. How much he'd needed her over the
last three months. She was the only person with
whom he didn't have to act confident and sure. He
could just be Luke.

Not the son who'd stood at his father's grave
and vowed to always look after the people who
depended on him. Not Lukas Kinsinger, who ran
the biggest business in Charm and was now responsible for hundreds of men's livelihoods.

Not the eldest brother whom his sisters and
younger brother now depended on.

But whether she'd pushed him away in order to
rile him up or because she didn't care about him
anymore, he didn't know. He'd been disappointed
when he'd realized that she wasn't as eager to mend
things between them. She was wrong to think that
keeping away from each other was going to help
their grief or heal their families' heartache.

Yes, everything was difficult right now—
beyond difficult, and painful, too—but that was
how he knew they should be reaching out to each
other, not pushing away. Not only did it make
sense, but it was the best thing for the lumber mill
and maybe even the town itself. Everyone knew
that there was a lot of tension between their families and it was causing a lot of talk.

There was no reason on earth that the two of
them couldn't continue their friendship. They'd

survived so much already: the summer they'd both gotten ringworm and neither had wanted to appear in public, Lukas's brief infatuation with Molly Miller and her alluring curves, and that one awful, hormonal-crazed year when Darla had turned thirteen and cried almost every day.

Still, recalling the afternoon he'd teased her about her moodiness, he winced. Darla had gotten so tired of his playful comments and jibes, she'd announced very loudly that it was her time of the month—much to his dismay and her embarrassment. He was sure he'd blushed every single time he saw her for a whole year afterward.

If they could survive all of that, plus a whole bunch of other catastrophes and minor arguments, he imagined that they could help each other get through almost anything.

Even the deaths of their fathers.

Lukas had hoped that they'd reached a point in their lives where they could ignore the rest of the world, reach out to each other, and offer comfort and care. Wasn't that why God had given them years and years of opportunities to gain each other's trust and affection? Only such a foundation would help them get through this year. After all, what was the point of a friendship surviving fifteen-plus years if not to have each other at times like this?

He didn't know. Worse, he didn't think Darla knew either. If only she would give him some time to talk to her, Lukas was sure they could finally, *finally* reach a point where the awful ache resting deep inside his chest would ease. If that happened, he'd be able to breathe easier and do everything he'd promised his father.

And if that happened, everything else that was worrying him would fall into place, too.

But until Darla stopped being so obstinate, he was going to have to give her a wide berth. And now, he was practically banned from the post office!

He kicked at a rock in his path. How could something he'd taken for granted for years now suddenly feel like it was the most important thing in his life? And for that matter, why did repairing the damage between them now feel as impossible as turning back time?

Frustrated beyond measure, he kicked at the rock again. This time, instead of merely skittering to a stop in front of him, it veered to the right, narrowly missing a pair of children.

Their mother glared at him.

"Sorry!" he called out before grumbling to himself again.

He needed Darla back in his life. He needed her friendship and she needed to understand that what had happened to their fathers—indeed, to all the men—had been a terrible accident. The fire hadn't been her father's fault and it certainly hadn't been his father's fault. It had been caused by spontaneous combustion—according to the fire marshal.

Lukas preferred to simply consider it an accident. An act of God, much like a lightning strike or a tornado. And because of that, he understood that it made no sense. But they didn't need for it to make sense. One day He would help them understand.

Lukas hoped so, anyway.

Still annoyed, he kicked another pebble blocking his path, earning him another glare from a pair of *kinner*.

"Ack, Lukas, stop with the rocks!"

Only his brother, Levi, talked to him that way.

Drawing to a halt, he turned as Levi approached, his brown eyes contrasting with his dark blond hair curling wildly under the brim of his straw hat. As usual Levi walked like a runner, his thin, wiry body moving in a constant fluid motion. "Hey, Levi."

"Hey, yourself," his brother snapped. "Did you see that you almost hit those *kinner* with that rock?"

"It wasn't even close."

Levi pulled his hat off and brushed back a chunk of hair from his forehead before slapping the hat back on. "What is wrong with you? Who burned your toast today?"

Lukas refrained from rolling his eyes, but just barely. "I canna believe you brought that up."

Levi slowly grinned. "Couldn't help myself."

His brother was referring to an episode when Lukas was eight, when he'd yelled and griped at everyone one morning on the way to church. When their mother had finally had enough of his surly attitude, she'd asked what had happened to set him off so badly. And because he couldn't really think of a reason why he was grumpy, he'd said the phrase of which he was now reminded with irritating regularity: that his toast had been burned.

Oh, but his family had had a time with that! Now, whenever he wore a frown, they brought it up with a teasing smile. Unfortunately, he didn't get as much entertainment from the constant reminder as the rest of them did.

"I'm never going to live that down, am I?"

Levi's lips twitched. "Nope. Especially when you're stomping down public sidewalks, scaring women and children by kicking debris in your path."

"I didn't mean to scare anyone. And the rock was in my way."

"They always are. Ain't so?"

Lukas refrained from saying a word about that, but it took some effort. That was the kind of response their father had liked, short quips that got to the heart of the matter. Like their *daed*, Levi was a master at it.

Himself? Not so much.

Leaning against the side of a brick building, Levi looked him over before he raised his eyebrows. "So, what has got you in such a lather? Did something happen at the mill today that I wasn't aware of?"

Since their *daed* passed, he and Levi had divided up their shifts. Now Lukas arrived around five in the morning and left in the early afternoon. Levi came in around eleven and worked until five or six. Their sister Rebecca managed the mill office from nine to four. That way Levi could help their sister Amelia with the majority of the farm work in the morning, and Lukas and Rebecca could help with the evening chores. None of them wanted their twenty-two-year-old sister to feel like she was stuck caring for the big property their family had lived on for generations by herself.

"Everything is fine at the mill." After debating whether to tell the truth or not, Lukas forged ahead, figuring he had nothing to lose. "I just got in a small argument with Darla."

All traces of amusement vanished from Levi's expression. "Why were you even talking to her?"

"I was in the post office. That's where she works."

Levi rolled his eyes. "There are a dozen people who could have run that errand for you. Even Rebecca. You need to keep your distance, brother."

That was the problem, Lukas realized. While there were a lot of people who could have run to get a sheet of stamps that he hadn't actually needed, he couldn't be assured that any of them would treat her as kindly as he had. Even Rebecca was keeping Darla and her family at arm's length, and that was saying a lot because at one time they'd been almost as close as he and Darla.

"I wanted to reach out to her. Mend some fences."

"For what? For her father causing the worst disaster in our mill's history? For killing our *daed*?"

Lukas winced. Levi's temper was still running hot. Lukas usually tried to calm Levi, to be the voice of reason, but at the moment, he just wasn't up to the task. He felt too raw, too vulnerable after being rejected by Darla.

"I even asked if I could stop by and see her tonight. She refused."

"Don't know why she would have done that. I'm sure Aaron would have loved to see you."

Again, there was Levi's heavy dose of sarcasm. Aaron was known for having a volatile temper. "I wasn't concerned about Aaron."

"You should be. He hasn't tried to curb his tongue at all when it comes to talking about us. Micah confided in me that Aaron has even been stirring up trouble in his department at the mill."

"Save your warnings, okay? She didn't want me to come over. Matter of fact, Darla pretty much told me that we needed to stay away from each other."

"Maybe she's more than just a pretty face after all."

"She's always been more than just a pretty face."

"Maybe." Almost grudgingly, Levi said, "Still, I never thought one grown woman could remain so petite."

"She's five feet, two inches. She is small, but not unusually so."

"What do you think she weighs? Even a hundred pounds?" Levi asked.

"Maybe a hundred pounds wet." In spite of his irritation, Lukas smiled. "She only seems small because you're tall."

"Hey, you're six-foot-two, too."

"I know. We could practically be twins."

"Not hardly. No one would mistake your red hair for mine."

"It's not red. It's strawberry blond."

"It's red, Lukas."

"Whatever."

Those brown eyes that had flashed irritation just moments earlier now studied him carefully. "Hey, I am sorry about how things are going with Darla. I know you're upset about how she wants to keep her distance, but it really is for the best."

"Maybe." He understood his brother's reasoning but he wasn't eager to lose another person in his life. He'd already lost his parents.

"I know she once meant something to ya, but you need to let her go, *bruder*. Her father was not only responsible for Daed's death, but he killed three other men. And caused thousands and thousands of dollars in damages. No matter how you might yearn to excuse him, John Kurtz nearly burned our legacy down."

"Even if he did such a thing, it's not Darla's fault."

"I agree. But no one in her family has ever even apologized. That's all I want."

"Why should they?" They started walking toward the mill.

"You are seriously asking me that? We all bear

responsibility for each other's actions, don't you think?"

"Not necessarily."

"We're family, Lukas."

"Is that what you think it's only going to take, Levi? An apology?"

"Of course." He looked disgruntled. "It's our way to grant forgiveness."

Lukas nodded, but he had already forgiven John Kurtz publicly. Privately, too. Well, he'd tried to. After all, the man was dead. There was no greater price to pay. But for some reason he wasn't sure if that simple act was going to be enough for any of them. Actually, he was beginning to think it was going to be far harder to forgive than he'd ever thought possible. "It's our duty to grant forgiveness, whether the person asks for forgiveness or not."

"That is true. And maybe one day I'll actually be able to do that, but not yet." Before Lukas could comment, Levi clasped him on the shoulder. "Before I head home to help Amelia, I'll remind you of something Daed always used to say."

"What was that?"

"We can forgive a man because that's the right thing to do. But the Bible never said a word about forgetting."

Feeling like that statement was rather prophetic, Lukas opened the front door of the mill with a bit of relief. As he turned the corner, he spied his good friend Roman sipping a bottle of water and chatting with a couple of workers on his team.

After greeting the other men, Lukas smiled at his friend. "It's good to see you. How are you?"

"Good enough," he said in his usual, easy manner. "I was just coming to talk to you. Got a second?"

"Always," Lukas said as he led the way into his office.

As Roman started telling him about the project he was working on, Lukas felt the muscles in his shoulders relax. This was what he needed. Now, more than ever, he needed to lose himself in work. No matter what else happened in his life, he could be sure that there would be plenty to do here at the mill.

Chapter 3

"Hannah, you can head on home now," Mrs. Ross said as she entered her spacious living room. Looking like she'd won a big prize, she added, "I was able to convince my boss that he didn't need me for the last meeting of the day."

Hannah Eicher glanced up at the modern grandfather clock located next to the family's entertainment system. It was a pretty thing, made of metal and bleached wood. It also happened to chime Christmas carols all year long. Mrs. Ross was a fan of the unexpected. "It must have been quite a meeting. You're home almost two hours early."

"It was going to be long and boring." Mrs. Ross grimaced. "I told my manager that I'd rather work on a project for a few hours than sit through another interminable meeting. When he agreed, I decided I could work just as easily here as in the office."

"I'm glad that it worked out for ya." Hannah got out of the rocking chair she'd been reading in, absently smoothing one of the ties of her *kapp* over her shoulder as she did so. "I'll get my things together then and get out of your way. Christopher is still napping."

"How was he today?"

"Wunderbaar."

Mrs. Ross's pretty green eyes warmed. "That's what I like to hear."

Hannah giggled. Christopher was all of four months old. He was just a tiny baby. She didn't think it was possible for a baby to ever be anything but wonderful.

Mrs. Ross set down her briefcase next to the couch, then opened up her pocketbook. "Is it all right if I write you a check today? I may work at a bank but I constantly forget to get cash."

"A check is fine. *Danke.*" She stood patiently as her boss quickly wrote a check, folded it once, and handed it to her. Without glancing at the amount, Hannah placed it in her purse.

"I paid you for the entire time you were sched-uled for, dear," Mrs. Ross said.

"*Danke.*" After slipping a plain navy cardigan over her dove-gray dress, she picked up her bas-ket of books and embroidery and placed her small purse inside. "So, I'll see you in two days?"

"Yes. I'm off tomorrow, but I'll need to be back at the bank bright and early the next day."

"I'll be here at eight then. Enjoy your time with Christopher."

"I will. You enjoy your day off, too." For the first time, Mrs. Ross's perky personality faltered. "Are you doing better, Hannah?"

This was why she loved working for Mr. and Mrs. Ross so much. They not only paid her well to watch a sweet-tempered baby but they were nice. Time and again, they did and said things that made her think they really cared about her.

Because of that, she replied with more hon-esty than she usually allowed herself to reveal. "I think I'm better. Some days are good, others not so much. But everyone says I'm doing as well as can be expected."

"Are you sleeping any better?"

"Some." Last night, she'd gotten almost five hours of sleep before she'd woken up in a cold sweat.

"I didn't know your Paul, of course. But knowing you, I can only imagine that he would want you to move on as best as you can."

Hannah didn't know what Paul would've wanted. All she knew was that he'd been her boyfriend, then he'd died in the fire at the mill, and now he was gone. "I better get to the bank," she said, purposely not continuing the conversation. Neither she nor Mrs. Ross wanted her to dissolve into tears. That had already happened once and it had been awkward for them both.

Mrs. Ross's expression softened. "Yes, of course." She walked across the wooden floor, her black patent-leather high heels making little clicking noises. After opening the door, she gave Hannah a small pat on the shoulder as she walked by. "Good-bye, Hannah. Thank you again."

"Bye, Mrs. Ross," she replied with a smile before starting the mile walk to the center of town.

The first time Mr. and Mrs. Ross had learned that Hannah walked back and forth from their house, they'd been very concerned about her safety. Mr. Ross had promptly devised some complicated plan so she could be picked up and brought home daily. Unable to help herself, she'd giggled when he showed it to her.

"This isn't necessary, Mr. Ross. I like walking," she'd said.

"But it could be dangerous."

"I don't think so. I've been walking around Charm all my life." They, on the other hand, had moved from Indianapolis after Mrs. Ross had gotten a promotion. They couldn't imagine living someplace where crime wasn't an issue.

After much discussion, they had ended up compromising. They would drive her in bad weather or if it was dark outside. But so far, that had only happened four or five times.

The truth was that she needed these moments to simply think about things.

She liked her job and she liked the independence it gave her. Being at home with her concerned parents had become extremely trying. They constantly watched her with looks of pity and asked if she needed anything. Though she loved them dearly and was grateful that they cared so much, their inability to see her as anything but Paul's grieving girlfriend was frustrating. Even though it had been only a little over three months, Hannah knew that it was time to move on, even if it hurt.

When she got to the bank on Main Street, Hannah deposited her check and then decided to sit at Josephine's Café for an hour. She could have some tea, eat a cookie or muffin, and read her new book until it was time to go home.

Just as she was about to open the door to the

charming café, she saw Aaron Kurtz walking up the sidewalk and braced herself. Aaron and Paul had been friends. Ever since the fire he'd sought her out, as if both of them, having lost people they were close to, now had something in common. Hannah, on the other hand, felt they had less in common than ever before. While Aaron was angry and seemed content to dwell on the loss of his father, she simply wanted to move forward.

The moment he saw her, he straightened his shoulders and puffed up his chest a bit. "Good afternoon, Hannah."

She nodded. "Aaron." Though it was a bit of a fib, she added, "It is *gut* to see you."

Immediately, his polite expression disintegrated. "If you think so, you're the only one."

She didn't want to have this conversation, but there seemed to be no choice. "I'm sorry to hear you so distressed. Did you not have a *gut* day?"

"How can it be good? I'm still working eight hours a day at Kinsingers."

She winced, hating how he emphasized the Kinsinger name as if it were a terrible curse word. "I got off work a little early myself. As you can see, I'm heading into Josephine's right now. I hope the rest of your day is better."

His expression cleared. "Hey, wait. Are you meeting anyone?"

She wasn't sure if he was being nosy or hoping to join her. If it was the latter, it wasn't an option. No way was she going to end her pretty good day by listening to him complain about Lukas Kinsinger. "I'm by myself, but I'm planning to read."

Gesturing to the glass door she was standing in front of, he raised his eyebrows. "You want to sit by yourself at the café? Just to read?"

"It's a real *gut* book." She smiled weakly. She'd spoken the truth. However, she knew most wouldn't understand. Her family had always thought she read too much. In fact, the only person who had ever seemed to understand how much reading meant to her had been Paul.

"I'm surprised you can read anything, what with Paul gone."

She refused to feel guilty. "I manage."

"Sorry. I didn't mean to hurt your feelings. But it's just that it's so unfair," he added quickly. Shifting his stance a bit, Aaron shoved his hands in his black wool coat's front pockets. "You and Paul would probably be engaged by now if not for the accident. If I lost Hope, I don't know what I'd do."

And . . . now she had reached the end of her patience with him. As far as she was concerned, he was being more than cruel to bring up Paul and what her life should have been like.

"I hope you never find out," she said, and even though she knew it was rude, she opened Josephine's front door right then and walked inside, leaving Aaron to stare after her on the street.

"Hannah Eicher, what a nice surprise!" Josephine, the Mennonite woman whose name graced the café's sign, said with a wide smile. "What brings you in today?"

"Do you have any soup?"

"Tomato basil and potato corn chowder. Either sound good?"

"Tomato," Hannah replied, already feeling more relaxed. "Any chance you have fresh biscuits, too?"

"Of course I do. I got a batch just out of the oven, as a matter of fact."

"*Danke.* I'll take two."

"Coming right up. Go pick a table and I'll bring everything right out. With a Coke?"

"*Jah. Danke.*"

After picking out a table on the opposite side of the room, far from the only other table that was occupied, Hannah sat down and took a fortifying breath. Thank goodness for this café. It was darling, decorated in a mishmash of antique tables and modern artwork. All the dishes were from different sets of china, and all the napkins were black-and-white gingham. None of it looked as if it would match, but it fit well together and never failed to make Hannah smile.

In addition, Josephine was friendly and polite and always had a smile on her face. And today she was the perfect antidote for a conversation with Aaron.

Oh, but that Aaron Kurtz exhausted her! He'd changed so much since the accident. Now it seemed that *everything* bothered him. She'd seen him lose his temper on more than one occasion with his sister Darla, too.

"Was that Aaron Kurtz you were talking to outside?" Josephine asked when she set the bowl of soup, basket of biscuits, and tall glass of Hannah's guilty pleasure on the table.

"Yes."

After glancing around the room, Josephine sat down in the booth across from her. "How is he doing today?"

Hannah put her napkin in her lap and shrugged. "The same. Angry." Then, because she had to tell someone, she said, "I think he wanted to join me in here."

"Really? I thought he and Hope were still courting."

"He didn't want to flirt with me, Jo. He wanted a captive audience to listen to him complain about Lukas and Levi Kinsinger."

Jo winced. "I do feel sorry for Aaron, Darla, and the rest of their family. After all, there's no shortage of folks who think it was John Kurtz's fault that the fire started in the first place."

"I know. But placing blame on someone doesn't help. I am hurting, too, but I don't want to talk about the accident all day, and I surely don't want to stand on the sidewalk and say mean things."

"That's because you are a nice girl." Smiling softly, Josephine added, "York and Melissa Ross can't sing your praises enough."

That news warmed her. "I love watching their *boppli*. Christopher is adorable."

"Well, they're grateful for you." Josephine slid out of the booth and said, "Enjoy your soup and your book, Hannah. I'll leave you alone for now."

"Thanks." After saying a quick, silent prayer of thanks, she sipped two spoonfuls of soup, ate half a biscuit, then settled in with her newest novel.

There, on the page, Annabeth, the brave and beautiful heroine, was trying to gain a sheriff's attention, but he seemed more concerned with rumors of an Indian attack. As she became engrossed in the story, Hannah thought that Annabeth was the one who really had problems. Big problems, since it seemed they were in need of a good rain to save their corn crop in addition to everything else.

Though it was silly, Hannah drew strength from reading about the characters' hardships. After all, if Annabeth could deal with so much at one time, why there was no doubt that Hannah could find a way to get through each day without falling to pieces.

She sure hoped so.

All she knew was that she had to continue to try. She made a vow right then and there to avoid Aaron Kurtz as much as possible. She needed happiness in her life, not more anger and stress.

She just hoped that she, too, would find happiness one day.

Chapter 4

"Hey, *shveshtah*. You're home a little late," Aaron called out to Darla from his position in front of the mailbox.

As she approached the foot of their driveway, Darla forced herself not to hesitate. If she did, Aaron would wonder what was wrong and then he would badger her until he got the information he wanted. Once again, she wished things could go back to how they used to be. Before the fire, before their mother had left, Aaron had been far more easygoing.

And far less interested in her personal life.

"I am home a little late, but only by an hour." She shrugged, struggling to pretend that she wasn't still smarting from both Mary Troyer's latest scolding and her conversation with Lukas. If Aaron discovered either of those incidents had taken place, it would likely send him into a tailspin. "I had a rush of customers just minutes before four. Things were so hectic, I decided to take the long way home so I could decompress."

"Hmph."

Though she dreaded his response, she forced herself to ask the obvious. "Why are you home already?" He should have only been clocking out now.

Looking her way, he lowered the brim of his straw hat. It now shielded his eyes, preventing her from seeing his expression. "It was quiet at work. Real quiet. They didn't really need me so I clocked out."

That didn't make much sense. She knew from both their father's long career at the mill and her friendship with Lukas that things rarely ever quieted down. Plus, Aaron usually took advantage of the van service that the Kinsinger Mill offered their Amish employees. If he'd left early, he would have had to walk home.

But instead she said, "It's nice they let you do that."

He straightened. "They didn't *let* me do anything. I simply told my team leader that I was leaving. I said my time could be better served out here around the farm than doing next to nothing at the mill."

With their *daed* gone, he wasn't wrong about there being a lot of work to do. Her father had been busy from sunup to sunset, repairing and maintaining almost everything on their land. Now, because their twin brothers were only fourteen and not quite able to do much without supervision, the bulk of the labor fell on Aaron's shoulders, just as the responsibility for taking care of their youngest siblings fell on Darla's and Patsy's shoulders.

But that said, it was painfully obvious that Aaron had not inherited their father's work ethic. It was also hard to believe that the Kinsinger brothers had decided to start allowing their employees to leave whenever they wanted to.

"So you are repairing the mailbox?"

"*Jah*. I noticed that this post was listing to one side. I thought I'd fix it before you got out here and attempted to make it better." After a beat, he added, "We both know that you would have only made it worse."

His criticism stung, but she forced herself to be grateful that he hadn't been too harsh. "I wouldn't have tried to dig another posthole, Aaron." But she might have if Aaron had waited much longer to fix it. Their home was her source of pride. It bothered her that her other siblings never seemed to care about keeping up the house as much as she did. Daed had used to say that she and he were cut from the same cloth. Now, Darla was hoping that one of the twins or Maisie or Gretel would show that they were cut from that cloth, too.

"You are constantly getting into things you shouldn't. You need to leave the hard work to me."

"Thanks for fixing it so quickly."

He gave her a sideways glance. "So quickly? What do you mean by that?"

Tensing, she took a step back. "Nothing."

"This *just* started listing to one side." His tone was clipped. Defensive.

"I know." Well, it had begun tilting a couple of days ago. More like a week. She'd actually been trying to figure out the best time to ask Aaron to work on it, but lately, he was always exhausted. He'd also become increasingly short-tempered and took offense at things that never used to bother him. It seemed he found almost everything she did to be annoying.

When they were younger, he'd often joked with her and teased her about her persnickety ways. Now she sometimes wondered if he even remembered how to laugh.

After smoothing the packed dirt around the post, he picked up the pail he'd been using to hold all his tools, and led the way back to the house. She followed slowly behind.

"So you're going to keep your thoughts to yourself today? You're not going to continue to pester me about why I left work in the first place?"

"You already told me your reasoning."

"*Jah*, but you rarely listen to me."

"That isn't true."

Straightening, he glared at her. "You know it is. Don't pick fights with me, Darla. You won't win," he said, his voice hard. When she simply stared at him, he breathed in deeply. "Just so you know, I left work early because I've got some news to share."

Darla adjusted her quilted floral backpack that was hanging loosely off one shoulder and eyed Aaron carefully. But she knew better than to push, so she stood still and waited.

"You look about to complain yet again," he muttered under his breath. "Ever the mother hen."

Darla knew that he meant that as a criticism, but she didn't actually take it as such. Since she was the eldest, she did feel like a mother hen. And though she'd always felt the need to take care of her siblings, now she had no choice. Ever since their mother had taken off, Darla knew someone had to be the person her siblings could count on. Someone needed to keep tabs on little seven-year-old Gretel, twelve-year-old Maisie, and most especially her busy, into-everything fourteen-year-old twin brothers. Of course, Patsy helped, too. But lately, her twenty-two-year-old sister seemed far more intent on finding a husband than being a mother figure to a bunch of siblings.

Pushing away the frustration, Darla smiled at her brother who, for once, seemed in a reasonably happy mood. "So, are you going to ever share your big news with me?"

"I've actually got two things to share." He took a deep breath. "First, Hope said yes."

"Said yes to what?"

"To marriage, of course."

"You proposed to Hope?" Darla asked weakly. He'd been courting Hope off and on for years, since they were barely teenagers, but he'd never acted ready for marriage. Now seemed like the worst time to get engaged; their family was in pain, his behavior was erratic, and he was having a difficult time with most everyone in town.

"I decided there was no point in waiting any longer," he said with an awkward smile.

"But it's only been ninety-nine days," she blurted before realizing that it was exactly the *wrong* thing to say.

He glared. "What does that have to do with anything?"

Though she knew she was liable to regret speaking her mind, she continued. After all, someone had to safeguard their father's memory and that included observing a mourning period. "We are all still recovering from Daed's passing. You know that."

"Daed's passing? You mean Daed's *murder*. You need to call it what it was."

"The fire was an accident, Aaron. An accident."

Tossing the pail on the ground, he stepped forward, his hands clenched into fists. "I'm sick of you defending the Kinsingers, Darla."

"I'm not defending them—" She was only trying to get him to see that there were two sides to every story.

"I'm tired of feeling like you're always on their side instead of with the rest of the family."

"I'm always on our family's side—"

"Here I finally have some good news for all of us, and you can't even allow yourself to focus on it. Instead, you have to bring up the mill." His voice rose. "I canna wait for the day I say good-bye to that place."

Say good-bye? He intended to quit his job at the mill? "I wasn't bringing up the mill, only Daed's memory. Are you . . . are you truly planning to quit?"

"I am. As soon as I marry Hope, I'm going to quit and farm her land." He stepped closer. Now he was towering over her, intimidating her. "You can't even unbend enough to tell me congratulations."

"Of course I wish you the best."

"You better. And I better not hear you ever say anything so rude to Hope."

"I would never be rude to her."

"Just me, huh?" he asked, his voice thick with bitterness.

"Aaron—"

He clenched her slim shoulder with a heavy hand, stopping her words, and squeezed, pushing painfully into the muscles and no doubt leaving five fingerprint-shaped bruises.

Ignoring her gasps of pain, he shook her. "Don't tell me what to do, Darletta." After glaring at her again, he turned and strode toward the barn.

Still trying to overcome the burst of pain radiating down her arm, Darla watched him go. She hadn't thought it was possible, but she now felt even more distraught about her life. It had been a horrible day and it was almost certainly about to get worse.

"Lord," she whispered. "How much more do you intend for me to take?"

March 21

"AARON, THIS IS a mighty nice surprise," Hope said as she stepped outside the fabric and notion shop where she worked three days a week. "I didn't expect to see you until tomorrow."

Feeling more than a little foolish all of a sudden, Aaron shrugged and attempted to sound composed. "I decided to pay you a quick visit since you were on my mind."

"Like I said, it's a nice surprise." Her smile wavered as she bit her bottom lip. "How were you able to come over? I thought you were working today."

"I am. This is my lunch."

"Shouldn't you be eating?"

Why was she asking him so many questions? "I, uh, ate most of my lunch during my first fifteen-minute break."

"Ah." She folded her hands in front of her. The contrast of her pretty skin against the cornflower-blue dress and apron only emphasized her beauty. It also highlighted what he found so appealing about Hope. She looked peaceful and sweet. To him, Hope was the perfect girl.

From the first moment he'd spied her sitting across the aisle at school, Aaron had thought she was the best girl he'd ever met. Now that she had consented to be his wife, he could hardly believe his good fortune.

He just hoped he didn't lose her to his mood swings and anger.

"Aaron," she said gently after another few seconds. "Is everything okay?"

"Of course. Why?"

"Because you, um . . . well, you keep staring at me."

Feeling his neck flush, he averted his eyes. "Sorry. I was just standing here thinking how glad I am that you said yes."

Her light brown eyes warmed. "Surely you weren't surprised. We've been courting for two years now." Lowering her voice, she added, "To be honest, my *mamm* was starting to wonder when you were ever gonna ask."

"I had to be sure."

"About me?" She looked hurt.

"Of course not, Hope. I was talking about me." He was talking about his temper and how he was having such a difficult time containing it.

She peered at him closely. "What about you? Is something wrong?"

"*Nee,*" he blurted. "I'm fine." And he was—well, as fine as he could be with everything that was happening in his life. There was only so much a man could take at one time, and he'd reached his limit weeks ago.

"Aaron, what is it?"

"All I meant is that things around our *haus* have changed."

The faint lines of worry on her forehead eased. "Oh. Well, *jah*, to be sure, much has changed. But I think much is also the same. You're still Aaron. Right?" Reaching out, she ran one slender finger down the folds of his coat.

Underneath the fabric, goose bumps rose on his skin. All it took was one touch from her and he was transformed. When he was near her, he was calmer. Happier. Better.

It seemed Hope was his exception. With everyone else, he couldn't hide his anger and grief. With everyone else, he felt vulnerable. Hope, however, brought out the best in him. Like her name implied, she made him imagine that his future wasn't going to be filled with regrets and disappointments. Instead, with her, it would be possible to find happiness.

"Would you like to come over tonight?" Blushing softly, she said, "We could sit with my parents and talk about the wedding. We could set a date."

As much as he wanted her to be his forever, he didn't trust himself enough to set a date yet. He'd only asked her on impulse. "As much as I'd love to do that, I should probably stay around the farm. There's always a lot that needs to be done. My family needs me."

Her smile brightened. "That's why I love you, Aaron. You are always thinking of others and helping your family."

"I love you, too, Hope," he said quickly before he gave in to temptation and admitted to her that he hadn't been acting that way at all lately. He'd been selfish and short-tempered. Actually, he'd done so many things he was ashamed of, he doubted the Lord would ever forgive him.

Needing a bit of space between them so he wouldn't catch another hint of her almond-scented shampoo, he took a step backward. "You know what, I'd better get back to work before I clock in late. I'll see ya tomorrow."

She stepped closer, lifting her chin so she could look at him directly in the eyes. "*Jah*, Aaron. I'll see you *meiya*. I'll even make you a chocolate cake."

"I'll look forward to it." He reached out and gently squeezed her slim hand before dropping it.

"*Gut*." After treating him to another beautiful smile, she went back into the store.

He stood for a moment, watching her talk to the women inside. From the way she kept darting glances his way, Aaron knew she was talking about his surprise visit. It was obvious that she was pleased and proud that he'd used his lunch break to see her.

Then he turned away, taking a moment to give thanks that the Lord had put her in his life. Without Hope, he would feel only frustration and guilt and anger. All of the things that reminded him of how he was failing his father.

Years ago, he'd promised his father to always look after his siblings and his *mamm*. Aaron had also vowed to stand behind his father and do everything he could to help him.

But of course, with the accident and fire, he'd failed.

Walking back to the mill, Aaron didn't see the tulips and daffodils that decorated the merchants' front porches in a riot of color. Instead, all he saw was his father on the floor of the warehouse, writhing in pain. Burned and dying.

Instead of the warmth infusing the spring day, he felt hands barring him from his father's side.

Instead of the sounds of *kinner* laughing, he heard shrill sirens as fire truck after fire truck raced toward the mill.

When Aaron wasn't surrounded by the goodness that was Hope Mast, all he felt was the bitter desolation of failing his father. He needed Hope in his life. He needed a future with her, a future away from the mill. He wanted to farm their fields during the day and watch her smile in the evening.

With her, he still was a person to be proud of. With everyone else, he felt out of control. For some reason, he simply couldn't help but take out his frustrations on Darla. He couldn't seem to stop yelling at the twins or ignoring his little sisters.

He'd even given up trying to hide his anger and pain at work.

Even now, by the time he walked through the main doors of Kinsinger Lumber and made his way to the break room, the anger that burned inside him constantly had lit itself once again.

As he punched his time card, one of the men standing by the coffeemaker looked at him curiously. "You left, Aaron? Where did you go?"

"That ain't none of your business."

He raised his hands in surrender. "Sorry. I guess it ain't."

Aaron felt his shoulders tense at the words, at how harsh he had sounded. His cheeks burned with shame. His father would be so disappointed in him now.

But it was too late to take back the sharp words.

Instead, he turned away and headed toward the back of the warehouse. Realizing, as he did so, that his transformation was complete. Without Hope by his side, he was practically another person. A man she would hardly recognize.

Chapter 5

March 25

Five days had passed since Lukas had visited Darla at the post office and said too many things he regretted. Every time Lukas thought about the words they'd exchanged and the tension that now existed between them, he felt both lost and hopeless. There was little that could be done to smooth things out, but he would've liked nothing better than to repair their relationship. Lukas was missing his father's guidance more than ever.

And maybe it was because he could hardly think about anything else, but for whatever the reason, Darla seemed to be suddenly everywhere.

For the first time in three months, he caught sight of her as he was walking through Charm. He'd been so taken aback that he'd simply stopped in the middle of the sidewalk, blocking everyone's way, and watched her approach. When she'd surprised him further by smiling softly, he hadn't responded. Instead, like a fool, he'd gaped at her. He could have sworn that she'd giggled at his expression.

Seconds later, when he'd finally broken out of his self-imposed daze, she was far enough past him that it would've created quite a stir if he'd hustled after her. Because of that, he'd simply gone about his day. But that didn't mean he hadn't wondered what had brought about the change in her.

Two days later, he was face-to-face with her again. This time they'd been sitting on opposite sides of the church, the men and women facing each other like always. He'd been more than a little shocked when Hope Mast's father had announced that she'd recently become engaged to Aaron Kurtz.

Hope and Aaron had been seeing each other forever, so Lukas supposed that their engagement shouldn't have been a surprise. But he'd certainly thought the timing couldn't have been worse.

Later, when he was told that Aaron intended to move to the Masts' farm, Lukas had felt even more dismayed. He knew for a fact that Darla depended on her brother around their small farm. Lukas didn't know how Aaron was going to be able to tend to the needs of a new wife, work at the mill, and look after his siblings—all at the same time.

Why, Lukas himself could barely keep up with things, and he had Levi and his two sisters all helping out as much as they could. How was Darla going to handle her five other siblings on her own?

Then, of course, there was her job and dealing with people like Mary Troyer. He had to guess that she was as taken aback by Aaron's engagement as he was. Was she handling it okay?

After the announcement in church, he'd gotten his answer when he'd scanned the crowd and saw Darla's face. She was smiling, but her expression was strained. Worry clouded her eyes.

And because he knew how things worked in her family, he had a pretty good idea that Aaron hadn't consulted Darla before he proposed. Most likely, he didn't care about her thoughts on the subject. Though Darla had no doubt been happy for her brother and Hope, Lukas was fairly sure she was losing sleep over how to keep her family functioning and the farm going. Darla was trying to figure out things on her own.

Just like she always had.

Lukas had never been more distressed about the lingering rift between them. He couldn't help but dwell on the situation as he ate breakfast.

Without complaint, Amelia always fixed a large breakfast for the four of them. She got up before dawn, milked Angel, gathered eggs, and made a feast. She was a good cook and had been blessed with the sweetest temperament of them all. Their parents had doted on her, and now he, Levi, and Rebecca did, too. She was the kind of girl who needed someone looking after her.

But instead of letting the rest of them take care of her needs, she seemed determined to mother the three of them. "What's on your mind this morning, *bruder*?" she asked as she placed a large platter of scrambled eggs and bacon in the middle of the table. Already there was a bowl of chopped fruit and some kind of blueberry coffee cake that she'd made early that morning.

"Only your fine meal, Amelia," he teased.

After filling his coffee cup, she rolled her eyes. "You say things like that every morning. It ain't necessary."

"Of course it is. You are a fine cook and you

get up before dawn to prepare our meal. We all appreciate it. I don't want you to ever forget that."

Her eyes—sometimes blue, sometimes silver, but always so striking against her pale skin and white-blond hair—lit up. "It's the least I can do. You, Rebecca, and Levi work at the mill."

"While we are there, you take care of everything here. Believe me, I know that's a lot," he said as he piled his plate high with eggs and bacon.

"It's not too much. I'm a grown woman."

"It's not that I don't think you can handle everything. I just don't want you to ever feel that I don't appreciate you. I do."

As was her way, she pushed aside his compliment again. "Before Becky and Levi come down, tell me what's put the line of worry between your eyes."

Fork in the air, he paused. "It's that noticeable?"

"It is to me." After pouring herself a cup of coffee, too, she sat down next to him, her pale yellow dress and apron falling softly around her.

As he debated whether to share his burden, Lukas couldn't help but notice that she looked pretty. She'd been a pretty baby, and her beauty had only grown stronger with every year that passed. But more important, her sweet nature matched her angelic looks. She was everything lovely, and growing up, Lukas had heard his parents comment at least once a week that she was their precious angel.

One might have thought her beauty, combined with their parents' obvious adoration, might have spurred some jealousy toward her, but in truth, none of them—not even Rebecca—felt that way. Mainly because the Lord had not only given Amelia beauty and sweetness, He'd also made her a bit timid. It had made all of them want to look after her, sometimes even a little too diligently.

Now that she was in her early twenties, many men in Charm had taken notice. Levi and he had already been approached by several of the men in the area, asking for permission to court her when their period of mourning was over. Lukas had decided immediately that he didn't care one bit for the look in some of the men's eyes when they spoke of Amelia. He'd even had to glare at some of his friends when they'd asked.

Lukas had told Levi that he now had a better understanding of what their father must have gone through when he'd been raising his two daughters.

Luckily, when Amelia heard about those conversations, she'd calmly informed him and Levi that she did not need their permission to have a beau.

"Lukas? Lukas!" Amelia called again, her

voice turning sharp. "Stop daydreaming and talk to me."

"Sorry." Bracing himself, he said, "It just happens to be Darla who is on my mind."

She tilted her head to one side. "What about her?"

"Well, we've grown apart since the accident, you know," he said slowly.

"To be sure."

He shrugged. He hated that he had so many feelings for Darla, none of which was easy for him to describe. But instead of attempting some convoluted explanation about how he felt, he stuck to the simplest one. "I guess I miss her."

"Of course you do. You used to see her almost every day."

Hearing Amelia's matter-of-fact acceptance made him bolder. "I went to the post office a couple of days ago and told her I wanted to stop by her *haus* one evening and pay her a visit."

Her brow wrinkled. "I don't recall you talking about that."

"Probably because I didn't talk about it."

"Okay. Well, how was she?" Her voice darkened. "How was Aaron? And what about their *mamm*? Has she returned yet? Do they have any idea where she took off to?"

"I can't answer any of those questions."

"Because?"

"Because I never went over."

"Why not?"

"Darla told me she didn't want me to."

"That's too bad." Amelia forked a bite of coffee cake. "Why didn't she?"

"I'm not sure." Remembering the conversation, he said slowly, "I know she's still grieving."

"We all are."

"*Jah*, but she's also hurting because of all the rumors." Shaking his head, he said, "Darla mentioned that there might be questions about the mill's practices. Like Daed and me or the other supervisors should have been more diligent about everyone's safety." After taking another bite of eggs, he said, "If you want to know the truth, I think she was quoting Aaron."

Pushing her plate away, Amelia leaned back in her chair, propping one bare foot on the seat of the facing chair. "I don't want to be mean, but I canna say that I am surprised. The way he's been scowling at most everyone and anyone . . . he'd scare off snakes in his fields."

Lukas couldn't help but grin at the comment. "You might be right about that. He has been mighty upset with the world."

"Which makes me wonder why Hope Mast said

yes to him. When I told Aaron congratulations after church, the look he gave me was lethal."

Indignation hit him, heavy and hard. "He had no call to be mean to you."

"Settle down, *bruder*. Aaron merely glared, and I can handle that. I could even handle him saying something mean. I'm tougher than I look."

"You shouldn't have to be. It's my job to look after you." He knew he sounded a bit overprotective, but he couldn't help himself. She was his little sister and their parents were gone. Their *mamm* had passed away from a heart condition. Now, with Daed gone, too, someone needed to make sure she was taken care of.

As was her way, she ignored his concerns. Glancing toward the stairs, Amelia leaned closer. "You know as well as I do that Aaron has always taken advantage of Darla. Furthermore, he works for ya, now. He should be respectful to her."

"I don't know if I should mention that to him."

"It doesn't matter. You are his boss. That's a fact. Just as it's a fact that Aaron has always treated Darla shabbily."

"You've thought that?" He was kind of shocked. Amelia was so kindhearted that he and Rebecca often teased her, saying she was far too sweet to be a Kinsinger.

"Of course. Who wouldn't think that?" she retorted. "You and I both know he's lazy."

Lukas set down his fork before he took a bite and choked. "You think Aaron's lazy?"

"To be sure. He was lazy in school, and more than once I heard him bully Darla into doing his work." Her voice hardened. "And now he's marrying that Hope Mast. Part of me feels like I should talk to that girl and try to figure out why she said yes. She's going to need to go into that marriage with her eyes wide open."

"Please do not. Aaron doesn't have anything good to say about our family as it is."

"Since when do you pay any mind to what Aaron Kurtz thinks?"

"That's kind of bold!"

"Lukas, you shouldn't worry so much about offending Aaron. It ain't like he is suddenly going to become nice if we don't say anything."

"Oh, I am so glad you are talking about Darla and Aaron Kurtz." Rebecca's voice floated down the hall. "Did either of you spy her expression when the preacher announced the engagement?"

"I did," Lukas said. "She looked upset."

"She looked more than that," Amelia interjected. "She looked like she was about to break in two, poor girl."

"I thought the same thing," Rebecca said as

she walked directly to the coffeepot and poured herself a generous cup. After taking a fortifying sip—she'd never cared for milk or sugar—she sat across from Lukas and reached for the blueberry cake. "It broke my heart, it did."

"I am starting to worry about Darla," Lukas finally said.

"It's no wonder. She has all the burdens of that family on her tiny shoulders," Rebecca added. "I imagine it's a heavy load, too."

Amelia shook her head. "Becky. That ain't kind."

"I'm not being unkind, merely stating the facts. Darla is a tiny thing. I often feel like a giant next to her. I can't imagine how you feel, Lukas."

Since he'd always felt like she needed him, needed someone to lift her burdens and look after her, he said nothing. There were some things brothers didn't tell their sisters unless they wanted to be made fun of.

After Rebecca stood up and refilled her cup— she drank coffee like it was a food group—she looked at Lukas curiously. "So, what are you going to do about Darla?"

"Nothing."

"That's the wrong answer. You need to reach out."

"He did. She didn't want his help," Amelia said.

"It's true. I did. She told me that we needed to stay apart."

Rebecca carefully cut a small portion of her coffee cake and speared it with her fork. "Lukas, do you remember when I was nine and went hiking with Darla and Aaron?"

They'd always run around together. Actually, he had so many memories laced with Darla that he could hardly recall moments in his childhood when she hadn't been present. "We hiked all the time. Are you referring to a specific instance, Beck?"

"When we were near that creek."

"I remember that," Levi interjected as he joined them, pulling the juice out of the refrigerator. "Aaron had crossed right away. So had Becky and me."

"I was trying to go across," Amelia said. "But it was kinda deep."

"You were too small," Levi said. "I met you halfway and held your hand."

"Even though you were younger, you were bigger," Amelia said with a grin.

"And even back then Daed would have whipped me good if I hadn't kept you safe." Levi chuckled. "I learned by the time I was five or six to always look out for you." He held up a hand.

"And before you go apologizing for that, stop. I didn't mind."

"*Anyway*," Rebecca said under her breath.

"Anyway, Darla started saying that she was going to go back home. Then you discovered she couldn't swim," Levi said to Lukas. "So you told her to hop on your back and you carried her across."

"And then, over the next few weeks, you taught her how to swim," Amelia said softly.

"Which I am still kind of surprised her parents let you do, seeing how it wasn't very appropriate," Rebecca said as she started measuring out coffee grounds for a fresh pot of coffee.

"I was eleven, she was just nine. Nothing improper happened," Lukas said. "And I had to teach her. Someone had to." He frowned, thinking of how brave she'd been, wearing an old T-shirt and shorts that Levi had borrowed from one of his English friends. The pond nearby had been cold in the early morning hours when they'd met, but she'd hardly complained.

Done eating, Lukas stood up and carried his plate to the sink. He felt mildly uncomfortable now. He'd never felt closer to Darla than when she'd lain in his arms in the water and put her trust in him. The moment she'd let go and floated by herself had been wonderful. Now he could hardly get through a conversation with her at the post office.

"This was a fun trip down memory lane, but it doesn't help me understand why you brought it up, Becky."

"To remind you that Darla doesn't do anything for herself. She's going to put everyone else's needs ahead of her own. She always has and probably always will."

"Unless she's with you, Lukas," Amelia said with a soft smile. "She's always trusted you more than just about anyone. And because of that trust and the friendship you share, she's also always put your needs ahead of her own."

He frowned. "But that doesn't sound any different from how she is with the rest of the world."

"There's a difference. You *always* put her needs first," Rebecca said. "You care about her happiness."

It all sounded convoluted, but on the other hand, it didn't sound unfamiliar. "So what you all are saying is that I need to go over and talk to Darla."

"No you don't," Levi blurted.

"Levi, stop," Becky said. "The fire wasn't her *daed*'s fault."

"I'm not saying you should be rude to Darla.

But I surely don't think you need to be the one to look after her. And you really don't need to go to her house and deal with her siblings."

"They aren't that bad," Amelia said.

"Oh, yes they are," Levi retorted. "They're a difficult lot, and that's putting it mildly."

"Then what should I do?" Lukas was starting to lose patience with this conversation.

"You need to ask her to meet you somewhere," Amelia said.

"Such as?"

After a moment, Rebecca said, "Take Darla to the creek."

"I am not taking her swimming." He gulped. Did he sound as stunned and embarrassed as he thought?

"Go walking, not swimming," Rebecca said. "Being there will remind her of how much you both have in common. She'll remember that she trusts you."

Levi nodded as he took the last of everything on Amelia's serving platters. "Becky has a *gut* plan."

"Wait a minute. I didn't think you wanted me to have anything to do with her."

"I didn't," Levi said. "But I also feel kind of sorry for her."

Amelia nodded. "I wasn't sure how I felt about

her either . . . until I saw her face when Aaron and Hope were celebrating after church."

"Wait a minute, I didn't see her then," Rebecca said. "What did she look like?"

"I saw her standing off in a corner," Amelia said. "Darla looked like she felt all alone."

"Maybe she is." Feeling guilty, Lukas added, "It's been so hard, dealing with the company and the funerals and Daed's loss. Because of that, I've kept my distance from her. Now I wish I had reached out to her more."

"I haven't exactly been friendly, either," Rebecca said. "But what we gotta remember is that what happened that day at the mill wasn't our fault and it sure wasn't Darla's."

Though he noticed Levi hadn't quite jumped to Darla's defense, Lukas was relieved to note that his brother hadn't seemed as angry, either. That gave him hope.

After washing and drying his dish, he nodded. "You all convinced me. I'm going to go back to that post office and ask her to walk to the creek with me."

"I think that is a fine idea, Lukas," Amelia said with a smile. "I'll say a prayer today that it goes all right."

"*Danke*." Then, just to lighten the mood, he

added, "Before I forget, Levi and I were approached by Ben Miller yesterday at the mill."

"About what?" Amelia asked.

"About you, of course." Looking put out, Levi said, "He wanted permission to come courting."

As Lukas expected, Amelia's cheeks turned bright red. "Ben? Isn't he old?"

"He's almost thirty," Rebecca said. "And a widower. With two *kinner.*"

Amelia bit her lip. "What did you tell him?"

Lukas grinned at Levi. "Absolutely not."

Her eyes narrowed. "You told Ben no without even talking to me?"

"He ain't the man for you, Amelia," Levi said gently.

"He's too old and he wasn't looking for *you;* he was looking for a babysitter. There's no way I'm going to let him even think that's all right with me," Lukas added. When he noticed that Amelia was still working her bottom lip in that way she did when she was stewing on something, he forced himself to sit down by her side and talk about things. "You don't mind that we told Ben that, do ya? I mean, I didn't think you had any feelings for him."

"She doesn't," Levi said, then paused and eyed Amelia more closely. "I mean, you don't, do you,

Amy? I sure don't recall you ever mentioning his name."

"I don't. Ben is a nice man, but he's not for me." Looking embarrassed, she darted a concerned look at Rebecca. "Did he ask about Becky, too?"

Lukas was confused. "*Nee*. Why do you ask?"

"Because she's worried about me getting my feelings hurt," Rebecca interjected with a smile.

Amelia blushed bright red. "I didn't mean—"

Rebecca cut her off with an easy laugh. "Don't get spun up, Amy. I promise, I'm not hurt in the slightest." She tossed her head.

"Are you sure?"

"Positive."

Amelia, always one to wear her heart on her sleeve, looked unsure. "Becky, I just wanna say that you are real special. You are going to make a wonderful wife."

"One day," Lukas muttered. "One day in the future."

"Hush, Lukas," Rebecca ordered with a grin. "The men at the mill know that I'd never court a man who couldn't approach me himself anyway. They also have a pretty good idea that I'd never be interested in a man who works at the mill."

"Oh?" Amelia nibbled that bottom lip again. "Do you think I shouldn't ever date a man who works at the mill?"

"*Nee*. Our situations are much different. I work there. I'm around those men all day. You are not."

Lukas winced. He'd known Rebecca had jumped into her work at the mill because Daed had asked her to and now because he and Levi needed her help. However, her heart was with *kinner*. If she had her way, she'd be Charm Amish School's newest teacher instead of Kinsinger Mill's main receptionist. "You won't have to work there forever, Becky."

"I'm happy to help in any way I can, Lukas. You know that." Turning back to Amelia, her tone softened. "Amelia, I know you get tired of it, but we're all used to looking out for you."

"*Jah*, but it ain't necessary. I am not a baby. I can look after myself, too."

"You are right. Furthermore, I reckon the day will come when you don't need us running interference between you and half the population," Levi said as he walked to the sink and washed his dish. "But that day ain't today. Let us fend off the men for ya."

"Men aren't as interested in me as you make it sound."

"Oh, yes they are." Rebecca smirked.

"Ignore our teasing and let us help you for a little while longer," Lukas said. "It makes us feel useful."

"Don't say no to all the men, Lukas."

Because she looked a bit dismayed, Lukas reached out and gently squeezed her shoulders. "Don't worry, Amelia. One day the right man will come along. It, uh, just ain't Ben Miller."

Chapter 6

March 25

If she didn't increase her pace, Hannah knew she was going to be late to her job. And if that happened, it would be a disaster. Mornings with Mr. and Mrs. Ross tended to be a bit chaotic. They ran around handing her Post-it notes and index cards filled with detailed instructions for Christopher. And if she wasn't there right on time, they started thinking something had happened to her.

They were rather high-strung.

Just as she was about to turn onto their street, she spied a dog running toward her. Realizing that it was all alone and not on a leash made panic rise in her chest. She was afraid of dogs. Large, small, noisy, quiet . . . it didn't matter. Her fear encompassed all of them.

But this one was large and black and had a silver chain collar. It looked stronger than she was. It could no doubt knock her over without a moment's hesitation. More than likely, it would do much worse than that.

Though her brain was telling her body to move, to seek safety, it didn't seem like her legs were of a mind to listen. She couldn't do anything but stare as it loped closer and closer. When it was about two yards away, it slowed. Its black eyes stared at her curiously, its black nose sniffing the air. It whined.

Glad that it wasn't baring its teeth, Hannah noticed twin red tags hanging from its collar. She took a deep breath. Perhaps, it wasn't prepared to eat her. Perhaps, it was lost.

"Easy, *hund*," she whispered as she took two steps backward.

Watching her, it tilted its head. Then, without warning, it started barking.

And just like that, Hannah froze in place again. What was she going to do?

"Rose! Rose, come here!"

Though Hannah hated to look away from the dog, her instincts caught hold of her and she looked around anxiously. Was there a little girl in the fierce dog's path? She didn't see anyone other than a man about her age trotting down the street, a bright red mesh leash in his hand.

"Rose! Come!"

The dog barked again. *This* was Rose? Then, to Hannah's amazement, it turned around and loped to the man.

"You stinker. You know you can't go off making friends by yourself." He ran a hand along the dog's head, then snapped the leash onto its collar.

As if he'd just realized she was standing there, the man turned to her with a wide smile. "Sorry about that."

She nodded.

His friendly gaze turned concerned. "Hey, are you okay? I hope Rose didn't scare you."

Hannah's mouth was so dry, she wasn't sure she could form coherent words. But since she couldn't simply stand there, she gathered her wits the best she could. "*Jah.*" Hopefully he wouldn't notice that she sounded hoarse.

He stilled, looking uncertain, then approached her with Rose now walking complacently by his side. He was wearing a knit cap and had eyes as dark as his dog's.

"You're not okay, are you?"

"I . . . I'm all right," she sputtered. Finding her voice at last, she added, "Your dog just caught me by surprise. That's all."

He stopped a few feet away from her. Farther even than Rose had been. "I'm sorry about that." Looking down at his dog fondly, he said, "She loves her morning walk. I was on the phone when I opened the door; she was off and running before I could grab her."

"Maybe . . . maybe you should put her leash on before you open the door." When his eyes widened, she grimaced. "I apologize. I shouldn't have said that."

He waved off her apology. "No, she scared you. You have every right to say that. Look, I don't know if you'll ever be around here again, but in case you happen to see her, I just wanted you to know that she's a nice dog. Rose doesn't bite or attack people." He reached down and scratched his dog between her ears. "The most she'll ever do is try to lean up against you."

"Lean?"

"Yeah. Like she's doing now," he said with a grin. "She really likes to get her ears rubbed."

Hannah realized then that Rose was listing to one side, her head resting on her owner's thigh. She was panting softly, her big tongue hanging half out of her mouth.

"She's a mighty big *hund*."

"She is. She's a Rottweiler. But like I said, she's sweet and she's very well trained, except for when it's time for her morning walk. Sometimes she gets so excited, she darts off before I can get her leash attached." Still looking at his dog fondly, he said, "She doesn't understand that I have other things I need to do besides chase after her."

As his words took hold, she gasped. "Oh! I've gotta go. I'm gonna be late for work."

He looked around in confusion. "Where do you work?"

"At the Rosses' *haus*."

"No kidding? Talk about a small world. York and Melissa Ross are my neighbors." He smiled softly. "I'm guessing you are Hannah, their Amish babysitter."

She didn't know how to answer that. Should she tell him that his guess was right?

At her hesitation, he smiled. "I'm Rob Prince. I just moved in two weeks ago. And yeah, I know. I don't look like much of a prince. Harry is a lot more handsome."

She didn't quite catch his joke. Because she was embarrassed by that, she backed up a step. "I better go, Mr. Prince." Goodness, but that was a strange name! "Mr. and Mrs. Ross don't like me to be late and I'm late now."

"Let me walk you over there, then, and explain to them that this is all my fault."

She wasn't so sure if that was a *gut* idea. She didn't know him and she was afraid of his giant dog—but she was just as worried about coming in fifteen minutes late and facing Mr. and Mrs. Ross. "That ain't necessary."

"Yeah, it is. I lost hold of Rose and she scared you." Reaching out, he said, "May I help you with your bag?"

"*Nee.* I mean, no, my backpack is fine," she said as they walked up the street.

When they got closer, she saw Mr. Ross standing on the front porch, a cell phone in one hand and a cup of coffee in the other. The moment he saw her, his whole body eased.

"Oh, no. Mr. Ross don't look happy," Hannah said. She increased her stride.

"It'll be all right," Mr. Prince murmured. "Like I said, I'll be sure to tell York that this is all my fault."

"At this point it doesn't matter who is responsible. I should have left earlier."

"I don't mind taking responsibility for my wayward dog," he said before calling out, "Hey, York. Look who I found on the corner."

Looking incredibly relieved, Mr. Ross came

down the drive. He was dressed in pleated khaki-colored slacks, a golf shirt, and a pair of tan loafers. "We were getting worried, Hannah. You're never this late."

"I'm mighty sorry, Mr. Ross. I promise, it won't happen again."

"I'm not mad; I was worried about you." Looking a bit chagrined, he added, "I was actually holding my phone, ready to call you before I realized that, of course, there was no way to do that."

"I'm so sorry you were so worried. I'll go right in."

"Wait a sec, Hannah," Mr. Prince called out. "York, Hannah arriving late is my doing. Rose ran out of the house before I could get her leash on and she stopped right in front of poor Hannah. She thought Rose was going to attack. Scared her half to death."

"That makes sense. Your dog is the size of a small pony." To Hannah's surprise, Mr. Ross reached out and rubbed the dog right between her eyes. "Silly girl."

As Rose closed her eyes in obvious enjoyment and leaned toward Mr. York, Mr. Prince added, "I told her that I thought she might be your famous babysitter."

Hannah stared at him in confusion. "Famous?"

"I'm afraid we brag about you quite a bit," Mr. Ross said. "Melissa and I think you're a wonder."

"*Danke.*"

"You're welcome. So, did Rob tell you that he lives next door?"

She nodded.

"I work from home," Mr. Prince explained, "so if you ever need anything, you only have to knock on the door or call."

"Oh." She couldn't imagine doing either but she smiled.

"I'll tell Melissa to leave out his number, Hannah," Mr. Ross said. "If there's an emergency, he's just a few feet away."

Now that she wasn't scared of Rose or a nervous wreck about getting in trouble with Mr. and Mrs. Ross, Hannah noticed that Mr. Prince was much closer to her age than she'd first thought. She wasn't sure why she was glad about that, other than the fact that he seemed nice.

Flustered by the direction of her thoughts, she stepped away. "I better go inside. Good-bye, Mr. Prince."

"It's Rob, okay?"

"Okay. Rob." Rose barked as Hannah darted inside, the sound followed by laughter.

"Rose says bye!"

Rob's comment was so silly, she found herself giggling as she faced Mrs. Ross and Christopher.

"Hannah, you're here! Hooray!" Mrs. Ross said.

"I'm sorry I'm late." She was just about to repeat her excuses when Christopher giggled in his mother's arms, then wiggled.

To her amazement, Mrs. Ross set him down and then he rolled over. And rolled again!

"Christopher, look at you!" Hannah exclaimed as she got on her knees and held out her hands to him. When he rolled again and treated her to a gummy grin, she laughed. "When did you learn to do this? What a smart boy!"

"Isn't he adorable? He figured out how to roll over on Saturday morning. Now, he doesn't want to be held, he wants to roll on the floor! Oh, Hannah, I hope you ate a good breakfast. You're going to get your exercise today."

Picking up the baby, Hannah set him in her lap and gave him a little hug. "*Jah*, I am, for sure. He is doing a *gut* job."

Mrs. Ross smiled and grabbed her purse just as Mr. Ross came in through the front door. When he noticed Hannah sitting on the carpet with Christopher, he laughed. "We should have told you to get some kneepads. He's a regular wiggle worm."

"I'll do my best to keep up."

"I know you will. And Hannah?"

She looked up at him. "Yes?"

"Rob really is a nice guy. You don't have to worry about him or Rose."

"You met Rose?" Mrs. Ross asked.

"I'll tell you all about it on the way to work. Bye, Hannah."

After going over her list of items for Hannah to do, Mrs. Ross said good-bye, too, leaving Christopher and Hannah sitting on the floor.

After the garage door closed, Hannah swore she heard a faint bark.

For the first time in memory, the sound didn't make her flinch. Instead she wondered if it was Rose.

And then, as she watched Christopher reach out a hand for one of his toys, Hannah wondered about Rob, what he was like.

And she realized, with a bit of surprise, that she wasn't filled with sadness and regret for the loss of Paul.

Instead, she merely felt at peace.

Chapter 7

March 25

"U h-oh," Amanda Jefferson called out from the counter of the post office. "Don't look now, Darla, but you've got company."

It was five minutes before the end of a very long day. In the back, Darla was just locking up the cash drawer and closing down the machines. She looked at Amanda curiously. "Tell whoever it is that we'll be open tomorrow at nine. I'll help them then."

Amanda poked her head into the room. "I don't think it's gonna be that easy."

Darla bit back a sigh of impatience with effort. Amanda was eighteen and rather enthusiastic.

She also was a little scared of making decisions or confronting anyone by herself. Darla understood that, and could even sympathize, but it was time for her to take some responsibility.

"Amanda, it will be all right. People know what time we close. They might not like having to come back, but they'll understand."

"But—"

Deciding that maybe it would be best to illustrate how to be firm, Darla pointed to the clock. "Amanda, as of right now, we are closed. Tell whoever is out there that I couldn't help them even if I wanted to. The postal machines have been turned off." With a feeling of satisfaction, she flicked the machine's switch and listened to its steady humming fade into silence. "There now. Our day is done. Go lock the door if you'd like."

Yet Amanda remained, wobbling on the balls of her feet and looking a bit like a small child in need of a bathroom. "Um . . ."

"Amanda, please do this. I'm ready to pack up and go home. It's been such a long day."

And it would have been just as long if Mary Troyer *hadn't* come in to inflict her daily dose of accusations and threats. But Mary had, and today her anger and screeching had risen to new heights. Darla had had to press her palms down on the countertop so Mary and the other customers wouldn't notice how badly she was shaking.

Amanda cleared her throat. "I hear what you're saying, I really do. But simply closing the door on our newcomer ain't gonna be that easy."

"Because?"

"Because I don't think your visitor is gonna leave just 'cause I told him he needed to."

Darla stopped sorting the papers on the counter. "Visitor?"

"*Jah*. That's what I've been trying to tell ya. It's Lukas Kinsinger who's here."

"Lukas?" She was surprised. The last time he'd been in, Lukas had announced that he wouldn't be back. And though she hadn't been entirely pleased that she'd gotten her way—she hadn't thought he would back down so easily—it wasn't like him to be back so fast.

"I'll go say you'll be right out," Amanda announced before Darla could ask her to send him away.

Seconds later, the girl's voice drifted to her. "Darla's in the back, Lukas, but I'm thinking she'll be out presently. And by the way, we're closed," she chattered on. "She turned off the machines, so we can't be doing any work right now even if we wanted to. Which we don't."

"Is that right?"

Darla pressed her hands to her cheeks as Amanda continued spouting off information. "Oh, yes. Now, you gotta step aside 'cause I'm gonna have to put on the Closed sign and lock the door."

"That's fine, do what you want. I didn't come to do business. I came to walk Darla home."

His voice was deep and sure. And, like always, laced with that quiet confidence that Darla had always found so appealing.

There in the privacy of the office, Darla felt a tremor run through her.

Shoot!

"Oh," Amanda said. "Well, I told her you were waiting on her, but she didn't say nothing about your walking her home. Do you think she knows?"

"I have a feeling she probably knows by now. Now, don't you worry about me, Amanda. I'll just stand here while you do whatever you need to do." Raising his voice a bit, he said, "I don't mind waiting here all afternoon for Darla."

"I think I better go tell Darla that," Amanda squeaked. "Um, I'll be right back."

Before Amanda could appear again, Darla snapped the drawer shut and picked up her purse. After locking her office door, she joined them at the front. Now Amanda was standing in front of the counter staring at Lukas like he was the most handsome man in Charm, Ohio.

Which he was.

Lukas, on the other hand, was leaning against the wall of post office boxes, arms crossed over his chest, looking for all the world like he had every right to loiter in the lobby.

His chin lifted when she appeared. And then, to her regret, he smiled. "Hi."

Aware that Amanda was staring at them, Darla smiled. "Hi. Just a sec, okay?"

He didn't reply. Merely smiled.

Now, why in the world did that make her shiver? She really needed to get a handle on both her reaction to Lukas and all those foolish dreams she used to entertain about him.

Practically pivoting on her heel, she turned to Amanda. "*Danke* for your good work today. I already locked the office door, so the next time you come in we'll note the time you left. You can leave now."

After looking from Lukas to Darla to Lukas again, Amanda went behind the counter and grabbed her canvas tote bag. "I'll see you on Saturday."

"I'll be here. See you then."

The minute Amanda walked out, Darla locked

the door behind her. Then she turned to face Lukas, who was still leaning against the wall of post office boxes as if he had nowhere else in the world he'd rather be.

His presence made the room seem smaller and her mind go blank. "Lukas, I thought we already discussed this. We canna spend time together."

"I decided I wasn't really on board with that."

"Why? What are you doing here? And why did you tell Amanda that you were walking me home?"

"I think that would be fairly obvious. Don't you agree?"

"But we agreed not to be friends."

"I know, but I changed my mind. Are you ready?"

"Nee." She needed to stand firm. He shouldn't be so bossy with her. He shouldn't ignore what she was saying. Just as important, he needed to understand that she simply wasn't going to drop everything whenever he asked.

Well, not anymore.

He looked around then, pointedly, at the purse on her arm. "What else do you still have to do?"

"It's not that." She took a breath and plunged forward. "Lukas, I don't think we should be seen walking together. People will talk."

"People are already talking." He stepped forward, getting into her space. "People are talking a lot. Actually, I don't think they want to stop talking about you and me and the mill and the fire. From what I hear, and I don't hear much, we seem to be the favorite topic of conversation around most every coffeepot in Charm."

"See—"

"In fact, I think the only people not talking about you and me are you and me. Therefore, it's time to change things."

Part of her agreed with him, but she was learning that what she wanted didn't always matter. "Lukas, my family won't be happy."

"I don't care," he said quietly. "I don't care about how they react. I care about what you think and how you feel." Every word seemed to have new emphasis.

And in spite of her best intentions, she felt a pull toward him. She wanted to agree with him. Wanted to believe that he was right.

Lukas crossed his arms over his chest and studied her. "Darla, I have decided that God placed you in my life to help me become more patient."

"Oh, Lukas, stop. And you mustn't use the Lord to attempt to explain yourself."

"I'm serious, Darla. I don't think the Lord minds

me bringing Him up in the slightest. What's more, I think He wants me to realize that I need to wait for the important things. That is why I'm determined to wait for you to change your mind. I'm gonna wait as long as it takes."

"God doesn't bully, Lukas." And yes, she did sound just a tad bit pious.

"No, God is good. So good that He is giving me the courage to push aside both of our doubts and wait."

"You might be waiting a mighty long time."

"I don't mind." Staring at her intently, he lowered his voice. "Are you really going to throw away years and years of friendship?"

They did, actually, have years and years of friendship between them. Wonderful years.

Was she willing to disregard them in order to keep peace within her family?

Warily, she eyed Lukas, noticed that he was leaning against the wall again. It seemed he was intent on proving to her this new patience of his.

She didn't know what to say. Well, she knew what she *should* say, but she wasn't going to say it. "All right. I've got the keys right here. Let me finish locking up."

Looking far too pleased for his own good, Lukas nodded. "Take your time."

Taking her time involved locking up two more drawers before leading him outside and at last locking the front door. "I'm ready now."

His lips curved up. "Is all that locking up standard procedure or did you put your own spin on it?"

"It's standard. Why?"

"Nothing. It's just that it seems like a lot of effort to guard some letters."

"The United States Post Office takes mail seriously."

"Obviously." His faint smile grew into a grin. "So, do you need to go straight home? Or do you have some errands to run? Or we could walk to the creek."

"Let's go straight home." Her family wasn't going to be happy that she was renewing her friendship with Lukas, but she was too tired to even attempt to sneak around.

"That's fine with me," he said easily.

As they walked together, Darla felt a curious sense of everything finally going right for the first time in months. For the first time in more than one hundred days.

"So, Aaron and Hope, huh?" he said after about a half a block. "That's quite the news."

"*Jah.*" She tried to smile. "They are happy."

"This engagement came up kind of suddenly, don't you think?"

She'd thought so but said, "Well, they've been courting off and on for two years, so I suppose it isn't all that sudden."

"I meant the timing of the engagement."

She glanced up at him out of the corner of her eye. He was being completely serious. More important—to her at least—she recognized that he wore a look of concern. For her. And because of that, she allowed herself to be completely honest. "Yes. I thought the same thing."

"How did your siblings react?"

"About how you would expect. Patsy was happy, Maisie asked about a thousand questions. Little Gretel asked if Patsy could make her a new dress for the wedding, and the twins acted like it wasn't a big deal at all."

"What about your *mamm*? How do you think she'll react?"

"Does it matter?" She didn't even try to hide the bitterness in her voice.

His tone gentled. "Is Aaron going to try to track her down and tell her?"

"*Nee.*" Thinking about all the pain her family had gone through lately, in some ways their mother's departure had been the hardest to accept. "If there's one thing we all agree on, it's that we don't even want to think about our mother. She left us. She left us when we were hurting and grieving. Even my seven-year-old sister."

Lukas lifted his arm, as if he were about to enfold her into a reassuring hug, but then, just as abruptly, he dropped it. "I'm so sorry, Darla."

"*Jah*. Me, too."

"Maybe she'll come back soon and be able to explain herself."

"Maybe." She shrugged. "It doesn't matter now. We're doing all right without her."

But she knew that wasn't true. None of them was doing all right.

"Sometimes life is too hard to manage," he said gently. "Sometimes we all need a little time to ourselves."

Because she didn't want to sound as bitter as she felt, she nodded. "I suppose." But she didn't actually think that Lukas meant what he said. No matter what was going on, Lukas would have made time for everyone. It wasn't his way to make things easy for himself.

It wasn't her way, either.

Hating the downward path of their conversation, she blurted, "It's best we all learn to be happy for Aaron and Hope, no matter how their timing might affect us. Aaron is mighty pleased about the whole thing, and life is a lot better when he is in a good mood."

"I bet."

Those two words expressed a wealth of information about Lukas's feelings. That thought was neither a welcome nor pleasant one. She didn't exactly want to see his point of view on anything. However, it was becoming apparent that a lifetime of compatibility overruled a hundred days of suffering.

She wasn't sure if that was right or wrong. All she knew was how she felt.

They turned right off Main Street. In another two blocks, they'd turn right again, and then they'd be just a few yards from her house. She knew she should brace herself. Her walking with Lukas was not going to be received very well. At all.

"Rebecca told me she heard that Aaron was going to move to Hope's house," Lukas said. "Is that right?"

"*Jah*. I mean, I believe it is."

"He's taking on a lot. More than I would have ever given him credit for."

She heard the sarcasm in his voice. Darla paused, unsure what to say about Aaron's plans.

If she said that he wanted to farm, she would be betraying Aaron's secret.

But if she didn't mention Aaron's intention, she worried Lukas would think she was supporting Aaron's actions.

She decided to err on the side of the truth. Daed had always said that the truth was worth bearing, no matter how hard it might be.

"Lukas, Aaron plans to farm Hope's land."

"Gonna be kind of hard to do that after work. Ain't so?"

"Um, well, he is planning to eventually quit the mill."

The amusement that had been playing on his lips evaporated. "I see."

She wondered what he meant. Darla said, "I know it ain't my place, but I'd appreciate it if you wouldn't let on that you know about that."

"First of all, it is your place," he replied, his voice hard. "You're his sister and my friend. You have a right to an opinion, Darla."

She'd made him mad. Wincing, she blurted, "I'm sorry, Lukas. All I meant was—"

He interrupted. "*Nee*, it's me who is sorry. I didn't mean to sound so harsh. Don't be upset."

"I'm not upset with you."

"I'm glad of that. Darla, you know I'd never

hurt you. Never." He took a deep breath. "Listen. I'll keep your secret. But I have to tell you that I'm not real pleased about this."

"I hadn't realized he was such a valuable employee."

"He isn't. But I'm not fond of the fact that he wants to work for me as long as possible before I discover that I'm going to have to replace him."

This was awkward. "If Aaron finds out that I told you, he will be upset with me. I'd rather not deal with that right now."

As if he no longer trusted himself to look at her, Lukas looked straight ahead. She sensed him tensing, noticed that a muscle in his cheek was clenched. Her own body tightened in response, bracing for him to throw her wish back in her face.

At last, he sighed. "I suppose I walked right into this, didn't I?"

"Maybe," she allowed. "But if I may be frank, it took me by surprise, too. I didn't know he had other plans besides working at the mill."

"How are you going to manage? You've got a big farm and a lot of animals. Too much for a woman to handle."

Truly, she didn't know. "Can we not talk about this? It makes me uncomfortable."

"The whole situation does, or talking with me about it?"

"Both. It's still fresh, and, well, no one at home seems too worried about it besides me."

"That's because no one in your house ever seems to worry about the future besides you." There was an edge to his voice. An impatience.

It wasn't a new thing. Darla had known for some time that neither Lukas nor Levi respected Aaron all that much. Sometimes, even in the quiet of the night, she let herself admit that she wasn't all that happy with how he handled things, either.

"He is who he is," she said softly. "He is Aaron."

"I disagree. He is who he is because he doesn't feel the need to be anyone different."

"That isn't my fault."

He stopped abruptly. Then to her surprise, he leaned a little closer. "Of course it isn't," he said. "I'm not blaming you, Darla. I'm not blaming your parents, either."

"Then?"

"All I am saying is that people change when circumstances force them to. When your *daed* died, Aaron had the opportunity to become someone different." He shook his head. "*Nee*. He had an *obligation* to become the man of the family. He should have willingly taken on the needs of your family. He should have decided to place his mother and siblings ahead of his own selfish wishes. He didn't choose to do that."

She forced herself to keep her mouth from dropping open. Lukas's words weren't exactly a surprise, but the passion with which he'd said them made her catch her breath and hold it tight. All she could think was how different her life would have been if anyone in her family had voiced such things.

Or if Aaron had felt that sense of obligation.

"Maybe he has," she said hesitantly—because if she didn't, she would have to admit that Aaron was so very far from the man that Lukas was. Even harder would be admitting to Lukas that her brother hadn't even tried. "Maybe this is why he's decided to marry Hope."

His eyebrows shot up. "Even if that is true, it doesn't mean that he made the right decision. He shouldn't be thinking about taking care of a wife when he can hardly take care of himself."

"That's not quite fair."

"Don't defend him. It neither helps him nor gives you the credit you deserve."

"I have to hope that he is doing the right thing. I have to, Lukas."

"I reckon you do." He sighed, looking up the driveway at her house. "Well, let's go get this over with so we can relax."

She didn't have to ask what he meant. Bringing Lukas to her house was akin to bringing the enemy home. Her whole family would see the action as a betrayal of their father's memory, instead of what it actually was: her need to have someone who was on her side. Who believed in her.

Chapter 8

As Lukas walked beside Darla up the long gravel driveway toward her home, he was painfully aware of the mistakes he'd made with her. He'd been absent when she'd needed him. Distant when he should have been near. Far too full of himself when he should have been concerned with her needs.

It would be easy to justify his neglect. In the days and weeks following their fathers' deaths, he'd had more on his mind than Darla's pain. He'd had his own grief to manage. Then there were the added responsibilities of the mill, compounded by the fact that virtually all two hundred of their employees were still reeling from the effects of the fire and the five deaths.

Every morning, he vowed he would work as hard as possible to ease the worry and pain of everyone there. And every night he realized that he hadn't even come close. He would toss and turn, sleeping fitfully before at last waking up and writing a new list of things that needed to be done.

But it was never enough.

In addition to the heavy burden at work, Lukas was doing his best to help his younger siblings recover as best they could. Of course, Rebecca, Amelia, and Levi were adults and would have firmly told him that they didn't need any help from him, but something inside him needed them to need him.

These were all very good reasons for not putting as much effort into his relationship with Darla.

But still, he should have known that she had been alone in many ways.

Even though there were more than a few clues that pointed to the fire having been started by John Kurtz's soiled rag, Lukas had steadfastly refused to publicly blame John. But Levi hadn't been as reticent. And in his efforts to comfort his brother, Lukas hadn't refuted Levi's grumblings like he should have. Therefore, he'd kept his feelings to himself, and simply worked hard to do everything that was expected of him.

But as the weeks passed, he'd begun to feel empty inside. He'd needed his friend. He'd needed Darla. He'd missed Darla's smiles, her bright attitude and her unwavering support. He'd missed her. Only after he'd visited her at the post office had he realized that she, too, had been going through many of the same things. But unlike Lukas, who had the support of his employees and his family, she'd had no one.

Instead of receiving a helping hand, she'd been the one supporting others. And now Lukas knew that Aaron had not only ignored her needs, he'd also selfishly added his own burdens to her slim shoulders.

Lukas would've said he couldn't fathom Aaron doing such a thing, but then he'd have to remember that Aaron had acted this way time and again. The only person whom Aaron had ever listened to had been his father. And now he was gone.

Of course, he also now had Hope. Hope was lovely and had always been smitten with Aaron, but whether she didn't see his faults or pretended she was unaware of them, she wasn't the type to change Aaron. At least, Lukas didn't think she was.

As Darla led him toward her family's old farmhouse, Lukas noticed that it needed a fresh coat of paint and the grass and bushes needed trimming. None of those things cost a lot of money or took a lot of time, but still Aaron had let the chores fall to the wayside.

Just thinking about how Aaron hadn't put his family's needs first made Lukas seethe.

Darla apparently noticed the tightening in his muscles. "Lukas? Is something wrong?"

"*Nee.* I, uh, was just noticing that the house could use some fresh paint. Would you like me to buy some for ya? It would be no trouble."

"There's no need. We have paint."

"Oh?" He let the word float between them. Hoping she would at last say how lazy Aaron had been.

Instead, she flushed with embarrassment. "I know it looks bad. I, um . . . well, I haven't gotten around to painting yet."

It took some effort, but he managed to keep his voice easy and patient. "You know painting ain't a job for a woman, Darla."

"Who says?" She pulled back her shoulders and playfully drew herself up to her full, unimpressive five-foot-two-inch height. "I can paint as well as you can."

"Maybe you could," he teased, "if you had a good ladder."

"Ha-ha. I've been making good use of ladders all my life, Lukas."

That might be true, but there was no way he was going to let her do more around this house than she was already doing. If he didn't step in, she was going to work herself to the bone. "I don't mind painting for you. Or I'll ask Aaron to get on it," he added at last. "He should be doing outside chores like this."

She raised her eyebrows but said nothing. Which was probably smart. Lukas knew Aaron didn't like to be bossed around, and especially not by him.

But that didn't mean he wasn't going to try.

In fact, part of him hoped Aaron would be there and would pick a fight. It would actually give Lukas a lot of pleasure to yell at the man and, for once, tell him everything he felt about him.

It wasn't just Aaron's intention of quitting his job that was irritating him so much. It was the man's complete refusal to see the position he was putting his sister in. Darla, who continually smiled to the world and pretended that she didn't carry what had to be a thousand pounds of burdens on her slim shoulders. Someone had to be on this girl's side. Someone had to look out for her.

Why was he the only person who realized this?

The moment they reached the front porch, Maisie appeared. At twelve years old, she already looked a lot like Darla. She shared Darla's blue eyes and small frame. In fact, they shared so many of the same features, it was uncanny. Except that their personalities were very different. While Darla was usually agreeable in nature and looked for the best in everything, Maisie always seemed to be in a bad mood. And had, for several years now.

Today she was dressed in a light gray dress that should have looked too somber for a young girl. Instead, it emphasized her wheat-colored hair.

"Hiya, Lukas," she said politely.

Glad that her grumpy mood might be a thing of the past, he nodded. "Good afternoon, Maisie."

She stepped closer, her hands restlessly twisting the side of her apron. "What are ya doing here?"

"I walked your sister home."

"How come?"

"Can't I walk her home without a reason?"

Maisie continued to treat him to a piercing stare. "*Jah*," she said slowly. "But you haven't spent time with my sister for weeks. What's changed?"

"Maisie, don't be rude," Darla admonished.

"Sorry, but I thought we didn't like the Kinsingers no more." Sheepishly she looked at Lukas. "Sorry."

Lukas said nothing. Instead he stared at Darla, wondering how the Lord had managed to give one girl so much patience.

"No one ever said that," Darla said.

Maisie narrowed her eyes. "But . . ."

After glancing at Lukas with a weak, contrite expression, Darla reached out and gently pulled Maisie's hands from her apron and held them in her own. "No one is upset and nothing is wrong. Lukas and I simply wanted to catch up."

She nodded. "Oh."

Darla's eyes lit up in approval. "Now, tell me who is home."

"Samuel and Evan. Gretel and Patsy. Now you. Everyone but Aaron."

"I see. Well, go get Lukas and me some glasses of lemonade, will you?"

After warily shifting her eyes to Lukas again, Maisie nodded and left.

"Lukas, I'm sorry about that. Ever since Mamm left, Maisie has been difficult."

"Nothing to apologize for. Maisie has always spoken her mind." After a pause, he added gently, "She has reason to be off, I think. You all have had quite the time of it. Ain't so?"

"*Jah.*" After motioning to the small grouping on the side of the porch, a trio of chairs nestled around a wicker table, Darla sighed. "Let's go sit down."

Lukas followed her, waiting for her to take a chair before sitting himself. Then he took off his hat and stretched his legs. The porch overhang kept the area cool. A light breeze blew in from the field beyond, bringing with it the scent of freshly mowed grass. He breathed deeply and felt his muscles relax. No matter what happened with her family, this moment made him glad he'd sought out Darla. This felt familiar.

Hoping to ease her tense expression, he murmured, "How many hours do you think we've spent right here?"

As he'd hoped, the faint lines that had appeared on her forehead lessened. "Too many to count."

"I'll try, though. I'd say at least two hundred. What do you think?"

At last, a genuine smile played on her lips. The first one he'd seen since before the accident. "Oh, more than that, Lukas."

"Really?" He pretended to look confused. As if he actually cared about having a right answer.

"Really. I know I'm right about this. I mean, if one insisted on trying to count them."

The front door opened again and out came Maisie and Patsy. Each was holding a Mason jar filled with lemonade and ice.

Patsy led the way. "When Maisie said you were out here, I couldn't believe it. I had to come out and see if she was telling the truth," she said as she set the jar in front of Lukas. Then she plopped in the empty chair between them.

"Why would I lie?" Maisie said, handing Darla her jar.

"No reason," Patsy said. "But your appearance here is something of a shock, Lukas."

"Hey, Patsy." He knew there was no need to say another word. In her own way, Patsy was as protective of her family as her sisters. She also was a bit bolder. If she wanted an answer, she never hesitated to ask for it.

"So, why exactly have you darkened our doorstep?"

Lukas raised his eyebrows. "I believe so far I've only darkened your front porch."

"Does this mean our dear sister is going to have her best friend again?" she asked.

"Oh my heavens, Patsy!" Darla said around a moan. "Stop."

"Don't get upset. You know I'm only teasing."

Still, Lukas knew that Patsy always had a reason for what she did. He glanced at Darla, wondering if she was becoming upset. However, she didn't look much different than she usually did when she was surrounded by her siblings. She was sipping lemonade and had one foot propped on the bottom railing of the porch. Just like she used to do.

"I wanted to spend some time catching up with Darla," he said at last. "It's been a while."

Patsy raised her brows at his statement. "Aaron ain't gonna be pleased that you're here. For that matter, I don't know if I'm real happy about it, either."

"I didn't come over here to make you happy, Patsy. I came over for Darla." Patsy's comment didn't come as a big surprise to Lukas. Though Darla was older, Patsy had always acted more protective of her brothers and sisters.

"If you think you're helping her by being rude to the rest of us, you're mistaken."

"I'm not being rude," he countered. "Just honest."

"Obviously some things never change." Darla pressed her hands to her cheeks. "Settle down, you two."

"I'll settle when your guest becomes nicer."

Lukas rolled his eyes. "Enough with the dramatics. I'm not your enemy. You and I both know that."

Instead of answering, Patsy glared at Darla. "Having him over was a mistake."

Only years of experience managing employees and keeping his emotions in check allowed Lukas to keep his patience. He instinctively knew that none of his siblings would put him down in front of others. But still it was amazing to see the family dynamics at play here. Nothing had changed. "What about your sisters and brothers?" he asked.

Patsy's eyes widened. "What about them?"

"Are they upset I'm here, too?" Lowering his voice, he added, "Are you really mad at me?"

After glancing at Darla again, Patsy met his gaze. "Not really." She shrugged. "I'm just tired. We've had some mighty long days since Mamm left. I simply don't want to deal with one more thing."

"None of us do," Darla said. "I didn't bring Lukas over to cause a row."

"I know." She sighed. "Lukas, no matter what Aaron says, I don't think you caused the fire."

"Of course I didn't. I lost my father, too, Patsy."

"Lukas and I have talked," Darla interjected quickly with a hard stare at both of her sisters. "We agreed that a lifetime of friendship should mean something."

"It does. Daed thought that, too, but now he's gone."

Darla inhaled sharply. "No good will come from clinging to hurts."

"No good will come from ignoring what is apparent to us all, either. Lukas, you are a good man, and I know you are doing your best. But being here isn't helping you or Darla or any of us. I think we should all keep our distance as long as we can."

But he was done with keeping his distance. He needed Darla in his life. He needed her friendship. "Keeping away from each other isn't really possible."

"Perhaps. But being over at each other's houses isn't the best idea, either." She moved her head, gazing out at the drive.

Following her gaze, Lukas watched Aaron approach. Even with the distance, it was apparent that his stride was angry. Maisie moved to Lukas's side. Her eyes were wide and she looked worried.

"It'll be all right," he murmured to her.

"I don't think so, Lukas."

"I'll make things better."

She wrinkled her nose. "How will you do that?"

"Trust me." When she stared at him in confusion, he smiled at her and hoped that she'd try to believe him.

"Maisie, go inside," Aaron called out.

Maisie slipped a hand on the top of Lukas's

chair and gripped it tight. "How come? I did my chores."

"You know why," Darla said. "Go on inside, dear."

Maisie looked panicked. "But all he's gonna do is yell at you, Darla. If I stay here maybe he won't get so mad."

Patsy pressed her hands on Maisie's shoulders. "I won't let him yell at Darla. It will be okay."

Fury burned deep inside Lukas. No longer caring who overheard their conversation, he turned to her. "Does Aaron yell at you a lot, Darla?"

Patsy rolled her eyes. "He yells at all of us."

"But mostly Darla," Maisie said. "Five days ago he grabbed her, too. Real hard."

Darla's cheeks flushed. "Maisie, there's no need to share this."

Lukas got to his feet. "He hurt you?"

"I'm fine." Standing up, too, she said, "Patsy, go take Maisie in. You know as well as I do what Aaron is going to say. There's no reason Maisie needs to witness it."

"Someone needs to stay with you."

Lukas stepped closer. "I'm not leaving her side."

Patsy took the twelve-year-old's hand. "Come on. Darla's right. We know what is about to happen."

The moment the two girls entered the house, Aaron walked up the steps. "You had no business bringing him here, Darla. Have you already forgotten what his family has been doing? What his father did? Are you stupid?"

Lukas stepped forward. There was no way anyone was going to speak to Darla like that in front of him. "I don't like how you're speaking to her. Watch yourself."

"Stay out of this, Lukas. I might have to listen to you and your brother at the mill, but I surely don't have to listen to ya at my own *haus*."

"If you are speaking to Darla in a way that I don't like, it's my business, no matter where we are."

Aaron glared. "Go home. Darla, what is wrong with you? How could you bring him here?"

Lukas stepped closer to Darla. "Do you really think I'd leave with you talking to her like this?"

"It's all right, Lukas," Darla said.

"*Nee*. It ain't," Lukas bit out. He was so angry with the situation and upset with himself for not being more attentive to her, he let his voice rise. "It ain't all right at all."

"Darla's none of your concern, neither. Now, get off my property."

"This is my house, too, Aaron," Darla said quietly. "You can't order people off the property."

"I can and I will." His chest puffed up. "I'm the man of the house."

Lukas was done having Darla fight this battle. Disdain coating his words, he said, "For only a few more months, though, right?"

"What I do is none of your concern, Kinsinger."

"You calling me Kinsinger now? You don't even want to say my name?"

"I don't even want to know you." Folding his arms across his chest, Aaron said, "Now, I'll only tell you this one more time. Leave. My family ain't no concern of yours."

"It is. I care about your siblings. And don't forget, you work for me."

"Are you threatening me?" Aaron asked. Before Lukas could say a word, he turned to Darla. "What did you tell him? Are you betraying me, too?"

"I have betrayed no one."

Only his aim of protecting Darla kept Lukas from getting up and walking away. "Aaron, I think it's time we all disposed of some of this anger we've been feeling. We have already lost so much. Why, both of our fathers are in Heaven. Isn't that enough?"

"Wasn't it enough that your family caused an accident and then decided to cover it up by acting as if it was my father's fault?"

"The mill is safe. It was safe then, too."

"My *daed* didn't cause the fire."

"No one in my family has ever said that he did. We paid for your father's funeral and have given your family a check to help with expenses."

"That wasn't enough."

"The amount?"

"Of course not. The amount was too small, and the deed was too little. At the end of the day, we are all burdened by the veil of accusations surrounding the accident." He turned to Darla. "And you. You are acting as if none of that is important."

Darla glared back. "Aaron, you are exaggerating everything."

Aaron clenched his fists. "Don't ever side against me again, sister. Especially not in front of him."

Lukas stepped forward, ready to place her behind him for protection. "Stop threatening her."

"It ain't a threat. It's a promise, Darla."

When Lukas saw her tremble, the last of his patience left him. Standing nose-to-nose with Aaron, he released all the pent-up anger that had been held hostage inside him for far too long.

"Hear me now, Aaron," he said, each word low and careful. "Hear me now and listen good. I will be watching you. And I'll be checking on Darla every day. If I hear or sense that you have been anything but respectful to her, I will find you."

"All you have to do is leave your office and find me on the line."

"Not any longer. You are fired."

Darla gasped.

Aaron looked stunned. "You canna do that."

"Of course I can. I would never keep anyone on a Kinsinger payroll who is not only back-talking me but telling lies about the factory."

Bitterness flashed in Aaron's eyes. "Why don't you admit that you will do anything you want, anytime you want to do it? The power has gone to your head."

Lukas knew that wasn't the case, but at the moment he didn't really care. He was tired of dealing with Aaron Kurtz. "Though you're wrong about my motives, you are exactly right about one thing. It's my mill. Mine."

"Since I'm no longer your employee, it's past time you left."

He had no choice but to comply. "Come walk me down the drive, Darla," he said quietly.

"Don't follow him, Darla," Aaron ordered. "You stay here."

"Oh, Aaron," she whispered before following Lukas down the steps—much to Lukas's relief.

He wasn't sure what was going to happen between them now. All Lukas did know was that he needed to say something to help her. As he waited for her to reach his side, he silently prayed that the Lord would give him the words he needed. Because he was fairly certain that what happened next between them was going to matter most of all.

Chapter 9

It was no doubt foolish to blatantly ignore Aaron's order and walk Lukas down the driveway, but as far as Darla was concerned, the time had come for her to follow her own instincts.

And she still wanted to be Lukas's friend.

After they walked a couple of yards, the gravel crunching under their feet, Lukas looked her way. "I'm sorry, Darla."

"It's not your fault. I knew if you came over, things wouldn't go well. I let you walk me home anyway."

"I knew it, too." Looking almost embarrassed, he added, "Maybe a part of me wanted to confront Aaron. I don't know."

"If we need to assign blame, it should be to all three of us. I knew better, you had an agenda, and Aaron . . . well, Aaron has no boundaries anymore," she said, though admitting such a thing was difficult. "He says and does whatever he wants without a care for others."

But instead of looking relieved that she wasn't taking the blame, Lukas looked shamefaced. "I had no idea things had gotten so bad. I should have been coming over here every day, checking up on you. I'm sorry I haven't."

"There is nothing to apologize for. I am not your responsibility." She also didn't like being thought of as a victim.

As they continued, Lukas absently kicking a couple of stones with each stride, he asked, "What do you think is going to happen now?"

"I guess Aaron will be staying home a lot more," she quipped. It truly was nothing to laugh about but she feared if she didn't make light of it, she'd cry. Though the mill had given them a sizable check to help pay for their expenses after her father's death and there was a lot of money in their savings, they'd also been counting on Aaron's paycheck to take care of their day-to-day needs.

How was she going to be able to take care of everyone now?

Her tears would only make Lukas feel worse and she didn't want to do that.

Abruptly, he stopped. "Will he hurt you?"

"Of course not."

"But Maisie said he grabbed you. Where did he grab you, Darla?"

His voice was so concerned, she answered before she thought the better of it. "My shoulder."

As she expected he would, he examined her carefully. "Where? Which shoulder?"

"My left one." When he reached out, she flinched. Not because she feared he would hurt her, but because she didn't want him ever thinking about her bruises. "Lukas, stop."

Looking pained, Lukas dropped his hand. "You're still hurting, aren't you?"

"Nee." And that was true. She wasn't hurting. Well, not too much.

He turned away, looking toward the front porch. Then, as if he had suddenly solved whatever problem he'd been tackling, he grabbed her hand and guided her farther down her drive, then directed her into a clump of trees surrounding the remains of her great-grandfather's cabin. The cabin was the first structure on their land and had served as both a reminder of their family's struggles and a fort to play in when they were young.

When they were hidden from both the house

and any stray passersby on the road, Lukas reached for the pin at her collar. "Let me see your shoulder."

Batting away his fingers, she stepped back. "Lukas, what in the world? Of course you cannot do this."

A muscle jumped in his cheek. "Darla, I canna leave you without knowing what he did. I'll stew on it and worry over it. You know I will."

Darla sighed. She absolutely knew he would. "Lukas, you're making too much of nothing."

"If I am, prove me wrong. Either unpin that dress enough for me to see your shoulder or I'll call Patsy or Maisie to come help you with it."

She didn't doubt he was serious. When he had a goal, he fixated on it, he always had. It was why he was now running Kinsinger Mill. It was why she'd always trusted him. Lukas didn't back down and he didn't change his mind.

After reminding herself that he was only wanting to inspect her bruises and that he'd seen far more of her body when he'd taught her to swim all those years ago, she pulled out the top two pins of her dress then spread the opening she'd made along her skin until it stretched across her bare shoulder. Hardly more than six or eight inches of her skin was visible to him. Hardly enough to feel embarrassed about.

Still, she closed her eyes because she knew what he would see.

"Oh, Darla," he whispered.

She shuddered and fought back tears. Not because of what he saw but because of his reaction. Pain and compassion laced his tone, reminding her that she wasn't alone. Not anymore.

As he carefully ran one calloused finger along what she knew were four dark purple fingerprints staining her skin, he glanced up. "You are hurting, aren't you?"

"They're just bruises, Lukas." She wouldn't dare mention that her shoulder had been sore for a good day.

"These are from his fingers. Where was his thumb?" Without asking for permission, he wrapped his hands around her hips and turned her like she was a mannequin. When she felt the tender brush of his thumb along the nape of her neck, tracing the last imprint, she lowered her head in shame.

Aaron wasn't a violent man, but it seemed he was becoming so. And she was letting him.

With her back still facing Lukas, she fought to keep her voice firm. "Now you have seen them."

"Jah."

"So . . . So, I need to refasten my dress. And

we need to get back on the drive before someone comes looking for us."

"Of course." He stepped back. Dropped his hands. She felt him standing rigidly behind her, whether to offer a tiny bit of privacy or because he was simply waiting for her, she didn't know.

She supposed it didn't matter.

After she got the last pin inserted and was covered modestly again, she turned to him. "Let's go. You need to get home and I need to get back."

Lukas seemed frozen. "I've never hit a man in my life, but I'm tempted to do so now."

"You know violence is not the answer."

"It might be."

"It's not *our* answer, Lukas."

Leading the way back toward the drive, he said, "I'm thinking that your *bruder* needs to remember that."

She hoped that would happen, too.

Walking again by her side, Lukas said, "Darla, how often does this happen?"

"Not too often."

After a small pause, he said, "What does that mean?"

It was tempting to lie, but she didn't want to do that any longer. She was so tired of pretending Aaron never hurt her. Keeping silent wasn't making her feel any better. Worse, her silence wasn't making Aaron change. "It means he grabs me roughly once or twice a week."

He inhaled, obviously attempting to control his reaction. "I don't like leaving you here. Why don't you come home with me?"

If this conversation wasn't so difficult for her to bear, she would have rolled her eyes. Lukas Kinsinger always, *always* tried to manage things. Tried to manage her. "And when would you suggest I do that?"

"Now."

The childish part of her was tempted. If she went to Lukas's house, she could escape Aaron's abuse and her younger brothers' and sisters' needs. She could rise without feeling the awful sense of panic in her chest that told her she wasn't going to get enough done, that she wasn't going to be enough for her younger siblings to forget that their father had died and their mother didn't love them enough to stay.

But because she was an adult and she'd never been one to run from responsibility, she shook her head. "Lukas, you're being ridiculous. Of course I canna do that."

"Think about it," he coaxed. "You know we have enough room."

"Running off to your house won't solve anything."

"Except keep you from harm."

"If I'm not there, I'm afraid Aaron might take out his frustrations on one of my sisters or brothers."

"Then we should contact the police."

"Absolutely not. This is a family problem. And Aaron isn't a criminal. He's just . . ." Her voice drifted off.

"He's just bullying and hurting you." He stopped and faced her. "Darla, you know I care about you."

"I know."

"Then you know how hard this is for me, too. I hate leaving you here. I hate you thinking you need to be your brother's victim in order to protect your siblings. That ain't right."

She lifted her chin. "Things aren't that bad, Lukas. I'm not going anywhere. I'm needed here."

"What is going to happen now?" he bit out, frustration evident in every word. "After I turn down the street and you head back inside, will he take his anger out on you?"

She hoped not. "I'll be fine. Aaron showers after work. Then he usually goes right over to Hope's house."

"Does Hope know he grips you so hard that

you bruise? Does Hope know that he yells at all of you?"

She doubted it. "Does it matter if she doesn't?"

His lips tightened. "If she accepted his proposal, she needs to know. She needs to know the real man she's planning to marry. Would you like me to talk to her?"

"Of course not."

"But she needs to know what he is capable of."

Darla was ashamed that they were speaking of her very own brother. That shame, combined with her frustration with Lukas's high-handed ways, made her speak a little too bluntly. "You can't protect everyone, Lukas."

"I can try."

She inhaled sharply, realizing how sincerely he meant those three words. He was willing to do everything he could to protect and support anyone who needed it. This trait of his was as much a part of him as his gray eyes and the defined muscles of his arms.

She knew he wasn't making an empty promise. He would never vow to do anything he didn't fully intend to actually put into practice.

They'd come to a stop at the end of the drive. His farm was less than a mile to the left, as the crow flies. In the other direction was the town of Charm.

They'd stood here together before. Many, many times.

As if reading her mind, he sighed. Little by little, the tension in his body eased, making him look far more like his usual self. Like the Lukas she'd come to know so well and loved. "This feels familiar. Ain't so?"

"*Jah.*" Letting herself relax enough for the memories to slip into the present, she said, "I remember waiting for you here when Maisie had just been born and Mamm put me in charge of Patsy."

He groaned. "Which was a thankless job. She never listened to you."

"We were twelve."

"*Nee.* You were twelve, I was fourteen."

"Anyway, Patsy, of course, had darted off to play instead of doing her chores."

"And you had done them instead."

"I did. Then I told on her, too, so she would have to stay around and watch the twins."

His lips twitched. "You always did tattle."

"I had to. Otherwise I never got a break," she said with a laugh. "Anyway, I was so happy to get away, I stood out here and waited for you." She was suddenly struck by how, even at twelve, she'd known that she could depend on him. And even at that young age, she hadn't been wrong. He had been everything trustworthy.

He grinned. "When I got here, we walked to the creek and waded in the water."

He'd kicked off his boots and rolled up his pants legs. She'd hiked up the skirt of her dress, feeling so daring. They'd walked for over an hour. And the one time she'd slipped, he'd wrapped an arm around her waist and held her close.

"That was a good day," she murmured.

"The best." His gaze met hers and she felt more than a little giddy.

Maybe it was because she wasn't in any hurry to go back to her family or maybe it was because she wanted to reassure him in some odd way— even though she had nothing at her disposal with which to reassure him—but whatever the reason, she didn't want him to leave.

"Even though your visit turned out so badly, I can't regret having you over here again," she admitted.

"I can't regret it, either. Especially now that I know exactly how tough it's been for you." Stepping closer, Lukas loosely wrapped his arms around her waist. The weight of his hands felt comforting. Familiar. She relaxed against him, even though they weren't children any longer.

He leaned closer. "Darla, I'm going to walk you home every day now."

There was only one thing to say. Only one thing she wanted to say, anyway. "All right."

"*Gut*," he said around a sigh as he tucked her closer against him.

She let her head rest against his chest, remembering how good it felt to have his arms wrapped around her. She felt protected and cared for. Like she belonged to him. Breathing deeply, she smelled his clean, masculine scent. Allowed herself to linger just a little bit longer.

And then remembered that it wasn't proper.

She needed to regain some distance. She wasn't his. She was his friend. Moreover, when he got home, he would no doubt realize that, too. Surely then he would have regrets.

Pulling away, she lifted her chin so she could meet his gaze. "If something comes up and you can't walk me home tomorrow after all, don't worry, okay?"

"I'm not going to change my mind. I'm going to walk you home every afternoon. And then I'm going to sit with you and we're going to talk like we used to."

"And then?"

"And then, I'm going to win each of your siblings over until they trust me again."

She tilted her head to one side. "And then what?"

"And then we'll see what happens next."

His words sounded like a promise. A vow. Something so deep and emotional and meaningful that she hardly knew whether to ignore it or grab ahold of that promise and beg him never to forget his words.

Running a finger along her cheekbone, he said softly, "Does that sound like something you could agree to?"

Before she doubted herself again, she nodded.

He sighed in relief. *"Gut."* Stepping away, he touched the brim of his hat. "See ya tomorrow, Darla."

"Yes. I'll see you tomorrow evening."

When he turned around and started walking again, his pace far faster than when he'd been by her side, she allowed herself to smile. Lukas Kinsinger was a part of her life again. And this time, it seemed he intended to stay.

Chapter 10

It was almost dark when Lukas finally got home. As he trudged the last couple of feet up the driveway, he wanted nothing more than to eat Amelia's supper, and take some time to sit quietly and pray about what to do next. He didn't know what to do about Aaron, and was still, frankly, a bit stunned by the new thoughts he was having about Darla. He'd always felt protective about her but now there was something else, too. Was it attraction? Was it love?

He wasn't sure. If he'd fallen in love, wasn't he supposed to feel sure?

"Hey, you. I wondered when you were going to come home," Rebecca called out.

Raising his head, he saw that she was sitting on the front porch in a light blue dress with what looked to be one of Levi's sweatshirts over it, holding a sleeping bulldog puppy. He almost groaned. She'd been after Simon, Lukas's best friend, to give her one of his dog's pups, and it looked like she'd gotten her way today.

"Looks like we have a new addition to the family."

She beamed. "We do. His name is Oscar. Isn't he cute?"

Oscar was in a little ball the size of a football on her lap. He was white with brown spots and tiny pink paws. Crouching in front of his sister, Lukas gently rubbed the pup's head with the back of one of his fingers. "He is, indeed. I didn't know you were going to get him today."

"I hadn't planned on it. But then when I got to talking to Simon at work, he asked if I had been serious when I'd told him I wanted a pup."

Sitting beside her, he chuckled. "Did Simon really imagine you weren't?"

"I think he was wondering if you were going to get annoyed with both him and me. You aren't, are ya?"

No way was he going to let her put him in charge of the household. "This is your home as much as mine, Becky."

"I know, but I don't want you to be irritated with me."

"You should be asking Amelia if she's irritated. She's the one who's home all day."

"Amelia ain't upset. She named him when Simon and I brought him over."

"Simon came over?" Simon was a good man. The best. However, of late, Lukas had noticed him gazing at Amelia just a little bit too often. On the one hand, Lukas couldn't blame him—even he could see how pretty his youngest sister was—but that didn't mean Simon was ever going to be good enough for her.

As he should have expected, Rebecca waved off his concern. "Simon gave us some puppy food and a little collar and bed. I couldn't carry it all home. He didn't stay long at all."

"*Gut.*"

"You can't stop him from liking Amelia, you know."

"Sure I can." Not willing to get into another discussion about Simon and Amelia, he switched subjects. "So, is there any reason you're sitting out here?"

"*Nee.* Well, not really."

"Not really?"

"Well, I guess I wanted to get a good look at you when you got home."

"Because?"

"Because I wasn't sure what was going to happen when you showed up at the Kurtz *haus*." After pausing to cuddle the pup when he squirmed and shifted in her lap, she looked Lukas over. "Hmm. You look okay. I half thought you'd come back with a black eye."

He waved a hand over himself. "As you can see, I've returned unscathed."

She looked at him skeptically. "So Aaron didn't have a problem with you walking Darla home?"

"Not even a little bit," he lied. He didn't want Rebecca to worry about him, and he sure didn't want to betray just how bad things were at Darla's house.

"What about Patsy? What did she say?"

"Nothing much."

Her voice hardened. "Did she flirt with you?"

"Becky."

"You know how she is, Lukas. She's always wanted to be your girl."

He worked to keep his voice light because they'd been over this a dozen times during the last two years. "You make that sound like a bad thing."

"It is, because she ain't in love with you, Lukas. She simply wants to be a Kinsinger *frau*."

He knew what she meant. He didn't think of

it often, but his family had a lot of status in the town. For a woman like Patsy, that would trump even the suspicion that it was his family's fault her father died on the job.

But did he want to talk about that? Definitely not.

"Patsy was fine. Maisie was fine, too. I didn't see the twins."

"But you did see Aaron."

"I did, for sure." Hoping to end the mini interrogation, he said, "We had words and then he quit." Again, he wished he felt more comfortable sharing the complete truth with his sister, but if he told Becky that he'd fired Aaron she was going to want the whole story and he couldn't do that to Darla. Until she was ready to be more open about her brother's treatment of her, Lukas was going to do his best to guard her secrets. For now.

"What?" Her reaction startled Oscar. Popping his eyes open, he whined.

Unable to help himself, Lukas pulled the pup from Rebecca and settled him on his lap. As he gently ran two fingers along the soft white fur, Oscar yawned and stretched. Soon, he was cuddled on his side snoring softly. "He really is cute, Beck."

"I love him already. I know you didn't particularly want me getting a pup right now. And while

I agree that there are a hundred reasons why you were right, this little guy has claimed my heart. I've needed him, I think."

"I know."

"So, are you going to tell me about why Aaron up and quit?"

"He was planning to quit anyway," he hedged. "Remember? You told me Hope's family wants him to farm their land."

"I see." Of course, the look in her eyes said the opposite. She knew he was evading and she was going to let him. For now.

Lukas debated the consequences of telling her the rest. Not only would she push and nag and cajole to get the rest of the story, he now realized that he had to tell somebody. The situation was too serious not to. "Becky, something's happened with Aaron," he said at last. "His temper seemed out of control."

She relaxed. "It's probably just because you were there, Lukas. You can't have imagined that he'd take your appearance at his house in stride."

He knew she had a point. But he also knew what he'd witnessed—and that he hadn't gotten it wrong. "*Nee*, there was more. He yelled at Darla."

"She brought you to their house, Luke. I'm not surprised he yelled at her." Looking faintly amused, Rebecca added, "You would've yelled at me, too. Or Levi."

"Darla has dark fingerprint bruises on her shoulder and the nape of her neck."

Rebecca stilled. "And you think they are from Aaron?"

"I know they are. Aaron grabbed Darla five days ago."

Her eyes widened. "That is bad, for sure. But—"

"I'm not wrong about this." He swallowed and then shared the rest. "Maisie said that he takes his anger out on Darla. A lot. This wasn't a case of him simply not knowing his strength, Rebecca. He tried to hurt her."

She tilted her head to one side. "Do I even want to know how you know about those bruises?" she asked quietly.

"Probably not."

After seeming to weigh his response for a moment, she said, "Since I'm likely to hear about it eventually, you might as well tell me now."

"I made her show them to me."

"Lukas, you shouldn't have done that."

"I didn't have a choice. I wanted to see what they looked like." When he noticed that she was looking scandalized, he waved a hand. "Settle down. We all used to go swimming together, remember? I didn't undress the girl, I just asked to see her shoulder."

"But still. What would Daed have said?"

Lukas both hated and loved that Rebecca brought up their father. He had been steadfast and true. The guiding light in all their lives, especially for Rebecca. For her to bring him up made it seem like they weren't quite so alone.

"Daed would have said that I should have known that Darla was getting manhandled by her jerk of a brother and done something about it earlier."

"Daed wouldn't have expected you to save Darla from Aaron."

"If Daed was around, then John Kurtz would be, too. And if John was still alive, this wouldn't have happened."

"Point taken."

"I think Daed would have been just as shocked by Aaron's treatment of Darla as I was."

"You're right."

Feeling the crushing weight of responsibility, along with the overwhelming desire to be the kind of man who lived up to their father's expectations, he added, "It was all I could do to not go back and give Aaron a couple of bruises."

"I'm glad you did not do that."

"I think Darla was, too. She already wasn't too thrilled about me witnessing his abuse."

"What are you going to do?"

Lukas liked that Rebecca assumed he would do something. "I'm going to start walking her home every day."

"Do you think that will help?"

He shrugged. "I hope so. Now her family knows I'm back in her life. Maybe it will remind Aaron that she's not alone and that he can't bully her anymore. I tell you what, Becky. Darla Kurtz is done taking care of that needy family of hers and being abused and taken advantage of. Now, if they want something, they're going to have to go through me first."

Amusement lit Rebecca's eyes. "Watch out, Lukas. If you ain't careful you're going to reinforce everyone's belief that there is something between you two."

He stopped himself before contradicting her.

Just in case she wasn't wrong.

Chapter 11

March 29

Though only a few days had passed since he'd been fired, Aaron was coming to realize that spending the majority of each day in his own company hadn't improved his state of mind. It was also painfully obvious that having too much time on his hands wasn't doing him any favors.

Though Aaron had never minded farm work, he'd never cared for the solitary days spent in fields with only a hoe or a pair of horses. The enforced quiet got to him. So did the number of tasks that were never-ending. Before he knew what was happening, the long hours with only his doubts and worries to focus on made every problem feel pronounced and every doubt magnified.

Today was no different. As he looked toward the barn, the sun's descent over the horizon making him squint, Aaron's frustration with his life grew.

Whether he liked it or not, he was going to spend the majority of his life ankle-deep in mud with only his dark thoughts for company.

After unhooking the pair of field horses from the plow, Aaron headed toward the barn, wiping sweat from his brow with a bandanna. The horses followed behind him complacently. They seemed to be as eager as he to end the day.

He didn't blame them. It had been a long, exasperating day. He'd made more than one mistake and his mistakes had cost him precious time. Though he'd plowed many an hour by his father's side, Aaron was beginning to realize that he'd never really watched and listened to what his father had told him.

He wished he had. But just like the rest of his hopes and dreams, it was a wish that was doomed to remain unrealized. The fire at the mill had taken that.

Now, because of Lukas Kinsinger needing to prove something to Darla, Aaron didn't even have his job at the lumber mill.

Farming was all he had.

When he opened the barn doors, he realized

that neither Evan nor Samuel had done their chores. Anger filled his heart. Though he was tempted to march into the house and force them, he was too tired to make the effort.

All he wanted was to pull off his mud-covered boots, take a long shower, and finally sit down with a big glass of water.

"Come, Jack and Jill." After guiding the horses to a pen, he cleaned their stalls and refilled their water and feed troughs.

Forty minutes later, the horses were settled and he was wiping more sweat from his brow and neck. Aaron smelled like mud and straw and a whole lot of other things he'd rather not name.

Coming into the kitchen, the first thing he saw was Patsy cooking and the twins sitting at the table doing homework. All three of them glanced his way.

"You're in late," Patsy said.

Knowing the reason why, his temper snapped. "It's your fault, boys. You neglected your chores in the barn."

Evan frowned. "Sorry, Aaron. I forgot."

"You forgot?"

"*Jah*," Samuel said, looking uncomfortable. "We had a lot of homework. Percentages and writing."

He hated that they had excuses. "*Daed* would never have let me get away with that. You two are

worthless. You should have been out there. I had
to do your chores for you."

"That's enough, Aaron," Patsy said as she
turned away from the pot she was stirring at the
stove. "They made a mistake."

"Don't make excuses for them. They are too
old for that." Pointing to the door, he said, "You
both go up to your room. I'll deal with you in a
while."

Without a word, the boys gathered their books
together and went upstairs.

"What are you going to do?" Patsy asked.

"What do you think? I'm going to teach them
to mind me."

Patsy's eyes widened. "Daed wouldn't have
liked you being harsh with them."

"Daed ain't here."

"Aaron—"

"Leave me be!" he cried before stomping to the
stairs.

He was so tired. Exhausted. Worries about how
he was going to take care of Hope had filled his
night, forcing him to spend hours staring at the
dark instead of getting the rest he needed. He had
far too many burdens and no one to share them
with. No one with whom he could be completely
honest. He was floundering, his family was suffering, and there was no end in sight.

All because their father died far too young and now Aaron had no job.

The minute he turned the corner, he spied Darla walking down the stairs. It made no sense, but he'd grown to hate the sight of her.

She was thriving while he was suffering.

She was going on about her life while he was still trying to pick up the pieces.

"Hello, Aaron," she said, stepping to one side as he started walking up the stairs.

"Who brought you home?"

Her blue eyes clouded with worry. "What?"

"You know what I'm talking about. Did Kinsinger walk you home?" When she nodded, looking almost defiant, the last of his patience evaporated. His temper boiled to the surface and he was as unable to prevent himself from exploding as he was from controlling virtually anything else in his life.

But still he tried.

Gritting his teeth, he said, "I told you I didn't want you near Lukas. I told you that."

"You don't get to make that choice, Aaron. I'll spend time with Lukas if I want to."

Clenching his fists, he glared at her. "He fired me."

"You were going to quit, anyway," she said, as if she had any right to talk to him that way.

"Now, step aside. I need to go help Patsy finish supper."

When he refused to move, she sighed and attempted to push by him. Reaching out, he grabbed her wrist. "Don't walk away from me. I'm talking to you."

"Let go of me, Aaron."

Though his heart was telling him to release her, he couldn't make himself do that. His actions felt beyond his control. Before he realized what he was doing, he pressed harder, until he felt faint indentions form on her soft skin. "Don't tell me what to do. Ever."

When Darla cried out, he pulled. His mind in a fog, he saw her opposite hand reach for the banister and try to right herself. And because he was so much stronger, he watched himself jerk her wrist again.

Darla's voice turned shrill. Panicked. "Aaron! Let go!"

Doors opened above them. He heard his sisters gasp and his brothers whisper to each other.

He didn't dare look away from Darla. "Mind me, or I'll make you."

Tears formed in her eyes. Those blue eyes that were so like his own. She was breathing hard. The skin around her lips was white, though whether from pain or fear, he didn't know.

And then, like a switch had just been flipped, reality returned.

Appalled with himself, he dropped her arm. While she sagged against the wall, he tore upstairs. Not trusting himself to look any of his siblings in the eye, he stared straight ahead and strode past them all.

After grabbing a towel from the hallway linen closet, he walked directly to the bathroom and slammed the door behind him. He pulled the shower curtain back, turned on the water as hot as he could stand it, and stripped off his mud-caked and sweat-stained clothes.

Only then did he let himself think about the damage he'd likely done to his sister's wrist.

How much he'd frightened his little sisters.

How disappointed his father would have been.

Only then did he step into the hot spray, close his eyes, and silently cry.

Chapter 12

April 2

Hannah hoped her parents never discovered that she was starting to feel more at home on Plum Street than she did on her own street. As she lounged next to Christopher on the blue-and-yellow-checkered quilt in the Rosses' backyard, lazily looking through one of Mrs. Ross's *Better Homes & Gardens* magazines, Hannah tried to tell herself that this was just a passing phase.

But it didn't feel that way.

Maybe it was because she now called Mr. and Mrs. Ross by their Christian names, saying hello to York and Melissa each morning when she walked through their front door. Now, she got herself a cup of coffee while Melissa darted around the kitchen, doing just one more thing before rushing out the door. York and she now teased each other about everything from his determination to never carry an umbrella to how seriously he took his Tuesday night softball league game.

Maybe it was because she was spending more time with Christopher and his life than she was in her own Amish world.

Whatever the reason, she no longer stared at Christopher's favorite DVD in confusion, wondering why he was so fascinated with the cartoon figures or their outlandish songs. She could now work their microwave as easily as their washer and dryer.

And she no longer felt shy or awkward whenever Rob stopped by in the middle of the afternoon.

He never stayed very long, but after double-checking with Christopher's parents to make sure they didn't mind, Hannah had discovered that she looked forward to his company.

No doubt it was because of his happy personality. Rob was completely ignorant about her loss and, therefore, didn't treat her as if she might break. Instead, he told her about his job, which seemed to mainly consist of staring at a blank computer screen and writing copious research notes.

He was also something of a cook, which had taken her by surprise. At least once a week he brought her a bowl of soup he'd just made or a slice of pizza or, once, a plate of cookies.

"Hey, Hannah?"

Startled, she glanced to the side, where the split-rail fence divided the Rosses' yard with their neighbor's. When she saw it was Rob, she smiled. "Hello."

"Hey," he said again. "I saw you were out here and that Chris was sleeping. Want some company for a half hour?"

He always did that. He always asked permission to join her. He never pushed too hard or stayed too long. The first time he came over, he stayed for only ten minutes. Then it was fifteen. Now it seemed that they'd reached the thirty-minute mark.

In spite of knowing that she shouldn't be growing so attached to an English man, Hannah found herself looking forward to his visits. Now she didn't even pretend that she wasn't happy to see him.

"I've been looking at the same magazine page for the last hour. I'd love the company," she said with a smile.

Grinning, Rob opened up the gate and slipped through the rather narrow opening.

As he walked closer, Hannah noticed that he was wearing baggy army-green shorts, a white T-shirt, and flip-flops in honor of the warm day. Though shorts were new, his casualness was not. She'd never seen him in anything as fancy as Mr. Ross's work clothes, and she was starting to wonder if he'd look the same or different in more formal attire.

"I see you've got on your summer sandals again," she teased.

"Yep." He looked down at his feet. "Even though I've been wearing flip-flops for the last three weeks, my feet are still pasty white. I'm working on my tan."

She grinned. "Maybe you should bring your computer outside so your toes can get some sun."

"I would if I thought I'd get anything done." Shrugging, he said, "Looks like I'm not the only person on Plum Street trying to get tan toes. You've got your tennis shoes off today."

Before she realized what she was doing, she scrunched her toes on the warm quilt. "I couldn't help myself."

"That's good. You need to enjoy today, Hannah. Why, tomorrow, it could be sleeting or something."

Rob always said things like that. He seemed to enjoy living in the moment as much as she was starting to. "I thought the same thing. After Christopher ate his snack, we came out here to look at books. Before long, he fell asleep." Belatedly, she realized that not only had she been sunning her feet, but she'd hiked the skirt of her dress up to her knees. Feeling her cheeks heat, she pulled the hem of her skirt down.

"Don't do that on my account. Believe it or not, I've seen girls' calves before." His voice was light-hearted and kind. Gently teasing.

Because she felt so comfortable, she spoke without thinking. "I bet you've seen more than that."

To her amusement, he looked embarrassed. "Maybe."

"Sorry. I spoke out of turn."

"No reason to apologize," he said as he stretched out by her side. "My life is an open book."

"Uh-oh. You better look out. Before you know it, I'll be discovering all sorts of things about your secret past."

He chuckled. "It's not so secret. You know I moved here from Chicago."

"*Jah*, but that doesn't tell me much. After all, Chicago is a big city."

"It is," he said agreeably. "Feel free to ask me anything you like."

"All right. Well, I know that you are from Chicago and that you have no family here."

He raised a brow. "What else do you need to know?"

"I am wondering why you decided to settle in Charm. Can you tell me about that?"

For once, his dark eyes were shadowed. "I, uh, had a girlfriend. We were serious. She was killed in an accident."

Well, now she felt worse than bad. She should have kept her questions to herself. "I'm so sorry," she said quietly.

"Me, too," he said, matching her tone. "Anyway, after a time, I realized that I needed a change of scenery. When my older sister, who enjoys staying in country bed-and-breakfasts, told me about Holmes County and how peaceful it was out here, I decided to come out here for a weekend."

Hannah tried to imagine what a city man like Rob had thought of Charm the first time he'd seen it. "And did you find it peaceful?"

"I did. The first night I was here, I slept through the whole night. I hadn't done that in months." He leaned back on his hands and crossed his ankles. "Next thing I knew, I was putting an offer on a house." Turning to face her, he said, "So that, Hannah, is how I ended up on Plum Street."

She felt both stunned and embarrassed. Here

she had been, thankful that she didn't have to face any prying questions, and she'd just done that very thing to him. "I am sorry. I didn't mean to pry."

"You didn't pry. We're getting to know each other. That's what friends do."

They were friends. She was spending more time with him lately than she had with many of her Amish girlfriends. Maybe it was time to share a little bit of herself, too. "I also lost someone close to me. A boyfriend."

Though it was obvious he was trying to appear relaxed, she noticed his body tense. "By lost, do you mean broke up?"

"*Nee.* I mean, no. I mean, he died." Taking a fortifying breath, she forced herself to be completely honest. "Paul died in that lumber mill fire about four months ago. Did you hear of it?"

He shook his head. "I'm sorry. I haven't been talking to too many people. Basically, I work on my computer all day, walk Rose, and talk about the weather with the neighbors—if I talk to them at all." Staring at her intently, he said, "So, what happened? I mean, if you want to talk about it, I'd like to hear."

She didn't want to talk about it but she didn't want to be rude. Hannah also supposed she needed to talk about the fire more if she was ever going to put all the pain from the incident behind her.

Reminding herself that Paul was in Heaven and no amount of talking was going to make her miss him any more or less, she began slowly. "In mid-December, a fire broke out in one of the back warehouses at Kinsinger Lumber Mill. A rag saturated with wood stain caught on fire inside a Dumpster. I guess there was some metal inside that had been heated, as well as a large amount of scrap wood, which acted as kindling. The Dumpster exploded and set the warehouse on fire. Five men died."

"That's incredible." Rob looked stunned. "I didn't know such things could happen."

"They usually don't, but lumber mills can be dangerous places, I guess." She swallowed, both hating and feeling proud that she was able to speak so knowledgeably about the accident that had claimed Paul's life. This, she thought, was a sign of how much she'd healed.

"Did they catch who started it?"

"He died. But it was an accident." She swallowed. "As best anyone can figure, a whole lot of factors came together, which didn't usually happen. No one knows why."

"I'm really sorry, Hannah. You're so young. That had to be hard on you."

Did her age really matter? Thinking about the Kinsinger family, about Darla and her little sister Maisie . . . Hannah knew none of their ages made death easier to handle or harder to bear.

Unable to look at Rob, she struggled to keep her voice calm and steady. For some reason she needed to be able to discuss Paul's death without breaking down. "The police and firemen said the men didn't suffer too much."

"I heard the same thing about Julia." He lifted his head. "Does that make you feel better?"

"Not especially. I, um, canna seem to ignore the 'too much' part."

"Me, neither." He stared ahead at nothing, his mouth set in a firm line. "Do you . . . Have you ever wished to get away and change cities, too?"

"*Nee*. Charm is my home. But, well, I have recently realized that I've changed my life, too. I took this job just a month after Paul passed away. Now, instead of being at home, I spend most of my time here in the Rosses' house. Melissa and York are nice. And, well, I think I needed to be around little Christopher here. He keeps me busy and doesn't ask questions."

He chuckled. "I bet he doesn't. Though now that he's rolling over, he seems determined to wear everyone around him out."

"Especially me."

"Maybe not especially you," he said quietly. "I'm beginning to think that maybe you are invincible."

His praise made her feel good but it was unwarranted. "Never that. I'm simply coping. Lately I have realized that I've put a lot of distance between me and my old circle of friends. I needed to start over fresh. I don't know if that is good or not."

After eyeing her closely, he shrugged. "Hannah, maybe it doesn't matter if what you are doing is good or bad."

"You don't think?" That sounded too easy.

"This is just me, but maybe all that matters is that being here helps you heal and cope."

She shrugged. "Maybe so." As she looked at Rob sitting next to her, his face a little scruffy from the beard he never completely shaved, the frayed hem of his shorts, his pale feet, Hannah realized that she had, indeed, learned to cope. "God is good," she said.

His brows went up, making her realize that there probably weren't too many people in his life who talked about God like she did.

But then he relaxed. "You know, a couple of weeks ago, I might have disagreed with you, but now I feel the same way. God is good."

She smiled at him before looking back at Christopher. As he continued to breathe softly, his little chest pumping up and down, and his mouth open into a tiny O, Hannah realized that if Paul had lived, she probably wouldn't have ever made the decision to get this job. Now she was getting paid to spend her days with a sweet baby and even a few minutes visiting with Rob. She was doing things she'd never imagined but managing to find joy in them. She couldn't deny that she'd been able to find a little bit of happiness.

"Hey, Hannah?"

"*Jah?*"

"Even though I've already been sitting here for thirty minutes, would you mind if I just sit here with you for a few minutes longer? We don't even have to talk."

"I don't mind." She leaned back on her elbows and closed her eyes, enjoying the warmth of the sun on her face and the faint scent of Christopher's baby lotion in the air.

And the quiet presence of Rob sitting next to her. He'd become her friend.

And now that she knew that he, too, had loved and lost so much, she thought that he might just be the best friend she'd ever had.

SHE WAS STILL thinking about Rob and their easygoing conversation when she walked home from work that afternoon. After stopping in the market to buy a bouquet of fresh flowers they had on sale for her mother, Hannah practically ran into Aaron Kurtz.

He held out his hands to steady her. "Whoa," he said with a light smile. "Are you all right?"

"*Jah.*" Looking a little sheepish, she said, "I fear I was thinking more about these daisies than where I was going."

"What's the occasion?"

"For the flowers? Oh, there is no occasion. I simply thought my mother might enjoy them. She loves daisies."

Something in Aaron's face altered, the relaxed expression he wore hardening. "It's a blessing you have a mother still. We lost ours when Daed perished in the fire."

Hannah didn't want to be unkind, but she was beginning to think that every single conversation with him centered on the fire and his father's passing. "I worked all day. It's past time that I headed home."

"*Jah.* You had better do that. Your parents will no doubt be worried about ya."

Slipping past him, she clutched the flowers against her chest and started back down the sidewalk. For a good fifty yards, she walked briskly, anxious to put some distance between herself and

Aaron's hurt and pain. Unfortunately, the distance didn't make her brief interaction with him any easier to bear. One five-minute conversation with him had removed her happy mood and the optimism she'd been feeling.

Right then and there she made a vow to keep her distance from Aaron Kurtz. Something felt off about him.

Since she couldn't help him, she had to help herself.

Chapter 13

It was almost becoming a habit. For a week now, Lukas had worked late, walked out of the mill's office a little after four in the afternoon, did what little errands needed doing, then proceeded to the post office.

Once there, he would either wait on one of the wooden benches lining the sidewalk in front until Darla finished serving customers or he would come inside. Whether he stayed inside or out depended largely on who was inside being helped. If they were friends, he might stop in and say hello, but Lukas was discovering that he didn't always feel like socializing with the whole community at the end of his workday.

Instead, he liked simply being around Darla and enjoying their quiet conversations. It seemed Rebecca was right; Darla Kurtz really did mean a lot to him, maybe more than he'd ever imagined. However, instead of being distressed by this, the notion entertained him. He liked that he was still getting to know a woman he'd known for the majority of his life.

That was why he couldn't help but smile when he peeked in the window and realized that, today, she was completely alone.

She was in one of the mismatched chairs that decorated the small post office lobby, her legs stretched out in front of her. The late afternoon sun was streaming in through the sparkling front window, and Darla had her eyes closed, obviously enjoying the warm rays of light shining on her skin. He was suddenly reminded of a cat lounging in the sun.

As he watched her, Lukas was struck by her innocent beauty. Darla's personality was so attractive to him it was easy to overlook her auburn hair and flawless skin. He certainly had. He'd always thought she was cute, and she was.

But really, she was more than that.

Or maybe it was just that his heart now realized she was so much more?

Not wanting anyone to see him staring at her

through the window, he opened the door and walked inside.

Darla started. Her eyelids popped open and she jerked her head to the side meeting his gaze with a guilty flush. "Lukas, please don't tell me that I've been sitting here with my eyes closed while you've been standing there."

Crossing the empty room, he smiled. "You haven't been sitting here with your eyes closed. I haven't been watching you sit in the sun like you were lounging on a towel at Siesta Key."

She squeezed her eyes shut. "I'm hopeless."

He chuckled. "You're human. It's a nice day and the sun feels warm. I'm glad you were letting yourself relax for a minute or two."

"Or ten," she corrected, looking embarrassed. After darting a glance at the clock on the wall, she got to her feet. "You're early today. Do you have plans for later?"

"Not really. It was kind of a slow day at the mill. I decided to get out of there and bother you until you got off work."

"Obviously, it's been kind of slow here, too."

"So, you won't mind if I keep you company for the next hour?"

"Not at all." Her puzzled expression warmed. "Guess what? Patsy baked this morning. I brought in two slices of chocolate zucchini bread. Want a slice?"

"Of course." Patsy was a flirt and flighty but she could bake better than just about anyone else in Charm. "What was the occasion?"

"Oh, I don't know. She made the bread because it's my favorite."

He was glad about that, he really was. But Patsy didn't do things for Darla without a reason. He began to study Darla more carefully. He hated that he was doing it, but he started looking for bruises and marks. He watched her turn to the white wicker basket she sometimes carried to work and carefully pull out two slices wrapped in waxed paper.

Then he saw her wrist.

Lukas was a man who'd worked all his life in a lumber mill. Accidents were common; it was the nature of the job. But little in life had prepared him for the sight of her delicate wrist swollen and marked with dark bruises. "Darla," he bit out, hardly trusting himself to remain in check.

"What? Oh." After noticing what he was staring at, she awkwardly pushed her sleeve down.

His temper flared and the only way he was able to contain himself was to remember that his anger wouldn't make her feel any better. "What happened?" he asked, though he felt foolish even uttering the question.

Her averted gaze told him everything he needed to know. Everything he already had known. Now all he had to do was figure out how he was going to be able to stop himself from going directly to her house and giving her brother a piece of his mind. Or worse.

He'd never believed in violence. He'd always believed in turning the other cheek and seeking to solve problems in a peaceful manner. But right now, at that moment, Lukas knew if Aaron Kurtz was standing in front of him, he'd hit him.

He'd hit him hard, and without a bit of remorse.

"THIS CAN'T CONTINUE, Darla," Lukas said through clenched teeth. "I promise you, I'm going to put a stop to this today."

Feeling the anger emanating from him, Darla had visions of Lukas throwing open the post office door, racing out to her farm, and attacking her brother.

Fearing that would happen, she hurried to his side. "Please, Lukas. Calm down."

"I don't know if that's possible."

Even though his body was fairly trembling with his anger, she rested her palm on his bicep. "Please?" she asked.

Her touch seemed to do what her words couldn't. With a shiver accompanied by a ragged sigh, he attempted to regain his composure. Gently, she squeezed his arm when he closed his eyes.

A second passed. Then two. Three. After taking another deep breath, he opened his eyes again and stared directly at her. Now his expression filled with concern instead of anger. "When did he do this? When did he hurt you?"

"I'm not hurt," she blurted automatically. When she saw his eyes flare, she realized she was now used to denying that she'd ever been hurt. It made her wonder who she was protecting—Aaron or herself? Did it even matter?

Instead of arguing, Lukas reached for her hand on his arm. As if she were made of spun glass, he gently slid up her sleeve until most of her forearm was bare. Then, just as methodically, he held up her wrist to the fluorescent light shining above them. In the unforgiving light, the dark marks shone on her skin like angry symbols. Representations of all the pain that was in her house. In her family's lives. She could hardly look at them. Not because they were so painful, but because the stark blemishes made her finally accept that she needed help. Lukas's help.

She'd really hoped to be stronger.

Though his grip on her arm was still gentle, his voice was gravelly when he spoke again. "If you ain't hurt, what do ya call these marks then, Darla?"

She couldn't answer him. Instead, she continued to stare at her arm.

At her continued silence, he rotated her wrist a bit. "If this ain't bad, what is?"

"Shtobb."

"Nee, I ain't gonna stop." He continued to push her. "If this isna him treating you roughly, what do you call it when you get marked up like this?"

His words embarrassed her. "Lukas, please . . ."

"Manhandled?" he asked sarcastically. *"Nee?* Hmm. What description sounds better?" he persisted, his voice thick with sarcasm. "Did he merely forget himself? Yet again?"

Tears pricked at her eyes. "Stop, Lukas," she said again.

Immediately, he did stop. He exhaled, and there before her eyes, the anger in his expression ebbed away. "I'm sorry," he said as he pressed both of his palms against her cheeks, cradling her face like it was dear to him. "I'm sorry. I . . . It's just that you have to know how hard it is to realize that you are getting hurt when I'm not around. It makes me want to keep you by my side twenty-four hours a day." Now, gently caressing her cheeks with his thumbs, he whispered, "It makes me want to do whatever it takes to keep you safe and protected."

Her breath hitched. She hated Lukas's anger. Hated how her wrist looked. Hated the memory of how she'd received the bruises last night. But most of all, she hated knowing that it had happened many times before and would likely happen many times again.

As a single tear escaped and trailed down her cheek, she pulled away. As she had known he would, he released her easily. Part of her yearned to run from his sight but there was nowhere for her to go.

Instead, she remained where she was, breathing hard, as if she'd run a race.

Lukas, too, was breathing heavily. His gray-blue eyes were stormy and it was obvious that he was determined to not frighten her. "This needs to stop, Darla. He could have broken your wrist," he said at last. Each word sounded as if it were being pulled from his soul.

She couldn't look at him any longer. "I know."

As if he couldn't resist touching her, he wiped her tears with a thumb. His callouses were rough against her skin, yet they didn't feel bad. Instead, it reminded her of how much she liked his touch. She shivered.

He noticed. There was a new awareness in his

eyes that had nothing to do with anger or worry and everything to do with the new intimacy that was forming between the two of them. "Do ya? Finally?" he asked.

She nodded.

Dropping his hand, he spoke. "I'm going to talk to him tonight, and this time I'm gonna make him listen. If necessary, I'm going to bring Levi with me. Or Simon."

She couldn't bear to let anyone else know. "Please, don't bring anyone with you."

Lowering his voice, he said, "We can contact the police, you know."

She shook her head. "*Nee*, we cannot. I am not going to involve the English in my problems."

"They could help you."

"I don't want them."

He sighed. "I know you don't want anyone else to know, but you may not have a choice."

"Not yet."

"All right. But then you need to let me speak to him." Looking somber, he added, "Darla, I want to make sure he understands that I'm not fooling around."

"He won't think that." Lukas was over six feet, had to weigh almost two hundred pounds, and was heavily muscled. His current expression was rather murderous.

"I've already talked to him once. He ignored me. If we don't put a stop to this now, Aaron could hurt someone else. What if he harms Gretel or Maisie?"

Even imagining Aaron taking out his frustration and anger on them made her feel sick. "He would never touch my little sisters."

"Are you sure?"

She nodded weakly because she was unable to tell him the truth. Aaron's behavior was so erratic, she wasn't sure what he would do next.

He lifted up her hand again. "What would you do if little Gretel's wrists looked like this? Would you tell her that they were only bruises?" His voice hardened. "Would you tell her that the pain didn't matter?"

She flinched. "Of course not."

"If he hurts you, he's going to eventually hurt Maisie or Gretel or Patsy. It's the way of abusers. If you stand up to him, he'll find someone who won't. Maybe he'll even harm Hope."

She shook her head. "He wouldn't. He loves Hope."

"He loves you, too. But, Darla, do you see we're out of options?"

Wearily, she nodded. "All right."

For the first time since he'd spied her wrist his body relaxed. "So, what brought it on?"

She closed her eyes. "We argued last night. He got tired of it."

"What were you arguing about?"

She didn't want to admit that Lukas had been the subject, but it was too late to try to hide anything now. "Our renewed friendship, Lukas. Aaron wanted me to stay away from you. When I told him that wasn't going to happen, he . . . well, he got upset."

Immediately, the tension in the small room heightened again. "He has a lot of nerve." Looking at the door, he said, "I'm tempted to go to the mill, get Levi and Simon and face him this minute."

What could she say? She had wanted to solve things herself. She had promised Lukas that she would tell him if Aaron harmed her again. Instead, she'd hidden her wrist under a long-sleeved dress and pretended her wrist wasn't marked.

"I understand your reluctance to get other people involved, but he needs to be stopped. It might be better if we have witnesses, too."

The idea of Lukas swooping in to help her was as appealing as it was scary. But then she imagined the further pain it would cause. "The three of you acting as my avenging angels isn't the way to handle Aaron."

"Patsy making you chocolate zucchini bread ain't gonna make things better, either."

She felt frustrated and tired. Oh, so tired. He was right, but sometimes she just wanted to forget everything. She wanted to go back to sitting in a sunny spot in the room with her legs stretched out.

"Darla, honey, you know I'm only pushing because I care about you."

"I care about you, too. You know that. But we need to come up with a better way to handle Aaron. Maybe we should speak to the bishop."

"The bishop will feel sorry for ya, but I don't think he's going to interfere right away. We need to do something tonight."

She could just see what was going to happen. He would walk her home, stewing and fretting. Then, the minute Aaron showed up, Lukas would say too much and possibly even threaten her brother. Aaron would lash out, lose that argument, and later, take it out on her.

She needed to put a stop to it before things got worse. "Please, Lukas. Don't be so pushy. Maybe . . . maybe I should go home on my own today instead of you accompanying me."

He flinched as if she'd slapped him. "I'm trying to help you—I'm pretty much the *only* person trying to help you—yet you're still pushing me away?"

It didn't matter that his words were true. They still hurt.

She needed to think about that and about what to do next. Most of all, she needed time to think about what he was offering and what it would mean to accept his help, as well as how it would affect Patsy, Maisie, and Gretel—and even Hope.

"If that is what you wish to call it, then yes."

Disappointment clouded his features. "I thought we were friends again."

He was more than just a friend to her. After all, she was fairly sure that friends didn't caress each other's cheek the way he'd caressed hers. "Friends don't interfere with each other's lives the way you are doing."

"They do, Darla," he countered. "At least, they should. No one can do everything. Not Aaron. Not you and not me."

He sounded so frustrated, so betrayed, that she admitted what she most feared. "If you come over and threaten Aaron, it won't make him afraid. He'll simply be angry. Then, after you go home, I'll have to deal with the consequences."

"Then . . . then come home with me."

"Go home with you." He might as well have asked her to begin work in the lumberyard. "What then, Lukas? What would you want me to do next? Move in with ya?" She rolled her eyes. "Now, that would go over well. What am I going to do? Be Rebecca's new best friend?"

Looking tense, he studied her. That muscle in his jaw seemed to work double time. Then he blurted, "Marry me."

"What?"

"If you marry me, it will solve all our problems. You can move in. The gossip will stop. The tension between our two families will ease."

"First, that's doubtful. Secondly, that won't help my sisters and brothers."

"Fine. I'll . . . I'll move into your house."

The idea of the wealthy, assured Lukas Kinsinger living in their ramshackle home and sharing the bathroom with her twin brothers was laughable. "Oh, for heaven's sake, Lukas. Stop."

"I'm being serious."

"I am, too. Even . . . even if we married . . . you couldn't live on my family's farm."

"Why not? Aaron is planning to move to Hope's family farm." He took a breath. "If I did that, I could take care of you, and your family's financial situation would ease."

She was a grown woman. She'd lived most of her life taking care of her siblings and trying to be everything to everyone. So why did the idea of Lukas taking care of her sound so appealing? Was she so needy? Or was it because she would be Lukas's wife and he would be hers forever?

Embarrassed by the direction of her thoughts,

she brushed off his words. "Lukas, you seem to forget that we would be *married*. To each other. For life."

"And what is wrong with that?" His voice was soft. Tender, even.

At the moment, she wasn't so sure. Except, oh yeah. He didn't love her.

Forcing herself to look cool and collected, she said, "*Everything* is wrong with that, Lukas. People don't get married for the reasons you are stating."

"Of course they do."

Feeling a bit like a broken record, she uttered, "Lukas, stop."

He didn't. Instead, he stepped closer, invading her space, invading her will. "Oh, yes. I forgot. Marriage is the product of romance and rainbows. Puppies. Kittens."

"I didn't say that."

"You implied it." Standing closer, close enough that she could smell the soap on his skin, he loomed over her. "But even though you have all the answers, you are forgetting that a marriage is also an agreement between two parties." Reaching out, he took one of her hands and pressed his palms on either side of it. "You know our grandparents surely didn't marry just for love. They were practical people."

She supposed that was true. When she was a

little girl, she remembered her *grandmommi* Mary sharing how she and Dawdi had been set up by their parents. In a weird, convoluted way, Lukas's reasoning made sense. She could understand why he thought a marriage based on need instead of love could work.

But that didn't mean she agreed with him. "I am not going to marry you to save my body from being bruised by my grieving *bruder*, Lukas."

His gray eyes, which had looked as cloudy as dawn on a spring day, now looked as hard as flint. "I am not joking, Darla. Something needs to be done."

"Lukas, I am grateful for your offer. You honor me," she added, meaning every word. "But a quick wedding between us is not the thing to do. When things get better with Aaron, you will regret your offer and resent my acceptance. We both know that."

"Think about it, Darla. Just think about it."

What he didn't realize was that there was a secret part of her that was actually considering it. He was her childhood crush. He was her best friend. He was the man she'd mooned over when she was a teenager and who could still make her breath catch now.

And, well, it was so tempting to allow him to protect her. She was tired. She'd love nothing better than to lean on him. To give him her burdens and simply be. To hold his hand. To take comfort in his arms. And, yes, to feel his lips on hers. To kiss him.

She knew these thoughts weren't right. She knew she wasn't supposed to think about any of it, and most especially not with a man whom her family now viewed as their enemy.

"Lukas, I cannot say yes to you." Not for the reasons he gave, anyway.

"You think a union between the two of us would be so terrible?"

She didn't. That was part of the problem, of course. Because of that, she lied. "I do."

Hurt filled his gaze. "I see."

Even though she knew she was doing the right thing for both of them, she felt so very bad. Rejecting him felt wrong. "I'm glad you do," she replied. Her voice was stiff.

"That's all you have to say?"

"There is nothing else to say." That, at least, was the truth. The rest of her felt so jumbled and confused, she knew nothing she could say would make a bit of sense.

"You know what? You are right," he replied, his voice as harsh and grating as sandpaper across her skin. "If that is the most you have to say, it's better if we say nothing at all."

"Lukas, I am sorry."

"I am, too. Let's forget this ever happened. And if you can, try and forgive me for wanting to look out for you. Especially since I'm still going to speak to your *bruder* tonight. I'd rather have you mad at me than be hurt again. What he is doing ain't right, Darla, and I'm going to do everything in my power to make sure he doesn't do it again," he added over his shoulder before striding out the door.

Darla tried to summon the courage to run after him, but she couldn't. He was right. Aaron had to stop. Especially because she'd never be able to live with herself if he started hurting her sisters or the twins.

As she stared at the shut door, she realized that another part of her life had just ended. No longer was she going to be able to depend on Lukas Kinsinger to be her friend and confidant. She was going to have to stop daydreaming about the man and secretly harboring a childhood crush.

Things between them had changed, and most likely for the better, too.

It was simply too bad that doing the right thing left her feeling even more alone than ever before. She hadn't known such a thing was possible.

Feeling bereft, Darla slumped against the counter and peered through the plate-glass window, unable to help herself from watching Lukas walk across the street and blend in with the smattering of pedestrians on the sidewalk.

It seemed he was now completely out of her life—because she had pushed him away.

Chapter 14

Lukas left for the Kurtz house three hours after he saw Darla. He'd gone home after his visit to the post office and checked on Amelia. She'd been exhausted after working all day on everyone's laundry. Lukas had felt so bad for her, he'd fed and watered the animals, then peeled potatoes and chopped vegetables for their supper. Though Amelia had protested that cooking supper was her job, not his, Lukas had been grateful for the mindless activity.

The truth was that he'd been smarting from Darla's rejection. He had needed time to mentally prepare himself for what he wanted to say to Aaron. For a moment, he'd even considered asking Levi to come with him to the Kurtz house, but he'd immediately disregarded that idea. Though Levi would certainly stand up with him, and be a good support, Lukas feared that his younger brother's animosity toward Aaron for John's role in the mill fire would only make things worse.

There was another reason, too. Lukas cared about Darla. Cared about her a lot. So much so that he didn't want another man solving her problems. He'd taken on the role of her defender and he wanted to be the one to make things right.

Therefore, he walked to the Kurtz house on his own, the vision of Darla's swollen and bruised wrist as clear in his mind as the wildflowers decorating the side of the road.

When he was halfway up the drive, the front door opened and Patsy and Maisie came out, along with one of the twins. He'd never had much luck differentiating between Samuel and Evan, though if he had to take a guess, he thought he was likely staring at Evan.

Maybe it was the forceful way he was walking or maybe they simply didn't get a lot of callers, but whatever the reason, the three of them stood in a row at the porch's battered white railing and watched him approach.

"Lukas? Everything okay?" Patsy called out when he was just a few yards away.

He didn't know how to answer that. Instead, he kept walking, silently rehearsing the words he intended to say to Aaron.

"Darla's inside her room," Maisie said. "Want me to go get her?"

"Not this time."

"Why are you here, then?" the boy asked.

"I need to speak to Aaron. Now, if you please," he added as he came to a stop at the bottom of the steps.

The three Kurtzes looked at one another. From where Lukas was standing, he could see various expressions of worry lighting their eyes.

"I . . . I don't know if he's here," Patsy sputtered at last. "You need me to take a message?"

He knew Patsy was lying, but instead of arguing, he nodded. "If he ain't here, I'll wait."

Looking down at him, Patsy frowned. "You sure? It could be a while."

"I've got time."

The boy looked perplexed. After exchanging a glance with Patsy, he went inside. Lukas wondered if he was going to speak to Aaron.

"You want a glass of water, Lukas?" Maisie asked.

"*Nee*. I'm good. I'll, uh, have a seat here on the steps and wait," he added, taking care not to ask permission.

To his surprise, instead of arguing or leaving the porch, Patsy walked over and sat down a few steps above him. Seconds later, Maisie hesitantly joined them.

"What did Aaron do?" Patsy asked after they sat in silence for a few minutes.

"I'd rather not discuss it with you. No offense, Patsy."

"You look upset, Luke," Maisie said.

Unable to help himself, Lukas eyed her carefully, checking for signs of worry or anxiousness. He already hated the thought of Aaron harming Darla, but to see that Maisie might have already been learning to fear a man's anger made him feel physically ill. Luckily, however, the little girl didn't look frightened, only curious.

"I'm upset, but not at you, May," he said. "I simply need to talk to your *bruder* for a few minutes."

"Is this about the mill?" Patsy asked.

"*Nee.*"

"Then it must be Darla."

With effort, Lukas remained silent.

"Is Darla all right?" Maisie asked. "When she got home, she didn't try to help me with my homework like she usually does. She just went straight to her room."

Lukas hated that. Hated that she had no one to lean on in her family.

"I saw her earlier," he bit out. He didn't want to ignore the girl's question but it was almost impossible for him to reassure her about Darla's state. All he could imagine was her hurting at night when she lay down to sleep. Or worse, having to guard herself against Aaron.

They heard a shuffle from the other side of the screen door, then it swung open with a squeak. Heavy footsteps marked Aaron's appearance.

Maisie brightened. "Oh, look! Aaron was here after all."

"So it would seem," Lukas said as he got to his feet.

Patsy stood up as well, but she remained silent.

Aaron stared at him, his arms folded across his chest. "Heard you came over to talk to me?"

"I did." Eyeing him carefully, Lukas was vaguely surprised to see that Aaron looked much the same. He wasn't sure what he'd expected. Maybe more angry? Maybe bigger? "I need to speak with you in private."

Aaron's posture stiffened, but otherwise he remained still. "Why?"

"I'd rather speak about that when we are alone."

Aaron's eyes flashed. "Patsy and Maisie, go on inside."

Though Maisie obeyed immediately, Patsy stared at Lukas with hope in her eyes. "I think

I would rather hear what Lukas Kinsinger has to say."

"Stay or go." Aaron shrugged. "Makes no difference to me."

Lukas was tempted to argue, but then he figured there really was no point. Maybe it would be better if Patsy heard what he had to say, too. If she was getting hurt, she would know she wasn't alone. Or at the very least, she would know that he was determined to help her.

After Maisie went inside and closed the door, Lukas looked Aaron directly in the eye. "I visited Darla today at the post office."

"Yeah? So?"

"I saw her wrist. I saw where you grabbed her."

After a momentary flash of pain entered his eyes, Aaron exhaled. "That's what your visit is about?" His voice was full of bluster. "You're upset because I gripped my sister's arm a little too tightly?" He smirked. "Don't you have anything better to do? Or are you simply looking for a reason to bother us?"

"This wasn't a case of you gripping her too tight, though I fail to understand why you would be gripping her in the first place. You hurt her. On purpose."

"She is fine."

"She is not. I've told you that this needs to stop.

Last time I saw her bruises, I let her handle it, but it's obvious that didn't work." Looking at Aaron directly in the eye, he said, "I've decided to get involved. Listen to me, and listen to me good, Aaron. You need to keep your distance from her from now on."

Aaron rolled his eyes. "She's my sister. I ain't gonna keep my distance." He faced Lukas directly so they were standing chest to chest. "Now *you* listen to *me*. You need to stop interfering in our lives. I don't work for you no longer. I've also forbid Darla to see you. So she ain't your business, neither. Get off our property."

Lukas noticed that Patsy hadn't said a word. Turning to her, he said quietly, "Has he hurt you, too?"

Seconds passed. Then, to Lukas's surprise, she nodded. "*Jah*. But only once."

Aaron clenched his fists. "Enough, Patsy."

Patsy looked at Lukas for a long moment before turning to her brother. "I saw you grab her wrist in the kitchen."

"It was an accident," Aaron mumbled. "She'll be all right."

After pursing her lips together, she said, "Lukas, tell me. How did you find out about her wrist?"

"I saw it when she was reaching for something. It's swollen. You could have broken it, Aaron."

Patsy stared at him hard. "Is . . . Is that what Darla said?"

"*Nee*. She tried to excuse you, Aaron," Lukas said, not even attempting to hide his derision. "I felt bad for her, I did. She was embarrassed about her bruises, though I can't imagine why she'd ever be embarrassed to show me. But then she went and asked me to ignore her marks. Her pain." He exhaled, doing his best to keep his voice steady. "But I couldn't. I care about her. And I care about the rest of you." Studying the man standing across from him, who was almost his match in girth and height, Lukas said, "Have you grabbed Maisie like that? Or Gretel?"

"I am in charge of this family. Because of your mill, I have no father."

"What about Hope? Have you hurt her?"

Pure pain entered his eyes. "Of course not."

"Only your sisters."

"Like I said—"

Lukas couldn't listen to another meaningless excuse. "You try to explain. Because of your inability to care for your sister, she is bruised." He stepped closer. "I'm telling you now, Aaron, it needs to stop. I don't know what happened to you. Right now I don't care. But you are going to need to figure out a different way to handle yourself."

He flinched.

And with that flinch, Lukas knew he'd at last hit a nerve. "Talk to someone. Talk to the preacher. Meet with the bishop. Chop wood, go for walks. I don't know. But stop taking out your grief and frustration on the people you love."

Aaron clenched his fists, looking prepared to lash out at Lukas. But then he slumped. "What's happened to me?" he whispered before turning away and walking toward the barn.

When he was out of sight, Patsy reached out to Lukas. Curling her hand around his elbow, she squeezed, then stepped forward and hugged him. "Thank you for caring," she said at last. "I knew Aaron was taking out the worst of his anger on Darla, but not to that extent," she said when she stepped away.

"He and I might not be friends, and we might never get past what happened at the mill, but I couldn't sit by and not do or say anything, Patsy." Because he felt that she was finally being honest with him, he uttered, "I even offered to marry Darla as soon as possible."

"You want to marry her?"

"I want her safe. I can't stand the idea of her being at Aaron's mercy. I can't stand the thought of her getting hurt again."

"Because you love her."

Maybe that was the reason. Maybe he always

had loved Darla. Or maybe it was because he couldn't stand the thought of little Maisie one day wearing the same marks. Or perhaps it was because the whole family seemed lost, and in spite of knowing that it wasn't his family's fault, he still felt that he had to do something.

But if he admitted any of that, it would be too much. So he shrugged. "Because I care."

"Sometimes caring is enough."

He shrugged. "I meant what I said, Patsy. Your brother needs to grow up and learn some self-control. If this happens again, I'll walk Aaron to the bishop myself, after I take Darla to my house. If you need me, just ask."

"You mean that, don't you?"

"Of course. I promise, if any of you need me, just ask. Ask and I will help. No matter what time it is. No matter what else I'm doing."

"Danke." She looked about to say more, then stilled.

When he turned, he saw who had caught her attention. And then he prepared himself to take part in another verbal battle.

Only this one would likely be far harder.

Chapter 15

He'd kept his word.

Lukas had come over and talked to Aaron. He hadn't lost his temper and he hadn't hurt anyone. He'd simply been the man Darla had always known him to be—stalwart, firm, impressive.

It was no wonder Lukas was the mark by which she measured every other man.

Ignoring the stares of Patsy and the rest of her siblings who were just steps behind her, Darla walked to him. As she approached, Lukas kept his expression carefully blank. Whether it was because he was uneasy or because he knew they were being watched, she didn't know. She was simply glad he was there.

"Hey," he said at last.

"Hi. Do you have time to talk with me, or would you rather leave?" She didn't want to keep him here if he needed some distance from her family.

His features softened some, as if he was slightly amused by her question. "Of course I have time for you."

Keeping her voice low, she gestured toward the porch. "I'd invite you into the *haus* or to sit here, but I'm afraid we'd get no privacy."

"Your brother is in the barn, so that's out, too."

She sighed. She wished Lukas was the type of man to ride around in a courting buggy, but he'd always preferred walking or riding his bike if he could. He used to say that he hated having to depend on an animal to cart him around town. Still, that would have been nice about now. She would love to leave her life for a few hours, and sitting by his side in a buggy would be the perfect solution.

"I'm not sure where to go," she admitted.

He shrugged. "It's still warm. Why don't you walk me back down the driveway? We'll take our time."

Luckily, she had on shoes. Bare feet would hurt on the gravel drive. "That sounds *gut*."

After glancing at her family behind her, Lukas pressed a hand to the small of her back and guided her forward. After they walked a bit, he moved his hand from her waist to her shoulders and settled it there.

He was a big man and she was small. The weight of his arm should have felt heavy or confining. Instead, she felt cared for and protected. Better.

"This is nice. Ain't so?" he murmured.

"*Jah*. We've, um, never walked like this before."

He smiled down at her, though his smile didn't quite meet his eyes. "You mean like a courting couple? Then it's about time, I think."

She hardly knew what to say to that. "Are we courting now?"

"I did ask you to marry me today, Darla. It ain't my fault you said no."

"I . . . I didn't think it was for the best."

"Maybe."

"You know I'm right."

"*Nee*, I disagree. And now that I've asked you, I intend to make you say yes. One day."

He looked as self-assured and confident as ever. Maybe even more so. As his words sank in, her mind started spinning. Again. She'd hurried out of the house, intending to stop a fight between him and Aaron. Instead, Aaron was gone and

Lucas had been talking quietly with Patsy. Now, here they were, walking side by side and discussing his marriage proposal.

"I didn't expect us to be talking about marriage. I thought you'd want to talk about what you said to Aaron."

He paused, looked down at her, as if he was weighing the pros and cons of that . . . then shook his head. "I don't think so."

"Lukas," she chided. "You can't simply make me wait."

"All you need to know is that I told him what I thought about him hurting you. I feel certain he's going to stop. If he doesn't, we'll take things further . . . and you'll be moving in with me and my siblings, whether we're married or not."

To say she was stunned by his high-handedness was an understatement. "Lukas Kinsinger, even if we were engaged, I wouldn't care for you to speak to me like this."

"No?" His brows arched.

"Definitely not."

"I'll remember that," he said.

His words were all that was proper, but there was a new light in his eyes. It was obvious that he liked the spark between them. It made her want to shake her head in wonder. Their interactions

A part of her had been so tempted to grab ahold
of him before he changed his mind. But then she'd
remembered her responsibilities and their very
different lives. Yes, they were both essentially orphans. They also had siblings to take care of. But
while Rebecca, Amelia, and Levi were all adults,
she had Patsy, Gretel, Maisie, and the twins. And
Aaron—who was so angry and hurt that they

her siblings had to trust
No matter what.
in case

were as complex and ever-changing as the night-
time sky during a lightning storm. "Lukas, about
Aaron . . ."

"Let's not discuss him anymore, okay? I need
a break."

"What do you want to talk about?"

To her surprise, he squeezed her shoulder,
bringing her closer to his side. "Tell me how to
tell the difference between Evan and Samuel."

"That's what you want to talk about?"

"One of them was outside. It struck me that
even after all these years, I still can't tell the difference. How do you know?"

She knew because she'd helped raise them. She
knew because she just did. But she gave him a
break. "Samuel now has a scar on his chin."

"Yeah?"

"*Jah.* It's pretty visible. It's a good-sized scar."

"How did he get it?"

"Horse kicked him."

He winced. "Ouch."

"Ouch, for sure," Darla agreed. "Sam was out
in the barn mucking stalls. Somehow he startled
Jack and got it good in the chin. Mamm had to
hitch up the buggy and get him to the clinic in
town."

"How many stitches?"

"Seven. Two of them were inside his cut! He's going to be scarred for life."

Lukas grinned. "His misfortune means I'll be able to tell them apart now."

"I guess that is a silver lining."

They had passed the thicket of trees where she'd shown him her shoulder. Now they were standing next to the mailbox. Too far from the house for any of her family to see them. No one was on the road. They were as alone as they'd ever been.

Carefully, Lukas shifted her so she was facing him, then linked his arms around her waist. She braced her palms on his chest. They were standing too far apart for her to reach his shoulders. This new stance felt unfamiliar yet so nice. His shirt was warm against her palms.

"Do you think you're going to be able to sleep tonight?"

"I hope so."

"I hope so, too."

There was something new in his tone, something intimate and caring. She liked it.

But of course, it also brought back their previous conversation. "Lukas, about this marriage proposal," she began hesitantly. "I don't know if you were just talking or—"

"I meant it, Darla," he stated, looking at her

intently. "One day you will say yes. One will agree that marriage between us is t   o thing. One day you'll want me as muc   want you."

"And then?"

"And then it will be a mighty good day. Well, least for me."

As she stared at him, he leaned close and pressed his lips to her brow. Pres   temple. Then her cheek. T   dering if he was   wonde were as complex and ever-changing as the night-time sky during a lightning storm. "Lukas, about Aaron . . ."

"Let's not discuss him anymore, okay? I need a break."

"What do you want to talk about?"

To her surprise, he squeezed her shoulder, bringing her closer to his side. "Tell me how to tell the difference between Evan and Samuel."

"That's what you want to talk about?"

"One of them was outside. It struck me that even after all these years, I still can't tell the difference. How do you know?"

She knew because she'd helped raise them. She knew because she just did. But she gave him a break. "Samuel now has a scar on his chin."

"Yeah?"

"*Jah*. It's pretty visible. It's a good-sized scar."

"How did he get it?"

"Horse kicked him."

He winced. "Ouch."

"Ouch, for sure," Darla agreed. "Sam was out in the barn mucking stalls. Somehow he startled Jack and got it good in the chin. Mamm had to hitch up the buggy and get him to the clinic in town."

"How many stitches?"

"Seven. Two of them were inside his cut! He's going to be scarred for life."

Lukas grinned. "His misfortune means I'll be able to tell them apart now."

"I guess that is a silver lining."

They had passed the thicket of trees where she'd shown him her shoulder. Now they were standing next to the mailbox. Too far from the house for any of her family to see them. No one was on the road. They were as alone as they'd ever been.

Carefully, Lukas shifted her so she was facing him, then linked his arms around her waist. She braced her palms on his chest. They were standing too far apart for her to reach his shoulders. This new stance felt unfamiliar yet so nice. His shirt was warm against her palms.

"Do you think you're going to be able to sleep tonight?"

"I hope so."

"I hope so, too."

There was something new in his tone, something intimate and caring. She liked it.

But of course, it also brought back their previous conversation. "Lukas, about this marriage proposal," she began hesitantly. "I don't know if you were just talking or—"

"I meant it, Darla," he stated, looking at her

intently. "One day you will say yes. One day you will agree that marriage between us is the right thing. One day you'll want me as much as I want you."

"And then?"

"And then it will be a mighty good day. Well, at least for me."

As she stared at him, he leaned close and pressed his lips to her brow. Pressed another kiss to her temple. Then her cheek. Then, just as she was wondering if he was going to kiss her on the lips—and wondering how she would respond—he brushed a light, quick kiss to the nape of her neck and pulled away. "Sleep well, Darla. See you soon."

"*Jah*," she said, feeling a bit breathless. "I mean, *gut nacht*. And thank you," she added as she watched him start down the street.

He looked back over his shoulder. "For what?"

"Everything."

He smiled. "I'll take that."

When he turned and started walking again, Darla was of a mind to stand and watch him. He'd been everything she'd been sure he could be today. He'd defended her against her brother. He'd protected her, too. He'd also been kind and earnest and fun. He'd teased her and talked to her and yes, he'd kissed her, too.

A part of her had been so tempted to grab ahold of him before he changed his mind. But then she'd remembered her responsibilities and their very different lives. Yes, they were both essentially orphans. They also had siblings to take care of. But while Rebecca, Amelia, and Levi were all adults, she had Patsy, Gretel, Maisie, and the twins. And Aaron—who was so angry and hurt that they couldn't trust him.

And because of that, her siblings had to trust that she would be there for them. No matter what.

What's more, she needed them, too. Just in case one day soon Lukas Kinsinger actually did change his mind and decided that she wasn't worth his trouble. Just in case.

TWO DAYS LATER, as Lukas looked around his office, heard the rumble of saws and sanders and the hundred other things that made the business run like clockwork, he decided the lumber mill was the last place he wanted to be. It was filled with too many people asking questions, too many people needing answers.

He was a man used to bearing a lot of responsibility on his shoulders. Back when he was eight or nine, he'd come to terms with the fact that he was the eldest and therefore had to look after his siblings. When he'd started working at the mill at fourteen, his father had constantly reminded him that the mill was his legacy, his responsibility.

Though Lukas had been proud of his father's words, a part of him had always felt guilty that their *daed* had said those words to him and not to Levi. Because of that, and because he needed his brother more than ever before, he and Levi were attempting to divide their responsibilities. It was hard, though. He supposed giving up control always was.

Now, too, he was consumed by Darla's needs. And her refusal of his proposal. Oh, he knew he hadn't asked her in a romantic way, but didn't she see that his offer was good for her? She needed to accept and let him take care of her.

Jah, they could go to the bishop, get permission to marry quickly, and he'd take her away for a bit. He would gladly let Levi handle everything for the next week. He could even ask some of his close friends to check on Patsy and the rest of Darla's siblings while they were gone. A week of freedom meant he could have a week without having to appear confident and in control. He could be himself with Darla. They could laugh about nothing and sit together late at night and simply enjoy the silence. She wouldn't expect him to have every answer. No, it was likely she would be telling him what to do!

A week's honeymoon would be a wonderful thing. *Wunderbaar*.

Since wishes and dreams were for children, he made due with a few hours. He needed it. Suddenly, everything in his life had become too much.

Keeping his head down, he walked right by the mill's entrance, steadfastly ignoring both the faint outline of Rebecca standing in the front window and the low hum of machines and men's voices. Harder to ignore was the strong smell of sawdust and pine that permeated the air. Usually those scents made him think of everything good and secure in his life. After all, he'd grown up linking family, work, and love with one specific place.

Now he was beginning to realize that he'd been sadly mistaken.

It was his father's presence that he'd been drawn to at the mill. It was his family and the friendships he'd had with other workers that he'd looked forward to each day.

And that comfortable sense of belonging he'd been so fond of had simply been his immaturity. He'd taken it for granted. It wasn't until his father was no longer there that he'd realized everything he felt for the mill had actually been the love he'd felt for his father. He missed him.

Lukas continued to walk beyond the town's limits. He pushed himself, increasing his pace, breathing harder through the hills and valleys of the countryside. Hardly aware of his surroundings, ignoring the dry creek bed to his right, the dense thicket of brush to his left. Finally, as sweat formed on his brow and his breath came in short spurts, he allowed himself to slow down. And in that moment, he remembered another walk he'd taken almost five years ago.

His mother had just died from a heart condition none of them had been aware she'd had. Everyone in the family had been mourning her loss, especially Amelia who had still needed a mother.

And his father, who they'd all known still needed a wife.

He and Levi and Rebecca had tried to help their father as much as they could, though their efforts had been dismal at best. No matter how much they'd tried, none of them could fill the gap in their father's life or comfort Amelia enough to convince her to stop crying.

And so, one day, feeling frustrated and sad and helpless, Lukas had pushed all his frustrations and needs aside and started walking. After wandering the fields, looking steadily forward, and ignoring everything in his periphery for almost an hour, he'd gotten winded. He'd stopped and stretched. Then glanced behind him and spied the green metal roof of their sprawling home.

And had felt nothing.

It was then he'd realized that their home hadn't meant anything anymore. It had been their mother's light that had illuminated the shadows and brought them so much joy. That realization had brought him to his knees.

There, kneeling on the ground, he'd cried at last. Though not for his little sister or his father's blank stare or even for their mother's pain. Instead, he'd cried for himself.

Yes, they'd been selfish tears, washing away nothing but his needs and wants and wishes. When they'd at last dried on his cheeks, he'd realized that he was going to simply have to try harder. He was going to need to work harder to help Amelia recover. He was going to have to wake up earlier and go to bed later so that he could help their *daed* complete everything that needed to be done.

Now it looked as if he was in the same situation. Though each of them looked as if they were handling things all right, he knew in many ways he and his siblings felt confused and adrift. He needed to make sure somehow he got everyone back on track.

And along the way, he also needed to take care of Darla. The burdens were going to be heavy. He wondered if he was going to be strong enough to bear them. It would be a terrible thing to take on so much that he ended up hurting others instead of helping them.

But wasn't it true that the Lord never gave anyone more troubles than they could bear? Or was that merely wishful thinking?

"Lukas!"

He turned to see Rebecca tromping across the field toward him with a determined expression on her face. Frustration, mixed with concern, filled him. He'd really wanted a few hours to himself. He'd needed that. He deserved that, too.

However, he knew that only something really important would have brought Rebecca out to search for him.

"What's wrong?" he asked. "Is someone hurt?" When he realized she didn't look panicked, he began to think of what else could have brought her out. "Did that semi come in early?"

"Nope."

"Oh. Well, is there a problem at the shop? Did we get that famous basketball player in today?"

Their master carpenters were often asked to do custom jobs for some people up in Cleveland and Columbus.

"It's none of those things."

"Then what's wrong?"

"You are, that's what." Before he could ask her to explain, she stepped to his side and nudged his arm with her shoulder. "I saw you walk by the office. When I peeked out the door, I spied you heading here."

That still told him nothing. "And?"

"When you turned, I got a good look at your face. I recognized that look you were wearing." Softening her voice, she murmured, "Lukas, you are troubled."

There was no sense in denying it. He shrugged. "Maybe."

"What's on your mind?"

"What isn't?"

She sighed. "I know things seem bad, but they're better."

"Do you really think so?"

"I do. Things are settling at work. The employees are looking to you and Levi now for guidance." She smiled wryly. "A couple have even come to me for help from time to time. Made me feel real important, it did."

"*Gut*. Answer all the questions you can," he

teased. Well, only half teasing. He would be grateful for any help Rebecca could give him.

"I already have. Levi said the same thing." She paused, then said, "So, is it work that has you so tied up in knots?"

"I thought it was," he ventured as they began walking side by side along a worn footpath to a fishing pond. "I thought it was Daed and work and everything. But now I'm realizing that we have each other and everything is going to be okay. Somehow or some way."

"Then what has gotten you so worked up?"

He didn't want to admit what—or rather, who—was bothering him, but he needed some advice. With a sigh, he made a decision. "I'm worried about Darla."

"She'll come around, Lukas. She's been grieving as well as dealing with Mary Troyer, and we know what Mary's like. What she's always been like." Her voice hardened. "Mary has always been critical of the mill and her son working here. She wanted him to stay home and farm."

"Mary has been especially hard on Darla. But that will ease. I'll make sure of it. But, Becky, Mary ain't the reason I'm so worried. It's because Aaron is still hurting her."

"Are you sure?"

He nodded. "Aaron is still angry at the world,

and for some reason, he's taking out all his frustrations on Darla."

"Lukas, you better tell me what happened to her now."

Briefly, he told her about the bruises he'd spied on her wrist and recounted the talk he'd had with Aaron the day before.

"I canna believe all this has been going on and I've had no knowledge of it. I should have reached out to her more."

"I doubt she would have told you anything. She's very private."

"Amelia and I might not have the close friendship with her that you do, but we care about her."

"I know that."

When she bowed her head, looking as if Darla's hurts were weighing on her, too, Lukas blurted, "I'm worried, Rebecca. I'm worried that these bruises aren't the only ones she's received. I'm worried that something else might happen and I won't be there to protect her." And then, feeling absolutely vulnerable, he said, "I asked her to marry me."

She stared at him in confusion. Then blinked slowly.

He braced himself, waiting for her temper to erupt.

But instead, she said softly, "Does she truly mean that much to ya, Lukas?"

"*Jah.*"

"Are you sure? Do you love her, or are you merely trying to protect her?"

In his mind, they were one and the same. "She's been my best friend for years. You know that."

"I know that you've been close." Not meeting his eye, she said, "I know that I've always been a little jealous of the bond you two have shared."

He was confused. "Jealous? Of Darla?"

"You've treated her like a sister. In a lot of ways you've been closer to her than you ever were to Amelia or me. Of course I've been jealous of that."

"My connection with Darla has never been like that." Though, if he hadn't thought of Darla as another sister, how had he thought of her?

Her expression eased. "It seems it wasn't. You haven't been thinking of her as a sister, but as someone special in another way. In a romantic way, Lukas."

"Maybe so." He wasn't sure how he liked the sound of that, but he supposed the Lord had placed them together all along.

"So when is the wedding?"

Her question startled a bark of laughter from him. Only Rebecca could accept news that quickly. "There isn't going to be one. She said no. Twice, now."

"Really?" She threw him a look over her shoulder as she strode forward, the hem of her dark purple dress cutting a path through the weeds and early spring wildflowers. "Did she give you a reason?"

"For sure she did. She gave me a mouthful," Lukas said with a smile. "But I suppose what matters the most is that she thinks we'd be getting married for the wrong reasons."

"Because she thinks you were asking out of pity. Because you were trying to save her."

"*Jah.*" He shrugged. "She wasn't wrong. I do want to help her. However, I'm not sure if she refused me because she's worried about love or worried about her siblings. She's always put them first."

"And they made sure of it," she quipped. "Of course, if she is worried about Aaron transferring his anger to another member of the family, I can't say that I would have said yes, either."

They were at Dawdi Pond now. It was just a little thing. Not big enough to do anything but sit on the bank and toss in a fishing pole in the summer or skate on in the middle of January or February. But most figured it wasn't all that good for those things, either. Though it was filled with algae, lily pads, frogs, and turtles, it never seemed to be very full of fish. And a skate around its circumference would take all of five minutes. He'd always secretly wondered if the folks who owned it wished they could fill the thing up with dirt and be done with it. Rebecca, on the other hand, had always loved watching all the turtles sunning.

She looked mighty happy at the moment to do just that. Plopping down on the grass, she beamed. "Look, Lukas! A bunch of turtles are out today."

He sat down next to her and gazed at the curious little creatures, their heads and tails poking out of hard green shells, their dark, beady eyes watching each other and Rebecca warily. When one slowly turned around so that it faced her, he grinned. "Becky, I swear, these turtles know ya. One would think you feed them every time you come." He turned to her. "Do you?"

She rolled her eyes. "Of course not. I don't feed them, but I think they know they've got a kindred spirit in me."

He burst out laughing. "I'm awfully glad you

showed up. I was feeling kind of blue and confused."

"Aren't you still confused?"

"Yes. But now, at least, I realize I'm not alone." Pulling his legs up so he could rest his elbows on his knees, he said, "You've made me feel better."

"Glad I could help."

He smirked. "Kindred spirits with turtles, indeed."

"I was serious about that." Looking almost hurt, she chided, "These turtles really do like me. A lot!"

He couldn't help himself, he started laughing harder. "That's what's so funny. Of course you're serious about them. I better tell Oscar to look out! Your puppy won't like discovering that your affections are so fickle."

Looking dramatic, she pressed a palm to her chest. "Oscar knows that he has my heart."

"Until a man comes along."

"Well, that is going to be a while, since I'm at the mill all day."

Her curt tone prompted him to stare at her more closely. Her light blue eyes had turned pensive. "You said you'd let me know when you've had enough," he said slowly. "Have you?"

"Not yet."

"Sure?"

"I'll tell you when it's time, Lukas."

She sounded certain. Relaxing again, he leaned back on his hands. "I'm gonna hold you to that promise."

"Hey, Lukas?"

"Hmm?"

"What are you going to do now about Aaron and Darla?"

"I'm not sure. I told Aaron he should talk to the bishop. I also told him if he wouldn't listen to me, I'd come down harder." Glancing her way, he said, "If he doesn't, finally, resolve his problem, I'm going to bring more men to talk to him. Maybe he'll listen to several of us."

"Surely he'll stop now."

"Maybe. Maybe not. All I do know is that I'm going to keep walking Darla home and asking her to be mine."

She swallowed. "Lukas, I hate to think of her being mistreated. Especially at home."

"I feel the same way."

"Do you think she might listen to me if I try to talk to her about marrying you?"

"What would you even say? That you don't want her *bruder* taking out his frustrations on her? She's the oldest in a very big family."

"But her *mamm*—"

"Has taken off," Lukas interrupted. "Who knows if she'll ever come back? And if she does . . . well, how can she ever repair the damage she's done? She left little Gretel."

"And everyone else." Frowning as she watched one of the turtles slowly make its way down a log, Rebecca continued. "Maybe we shouldn't have been all that surprised. She was a nice woman, but overwhelmed. I always thought that she acted like keeping tabs on her *kinner* was all she had to do. It was odd."

"I don't think she ever truly ran the house. John did, and now Darla and Patsy."

"I suppose you're right." She rested her chin on her knees.

He leaned farther back, enjoying the moment.

"Hey, Lukas?"

"*Jah?*"

"What would you have done if she'd said yes? I mean, how would you have felt? Would you have been happy?"

He thought about that. "I would have been re- lieved to know I was helping her. I would have been anxious to get her someplace safe." He would have been eager to care for her, too.

"But would you have been happy that she would be your wife for the rest of your life?"

"*Jah*," he said before he even allowed himself to think about it. "I love her."

"That's something, then."

"I suppose it is."

He just wasn't sure if it was enough.

Chapter 16

April 6

Just as Darla handed Mr. Carson his mail, Mary Troyer pulled open the front door to the post office. Knowing what was about to happen, Darla braced herself. Funny how her body automatically stiffened at the sight of Mary Troyer now. The woman had affected both her mind and her spirit.

Mr. Carson looked at her curiously. "Everything okay, there, dear?"

"What?" Belatedly, she realized she was clutching his *Popular Mechanics* magazine in a death grip. "Oh, *jah.* Sorry about that," she said as she attempted to smooth the wrinkled cover. "Well, here you go. I'm real glad you're back from Florida safe and sound."

Mr. Carson gave her a toothy smile. "Me, too, Darla. See you soon."

"Yes, sir." She smiled at him before meeting Mary's hard gaze. Mary was standing next in line and glaring at her. As usual. "What do you need?" Darla asked. She was beyond trying to be polite in the midst of Mary's mean tirades.

"Is that all you have to say to me?" Mary nearly yelled, causing Mr. Carson to pause on his way out the door.

It was an effort, but Darla kept her voice low. "I don't seem to have anything to say that you want to hear."

Mary stepped forward and braced her hands on the counter. "My Bryan is buried in the cemetery. Yet, here you are. Working, talking, and flirting with everyone in Charm most every day."

"I'm hardly doing that."

"You are moving on with your life, Darletta Kurtz, just like nothing happened."

"I don't need to cause scenes to remember the accident."

"Don't you, though? Because now you not only have to bear your father's shame, but you have insinuated yourself back into Lukas Kinsinger's life, much to everyone's shock."

"I don't see how my friendship with Lukas is any concern of yours."

"It's impossible to avoid. Why, it's all anyone can talk about." She shook her head. "I don't know how you can live with yourself."

Mary's speech was nothing unusual yet there was a new, firm, frantic thread to it now. Almost as if she was on the verge of a breakdown or becoming so desperate that she was willing to cast away her last bit of control. This change made Darla even more uncomfortable.

She was so, so tired of Mary's unreasonable anger toward her. She felt as if she were the lone soldier in Mary's firing line; every day she got shot down, only to be propped up again.

Darla was vaguely aware of the door opening and shutting. No doubt that was Mr. Carson rushing out. Mary's tirade had probably blistered his ears. She hated that sweet Mr. Carson had had to hear Mary's ugly accusations but it couldn't be helped.

"You have no reason to be so mean to me, Mary," she said, though she knew her face was burning with embarrassment. "I've told you time and again that not only was my father's part in what happened an accident, but that I, personally, had no more to do with what happened at the mill than you did."

Mary inhaled and looked like she might burst. Darla couldn't help but be glad about that.

"Now, if you don't need anything to do with packages or letters, I suggest you leave the premises."

"I'll leave when I feel like you have heard me," she retorted. Now, however, her voice had a tremor of doubt in it.

Was this all it had taken? Darla wondered. Had she simply needed to stand up for herself?

"I believe we've all heard you," Mr. Carson said, surprising Darla. "What's more, I think you need to rethink the way you are talking to Darla."

Darla popped her head up. She was dumbfounded to see Mr. Carson standing against the back wall glaring at Mary, as were two other customers, one of whom was Hannah Eicher.

Mary looked just as shocked about the audience as Darla. After a momentary look of discomfort, she faced them. "You might not know this, but her father is John Kurtz. He's the one who caused the mill accident."

"I know exactly who Darla is. And of course I knew John Kurtz," Mr. Carson retorted. "I don't work at the mill, but I did follow the investigation in the papers. John was cleared of any wrongdoing, as was the mill. It was simply a terrible accident."

Mary shook her head. "*Nee*. It was his fault."

Hannah walked to stand in front of Darla, as if she were trying to shield her from Mary's harsh words. "Mary, you know my uncle works at the mill. He knew John well, and said he was a *gut* man. A kind man. You must stop these visits here. They are serving no purpose except to hurt Darla's feelings. And if you want to know the truth, they make the rest of us wonder what has happened to you."

"Me?"

"You have lost your compassion, Mary. Your son would hardly recognize ya, what with the way you are acting."

Staring at her intently, Mary said, "Your Paul died there."

"I haven't forgotten. Don't assume that I have."

"I canna believe you, of all people, are sticking up for Darla Kurtz."

Hannah shook her head, her brown eyes full of sorrow. "And I canna believe you are ignoring our faith. It is time to forgive, Mary."

"Forgiveness is not that easy."

"Maybe you simply need to try harder," Mr. Carson interjected with a glare. "Everyone has been talking about these visits of yours. They are unkind and bordering on cruel."

Mary turned to Darla, "Is this what you have been doing? Telling everyone how mean I've been to you?"

"Your visits have been pretty hard to miss," an English lady in jeans and tennis shoes blurted. "I've been trying to avoid the post office because you are here so much."

"I haven't told anyone," Darla replied. "But like I told you the first time you came in, no matter how much I wish I could change the past, it is beyond my control. We all must move on."

The door opened again and this time it was Rebecca Kinsinger who walked through. She stopped and stared at the scene. "What's going on?"

"All of us thought it was time Mary stopped yelling at and taunting Darla," Hannah replied.

"Oh, thank heavens. Someone just came in the mill saying the same thing. I got here as quickly as I could."

Darla couldn't believe it. "That was kind of you."

"That was the least I could do," Rebecca said. Turning to Mary, she raised her voice. "Mary, it is time to mourn your Bryan. Cast away your anger and focus on him. That is how he would want you to behave."

Tears filled Mary's eyes as she looked from one person to another. "I never thought all of you would ignore what I'm feeling. None of you understand my pain."

"I've lost both of my parents. I know that pain too well," Rebecca said. "That is why I must say once again that it is time you stopped these visits."

"You all will regret siding against me." With one last glare around the room, she pushed her way out past Mr. Carson and Rebecca. At last the door opened and she was gone.

A fierce, tense silence filled the room in her wake.

Darla walked around the counter, her hands clasped together. A lump filled her throat and emotion infused her words. "*Danke*. Thank you, all of you. I never wanted to ask for help with Mary, but I truly appreciate all of your support."

"I know why you never said anything, dear, but that doesn't mean how she was acting was right," Mr. Carson said.

"She doesn't speak for everyone else, either," Rebecca added. "You are right, Darla. It was a terrible accident, but it is in the past. And even if someone there had caused it, no one can take on the sins of one's fathers."

Hannah nodded. "Mary's constant anger is causing a rift in our community. We need to concentrate on healing, not making things worse. I really hope she stops soon."

"Me, too." Looking at Rebecca, Darla lowered her voice. "Thank you so much for coming here. I think your words might have finally caused Mary to rethink her actions. Please let me know if I can help you in any way in the future."

Rebecca smiled. "It was nothing. But if you meant what you said, you can thank me by coming over this evening."

"To your *haus*?"

"To be sure."

Feeling as if everyone there was shamelessly waiting for her reply, Darla did the only thing she could do. She nodded. "I will do that. I'll be over after I get off work and check in at home. Maybe around seven?"

"Seven is a perfect time. You can meet my new puppy, Oscar. He's a bulldog."

In spite of the tension, Darla smiled. "I'd love to meet your puppy."

"You're gonna love him. He is so cute. He's a good cuddler, too."

Thinking that cuddling a puppy would definitely make her day better, Darla relaxed a bit. Then, as she looked around at everyone in the room, she called out, "Is there anyone here who needs something from the post office?"

"I do," Hannah said. "I need to get some stamps and then hurry to work."

As Darla walked back around the counter, the other people left. And for the first time in a long time, she realized that she was stronger. She'd been able to stand up for herself. Sure, she'd had help, but that was okay.

She'd needed it.

"She's coming over tonight at seven," Rebecca said to Lukas the minute she walked inside their house.

"Who is?" Amelia asked.

"Darla. After Ed told me he saw Mary in the post office, yelling at Darla once again, I ran over there to try and put a stop to things."

If Lukas wasn't so pleased about his sister's efforts, he would have rolled his eyes. It seemed Rebecca had healed a bit, too, and was now back to making sure everyone in her world was doing what they should. Or at least, what she thought they should. "*You'd* had enough, hmm?"

"I did. Besides, someone needed to intervene," Rebecca added as she crouched down on her knees to greet little Oscar, who was waddling his way over to her. After stroking his belly, she picked him up in her arms. "When I walked in there, poor Darla was getting an earful. She looked a bit like she'd reached her limit."

"I already spoke to Mary. I thought that would have helped."

"It didn't."

Leave it to a little sister to put things bluntly. "Good to know that Mary will listen to you, at least."

"I don't think it was me she was hearing. I think it was everyone else joining in. She was outnumbered. Maybe she realized that it was finally time to move on, too."

"Perhaps that was it." As hard as it was to come to terms with, all things happened at the right time. "How did Darla react?"

"I think she was surprised that we came to her defense, if you want to know the truth."

"That does not surprise me."

"There were four of us, and we all told Mary that we weren't happy with the way she'd been saying such hateful things to Darla. Mr. Carson even told her that he had heard enough!"

"Thank goodness he spoke up. And you, too."

Rebecca waved off his compliment. "Perhaps now we can finally move forward."

"So, how did you go from defending Darla to inviting her over here?"

"I took advantage of the fact that everyone was looking at her, as well as the fact that she owed me."

"Becky."

"You know I had to use some kind of advantage, Lukas. She couldn't exactly refuse me in front of everyone."

Lukas winced. "I'm not sure if that was the best way."

"I am. Plus, I mentioned Oscar. He's cute enough to convince anyone to pay us a visit."

Lukas waved a hand. "Anyway . . ."

Rebecca rolled her eyes. "Anyway, Darla promised me in front of Hannah and Mr. Carson that she'd stop by after she checks in at home."

Remembering how chaotic things were at the Kurtz house, he said, "Don't be too surprised if she doesn't make it over."

"Oh, she'll come. Now all we have to do is see what happens next."

"Do you think we need to worry about Levi?"

For the first time during the conversation, Rebecca looked unsure. "I don't think so. He's been working late this week. They won't see each other."

"He'll still find out about it and he's not gonna be too happy."

"He ain't going to be happy at all. But like Mary, he needs to get over what happened, Lukas."

Lukas wondered if it would ever be that easy for Levi. Unlike everyone else in the family, Levi had been in the room where the men had died. He'd witnessed the explosion and had tried his hardest to save John. Later, after much of the warehouse had caught fire, he led the fight to try to save the others as well.

They all knew part of Levi's anger toward John was a reflection of his own anger at himself. He felt guilty and wasn't eager to forgive others because then he'd have to forgive himself, too.

"Lukas, you know I am right, don't you?"

Feeling weary, he nodded. He did know Rebecca was right. Besides, he was eager for Darla to stop by, just like she used to when they were in school. At least two or three times a week she'd walk home with him and Rebecca after school and stay for an hour or two.

"It will go okay, *bruder*. I'll make sure of it."

Sometimes he wished God would have given him even an eighth of Rebecca's self-assuredness. He would like to know what it felt like to go through his days knowing that he was right.

Lukas glanced at the clock. "I think I'll go shower, then."

Rebecca smiled at Amelia, who had just entered the kitchen with a fresh load of laundry in her arms. "That's a mighty *gut* idea, Lukas. You don't want to scare Darla away before she even has time to settle in."

He would have acted annoyed about her teasing except he kind of thought she might be right. He was a stinky mess after working at the mill all day, followed by another two hours outside in the fields and in the barn.

"I'll be back down soon."

Handing him a stack of towels, Amelia said, "Put these away while you're up there, would you? And take your time. Supper is just soup and sandwiches tonight."

Grabbing the pile of towels, he went to do as his sisters bid. He not only needed to get clean, he needed to prepare himself for whatever was going to come next.

Chapter 17

By eight o'clock that night, however, Lukas was wondering why he'd gone to so much trouble.

Darla had come over as she'd promised. After shyly saying hello to him, she'd been claimed by his sisters, a sleepy Oscar, and a plate of coconut cupcakes that Amelia had somehow found the time to bake.

Lukas had sat in his father's old easy chair in the living room and feigned interest in the latest edition of *The Budget*. That didn't last long.

Now, feeling restless, he thumbed through two magazines, one on farming and one on lumber. He wasn't surprised that neither was as interesting as the sound of Darla's voice floating in from the kitchen.

After tossing the magazines on the side table, he gave up all pretense of doing anything but eavesdropping on the girls' conversation. He was more than a little curious what they had to talk about that couldn't involve him. Again and again, he strained to hear what, exactly, they were saying but he only caught Rebecca's words and Amelia's shy quips. Never Darla's responses.

He didn't want to remain apart from them another minute. Opening the door, he smiled at all of them. "I couldn't wait any longer for dessert," he announced.

Amelia, who'd been in midconversation, stopped abruptly. Darla blinked while Becky raised her eyebrows.

"You're too hungry to wait, Lukas?" Rebecca asked.

"Maybe." Feeling foolish, Lukas gestured to the cupcakes arranged on a serving plate. "These look mighty *gut*. I don't remember having them before."

"I made them last month," Amelia said.

"Huh. Well, these look different." Inwardly, he winced. It seemed he could no more casually enter the women's conversation than one of them could have joined him and his buddies on a fishing trip.

After a long, awkward moment passed, Darla saved the day. "You should take one, Lukas, they're wonderful—*gut*."

"They look good." He put two on a plate. "Real, um, coconutty."

Rebecca groaned as she sipped her coffee.

He sensed the girls' surprised reactions when he pulled out a chair and sat down. Lukas felt a little guilty but not enough to regret joining them. He'd wanted to spend some time with Darla as well. "Sorry, but I don't want to sit alone in the living room any longer."

"Obviously not," Rebecca murmured.

As his sisters smirked at each other, Darla cleared her throat. "We were just talking about Hannah Eicher."

"Really?" They all knew Hannah, of course. Amelia and she were close, though Lukas couldn't recall if Amelia had been spending much time with her lately. "Is she all right? The last time I visited her and her parents she seemed to be over the worst of her grief."

"I think she is, indeed," Darla said. "She's an Englisher couple's nanny now."

Picking up a fork, Amelia delicately speared a bite-sized section of her cupcake. "She's been working there for a while. She told me about the baby boy she watches. She says he's sweet."

"I got the chance to talk to her at the post office earlier today," Darla added as she stood up and set the sleeping pup in his dog bed by Rebecca's chair. "After everything settled down with Mary, we chatted for a couple of minutes. She said she was unexpectedly happy."

"I like that phrase," Becky mused as she reached for another cupcake. "Unexpectedly happy sums up a lot."

Darla nodded. "I'm so glad she is getting over Paul."

Lukas was a bit surprised that the ladies were talking about anything that had to do with the accident at the lumber mill, but he supposed he shouldn't have been. Almost every conversation he had with his friends had something to do with either the mill, the fire, or one of the men who'd passed away. "Paul was a *gut* man and I think they could have been happy. But they weren't engaged, were they?"

Amelia shook her head. "They were serious, but I guess not that serious."

"I brought Hannah up because she said something that struck me as meaningful," Darla said shyly. "She said she was feeling more at home at the Englishers' *haus* than her own. I wonder if that's because of work or the people she's working for."

"Maybe it doesn't matter," Amelia said. "I don't like to second-guess happiness."

"I agree," Rebecca said with a fond look at all of them. "We've already lost both our parents and several other people we care about. You never know what God has in store for our future. It's best to be happy when we can."

After they talked a bit longer and Lukas ate both cupcakes, Darla got to her feet. "I hate to eat and run, but I had better get home."

At last Lukas was going to get a chance to visit with her privately. "I'll walk you home, Darla."

"It's not necessary."

"Of course it is. It's as dark as tar out there," Lukas said.

"I think the phrase is dark as pitch," Amelia said with a smile.

Rebecca cocked her head to one side. "Hmm. Or one could say it's dark as ink."

Lukas smirked. "Or dark as sin."

"Oh, you all." Darla laughed. "That's why I've missed you all so much."

"Because we make terrible similes?"

"Because you all laugh." Looking more serious, she said, "I guess that's really why I brought up Hannah. I think I understand why she feels so comfortable in someone else's house. That's how I've always felt about this *haus*."

"We've missed you," Amelia said. "I hope you know that you're always welcome here."

"*Jah*. We are glad you came over," Rebecca added.

"Thanks for inviting me. And thanks again for what you did at the post office, Rebecca."

"You're my friend. I was glad I could help. Now, let's not mention it again."

Grabbing a flashlight from the kitchen drawer, Lukas gestured to the door. "I'll be back after a while," he told his sisters.

Rebecca grinned as she took a third cupcake. "Take your time, Lukas."

DARLA COULDN'T BEGIN to count the number of times Lukas had walked her home over the years. Easily dozens. Sometimes they'd been part of a group. Sometimes it had been just the two of them. But rarely had it been so late at night.

As they walked across the fields, choosing to stay off the curvy, winding road that led from one of their houses to the other, she realized that she seemed to feel everything more strongly than before.

Before what, she wasn't sure. Was it before she and Lukas had gotten so old?

Before the accident?

Before both of their fathers had passed away?

Before this evening?

"You scared, Darla?" he asked as his flashlight continued to cast a faint yellow glow in front of them.

"Not at all."

"Sure? I bet there might be snakes out in the grass."

Of course, just that moment she heard a rustling around her ankles. And she shrieked like a girl.

"Lukas, you did that on purpose."

He chuckled. "I did not. But I should have. I haven't heard you squeal like a baby pig in ages."

Though she was fairly sure he was just getting her riled up, she took the bait, hook, line, and sinker. "Please tell me that you did not just compare me to a fat piglet."

"I didn't." After a pause, he said, "I never said you were fat, Darla."

"Oh!"

He laughed again. "You always were too easy to tease."

"Probably. And I've always jumped right into your traps."

"They were never traps, Darla. I'm just having fun with ya. You know I canna help myself." His voice sounded tender in the darkness. A little deeper, his cadence a little slower. Sweeter.

She shivered.

"You cold?"

"Nee. I am fine." She looked at him in surprise, wondering how he could have seen her reaction. Then she realized that he had the light beaming near her feet. It cast a faint glow over the majority of her body, enabling him to see her far more clearly than she could see anything.

He stepped closer. "You sure? I saw you tremble."

"You are holding the flashlight. I can hardly see my feet."

He waved the flashlight. "That's why you need to stay by my side."

She was just about to comment on that when she stepped into a hole and tripped. Immediately, his hand gripped her arm.

"Easy, now." He drew them to a stop. "If you're not careful, you're gonna get hurt."

She tested her ankle, rolling her foot this way and that. She probably wouldn't have even done that much checking except for the fact that he looked so concerned. "I'm fine. I just stepped in a divot or something."

"Probably a snake hole."

"Lukas, halt!"

He chuckled as he wrapped one strong arm around her shoulders. Just like he had the other day, except this time he curved his fingers around the cusp of her shoulder, effectively holding her tight against him.

Because it was dark—or maybe because so much had happened between them that she couldn't really help herself—she carefully slid her arm around his waist. His skin was warm underneath his blue cotton shirt. But she also noticed how different he felt. Where her waist was soft and curved, his felt more like a solid wall.

It felt nice. Slowly her hand relaxed but stayed put.

In response, Lukas squeezed her shoulder a tiny bit. Maybe just enough to let her know that he was there and approved of her arm around him.

"Hey, Darla?"

"*Jah?*"

"What . . . what do you think would have happened if we tried again?"

Was he talking about their friendship? That worried her. Did he still not feel that they'd made great strides? "Tried what again?" she asked hesitantly.

"That kiss."

"That kiss?" She was just about to say that he must have gotten her confused with some other girl because they sure hadn't kissed . . . when she remembered. "I canna believe you mentioned that," she said around a groan.

"Why not? It's dark. We're walking arm in arm . . ."

"We're walking with your arm around me." She pulled her hand away from his waist, but to her surprise, he grabbed at it and placed it back around him.

"Don't get so spun up. There's nothing to be embarrassed about."

"You know there is."

He was talking about when she was thirteen and they'd played some awful game of truth or dare with his siblings, some of hers, and about five other kids they knew from school.

Lukas—being Lukas—had always picked dares. That one had surely been a doozy. He'd practically been forced to pull her behind a barn and give her a peck on the lips. Unfortunately, she hadn't known how to kiss and neither had he. They'd been nervous wrecks—their noses had smacked into each other and somehow she'd managed to bite her lip in the process. Next thing she knew, she'd been scurrying back to everyone, but someone had seen blood on her lip.

And then, of course, the teasing had begun. Most everyone had assumed that he'd bitten her instead of kissed her. Lukas had taken it good-naturedly, but she'd been mortified, both by their awkward nose-knock and the blood. But also by the fact that everyone in their circle of friends knew that she'd been kissing Lukas Kinsinger . . . and that her wonderful, most-anticipated moment had been such a terrible, terrible disappointment.

"Darla, it wasn't anything to be embarrassed about. After all, you were only twelve," he said patiently as he pulled them forward, their ankles brushing against the dark, cool grass.

"I was thirteen." She remembered, because her parents would have never let her join those kids if she hadn't been a real teenager.

"We were young. I didn't know how to kiss."

"Obviously."

"For the record, I never actually bit you. Just saying."

"I never said you did. Just, um, everyone thought you did."

He chuckled. "Guys called me all sorts of names after that. Ferret-mouth was the worst."

She giggled. "Ferret-mouth? That's terrible."

"Simon had heard ferrets had terrible teeth."

Simon had always been Lukas's best friend. Even then. And even then, he'd had quite the reputation. "I bet Simon knew how to kiss back then."

"Probably," he said good-naturedly. "Though . . . I assure you that I'm much better now."

Because they were now walking so slowly and he was holding her so securely against his side, she closed her eyes, trying not to think about why he would be better. "I guess that means you've had a lot of practice?"

"Well, some."

"Huh."

"What? You're actually going to try to tell me you haven't kissed anyone since you were twelve?"

"I was thirteen, Lukas."

"Whatever."

"Not really."

"Come on, twelve, thirteen . . ." He drew to a stop. "Wait a sec. Are you telling me that *that* was your only kiss?"

"Maybe." She yanked away from his arm, and looked down at her feet.

The flashlight hung limply from his hand, illuminating her black tennis shoes and his heavy work boots.

Then, to her surprise, he bent down and set it gently on the grass.

And pulled her into his arms.

"What are you doing?" Oh, but she hated that her voice was suddenly as high-pitched as it had been back when she was thirteen.

Thank the Lord, Lukas couldn't see her face.

Instead, he gripped her arm with one hand, curved a hand around her cheek and jaw with the other, bent his head, and brushed his lips against hers.

After the briefest of pauses, she reached out and gripped his arms. Kissed him back. And then kissed him again. There, in the dark, in the field in between their two farms.

She was old enough to know better, old enough to fear consequences of their actions. Yet young enough not to care.

Lukas's kiss was sweet and perfect and everything she'd once hoped it would be.

And then, all too soon, it was over.

After pulling away, he bent down and retrieved his flashlight. "I had better get you home," he said after a pause.

"*Jah.*"

"You want to marry me yet?"

"After one kiss in a field? *Nee.*"

He sighed. "At least I didn't bite you."

"At least there's that, ferret-mouth."

When he reached out and took hold of her hand, she clasped it. And couldn't help but think that Lukas Kinsinger had been right yet again.

He had learned an awful lot in the past eleven years.

Chapter 18

April 12

Hannah, are ya leaving for work already?" her mother called from down the hall.

After carefully spreading mayonnaise on her bread, Hannah added two slices of smoked turkey, a slice of Swiss, and a piece of crisp lettuce on top, then neatly sliced it. "*Jah*, Mamm. You know how Mr. and Mrs. Ross don't like me to be late."

"Well, I know how you like to get over there early," her mother reproved as she appeared. "I haven't had the pleasure of meeting your Englisher bosses yet."

Hannah shook her head. "I've said that you can always walk over to their *haus* any morning you like. They wouldn't mind."

"That doesn't seem quite proper. I wouldn't want to make them uncomfortable."

"They won't be. They're simply Mr. and Mrs. Ross, Mamm. They're nice." Actually, they were simply York and Melissa now, though she wouldn't tell her mother that. Her mother liked her to show respect to the people who paid her money.

After slipping an apple in her lunch sack, she eyed the clock hanging above the window that held her mother's herb garden. "Now, I'd best get going."

As always, her lovely mother eyed her with sweet compassion and just a little too closely. "Hannah, maybe you should tell them that you need some time off soon."

"Why? You know I am making good money there."

"I do know. But I fear you are working too hard. You have no time for anything but work now."

"That isn't true. I am helping out at home with my chores just like always."

"I'm not talking about chores," she gently corrected. "Dear, I'm startin' to worry that you have thrown yourself into your work for those Englishers with a bit too much enthusiasm. Is that the case?"

This was the first time her mother had ever said a cross word about her work. It took Hannah by surprise, though perhaps she shouldn't have been shocked. After all, they were a close family, and ever since the fire, Hannah had been pulling away from them.

Not intentionally, of course. She'd simply been trying to find some solace in her life. And she'd found that sense of peace away from her mother's constant fretting, her father's worried eyes, and the group of letters locked in a box under her bed. Paul had so enjoyed writing her short, sweet, silly notes.

Her need to immerse herself in different surroundings must not have escaped her mother's notice.

"I'm fine, Mamm. Mr. and Mrs. Ross are simply busy. They need me and I like being needed."

"We need you here, too."

"For what?"

Her mother blinked. "For everything. For you to be part of this family. Your sister and brother are missing ya."

Her brother, Calvin, was sixteen and Malinda was seventeen. Both were in the midst of their *rumspringa* and busy with their friends. In addition, Calvin had just gotten a job at Kinsinger's in the mail room. He loved his new job and being around the older men. And Malinda? Well, Malinda was always either sewing for some Amish families or giggling with her girlfriends. Neither of them was fretting about their older sister's absence. Hannah knew that for a fact.

But telling her mother that was another story. As she contemplated how to best alleviate her mother's worries, Hannah fidgeted with the seam of her raspberry-colored apron.

Oh, but she really needed to leave!

Still eyeing her closely, her mother placed a hand on one of her hips, a sure sign she was peeved. "Hannah, do you not have anything more to say?"

"I'm sorry, Mamm, but I really need to get going."

"Oh, you. Work isna going to make Paul come back."

Hannah winced. "I know that." Nothing was going to make him come back. Not even spending time at his grave or rereading his letters or staying by her mother's side. She edged toward the door.

Her mother noticed and moved closer. "Dear, maybe you should speak with Eli again."

"I don't need to be counseled, Mamm. I simply like working for the Ross family. I enjoy taking care of Christopher. Please don't invent things to worry about. I am fine."

"All right. Do you have your lunch?"

She held up her lunch kit. "I do."

"Is that enough?"

"There's always food there. Mrs. Ross usually leaves me something to eat."

"*Jah*, but is it any good?"

"It is wonderful. She's a good cook." As a bit of dismay flashed in her mother's eyes, Hannah reached out and gave her mother a hug. "I love you, Mamm. Please don't worry about me."

She held her tightly. "I can't help it. I miss you and love you."

"I miss you, too, but I'm growing up. It's time I find my own way."

"I know." But the expression in her mother's eyes told a different story. Hannah could practically feel her disappointment.

After grabbing a yellow cardigan, she slipped it on, picked up her canvas tote bag, and hurried off to the Ross house.

She'd just passed the market and the notion store when she heard Aaron Kurtz call out her name.

"*Jah*, Aaron?" she asked, barely containing her impatience.

He jogged closer. "*Danke.* I didn't think you were going to stop."

"I must get to work." She was only about five minutes away. If she hurried, she would arrive a good fifteen minutes early, which meant she could visit with Mrs. Ross and hear about her latest book club party.

"You're still working?" Before she could answer, he shrugged. "Well, that's all right. I'll walk with you."

She didn't want to walk with him. And though the right thing to do would be to let him have his say, she was frankly tired of his anger. "I'd rather we didn't walk together."

"Why? No one will think anything of it. I'm engaged, you know."

Hannah knew that. Besides, she and Aaron couldn't have been a worse match. No one who knew her would think that she'd ever harbor special feelings for him.

But instead of sharing that, she remained where she was. "If it's important, we can talk right here. Was there something you needed?"

"You mean besides my father?"

There he went again. Dwelling on his loss and bringing it up at every opportunity.

Furthermore, she didn't like how he seemed to think they were friends now. They'd never been close. Paul had never especially cared for him. And she? Well, Aaron Kurtz was everything she *didn't* like in a man.

All of that was why, she supposed, her temper snapped. "Oh, for heaven's sake, Aaron. *Shtobb*."

A muscle in his cheek twitched. "Stop what?" he asked bitterly. "Stop caring? Stop questioning? Stop grieving?"

"Yes. Stop everything. Stop bringing up your pain and sorrow to me all the time," she blurted, not even attempting to watch her words or her tone. "You are sounding like . . . like a petulant child. I am tired of hearing about it."

His fists clenched at his sides as he inhaled sharply.

Suddenly, Hannah didn't think he looked weak and pitiful. Instead, there was a new glare in his eyes. He looked dangerous and more than a bit frightening. She was tempted to step away.

Reminding herself that she had nothing to fear from him, she said, "Aaron, though I, too, lost someone I loved in the fire, that is where our similarities end. I don't wish to keep talking about the fire or listening to your suspicions."

"They are not suspicions," he bit out. "The Kinsingers should have checked the Dumpsters more regularly. You know that. I know that," he continued, his voice rising with every word. "Hannah, they should never have allowed that Dumpster next to the warehouse. Furthermore—"

He was causing a scene. More than one person was staring at them. Listening. Worse, he was making her feel nervous and anxious. And making her even later for work. "Stop! You're yelling at me and I don't care for it. Now, I must go—"

He reached out and gripped her upper arm. "Do not walk away from me."

"Aaron, we have nothing to speak of. Let go." She jerked her arm, but instead of releasing it, he dug in his fingers. And pulled.

She stumbled, attempting to keep her balance. Shocked by the way he was holding her, she slapped at his hand. "You are hurting me. Stop."

"Stop? That seems to be all you can say."

She was becoming frightened. "I canna help you, Aaron," she said in an effort to find a way for him to see reason. "Making me stand here and listen to you isn't going to change my mind. Instead, all you are going to do is make me want to avoid you."

"You'll listen. I'll make sure of it."

"I don't know how. Now, let—"

His slap across her face halted the rest of her words.

She cried out in pain, just as a voice in the distance called her name. "Hannah!"

Instantly, Aaron released her. Shaking, she pressed her hands to her cheeks and tried to catch her breath.

Then she became aware that Rob had been the one to come to her rescue. The expression on Rob's face was one she'd never seen before. He literally looked like he was about to grab Aaron and hit him. Rose, standing by his side, looked fierce, too. Her muscles looked ready to spring and a thin line of fur was standing up along the middle of her back.

But instead of being cowed by Rob, Aaron scowled. "Move on, man. This ain't no business—"

"This *is* my business. *She* is my business," Rob said.

At last Aaron stepped away.

The relief that Rob was by her side was so welcoming, Hannah felt tears spring to her eyes.

"Hannah," Rob murmured, "are you all right?"

"I am fine." She was about to add more when Rose sidled up next to her and leaned close. Before Hannah knew what she was about, she got down on her knees and hugged the dog's neck.

Rose responded with a wet lick.

As she attempted to get her bearings again, she heard Rob speak, each word cold and spoken with such clipped force it sounded as if he was struggling not to lose his temper.

"You listen to me, and listen well. You do not go near this girl again. You do not touch her. If you do, I will find you."

"And do what?" Aaron taunted.

"I'll make sure you hurt as much as she does," Rob replied, his expression completely serious. "I don't care who you are or what you are—Amish or English or French—if you hurt her again, I will retaliate. Hannah has me looking out for her now."

Aaron spit on the ground, his posture all bluster. "Is this why you didn't want me walking with ya, Hannah? Because you've already found a new man?"

She didn't say a word. Though it was cowardly, she simply just wanted him to go away.

"Now I understand why you don't care about Paul or what I've discovered about the accident. You've already moved on," Aaron called out loudly over his shoulder. Loud enough for everyone on the street to hear. Loud enough for Hannah to wince in shame.

Ignoring Aaron's last outburst, Rob crouched down by her side. "Hannah, honey, he left. Can you get back on your feet? Will you be okay to walk? Or would you rather I carry you?"

After wiping her eyes and taking a fortifying breath, Hannah climbed back to her feet.

"Easy, now." Rob grasped her elbow to steady her.

His touch felt comforting but she needed to show both him and herself that she was okay. "I'm all right," she said. "I can walk." She tried to smile but she feared it was as unsteady as her voice. "I, uh, was just shaken up."

"I can imagine." His expression was hard as his eyes skimmed over her. "Were you on your way to work?" When she nodded, he carefully placed a hand on the small of her back. "Come on, then. Let's get you to the Rosses'. We'll talk there, where there's some privacy. And put some ice on your cheek."

Conscious of the fact that at least a dozen people were staring at her, she nodded. She did need to get off the street and somewhere private. She was so rattled and confused.

Rose seemed to understand that Hannah needed her support because as they walked along, the big dog kept looking at her with what she was sure was a worried expression.

When they at last turned on Plum Street, Rob spoke again. "I can't tell you how freaked out I was when I saw that guy grab you." After a pause, he added, "And I don't think I'll ever be able to tell you how I felt when I saw him strike you."

"I'm glad you were there." Belatedly, she realized that she hadn't even thanked him. "Thank you for coming to my rescue."

"Don't ever thank me for that. I'm just glad I

was there." Looking at her closely, he added, "More than that, I wish it had never happened."

"Me, too." When they got to the Rosses' driveway, she pulled away from his reassuring hand and attempted to look more put together than she felt. "Well, thank you again. I'd best get inside and see to Christopher."

"Not so fast," he murmured. Instead of turning away, he walked her right up to the front door and knocked twice.

Melissa opened the door. She blinked when she saw Hannah standing beside Rob. "Good morning. Hannah, do you have an escort now?" she teased.

Hannah tried to smile, she really did. But instead of smiling, she felt her lip tremble.

At once, Melissa's happy expression turned concerned. Then horrified. "Oh my gosh! Hannah, honey, your cheek is swollen and I think you have the beginnings of a black eye. What happened?"

Her question brought forth York, who was holding a squirming Christopher. "Hannah? Hannah, why is your cheek bright red?"

Her eyes filled with tears. "Um . . . well, I . . ."

Rob wrapped an arm around her shoulders. "She's had a tough morning. I was taking Rose for a walk when I saw some guy not only grab Hannah's arm and yank her, but he slapped her face, too. She's hurt."

Both York and Melissa were staring at her, stunned. Though tears were streaming down her face, Hannah knew they deserved some kind of explanation. Still, she had never felt more unsure or afraid of what to do or say. "Aaron Kurtz grabbed me . . . because I wouldn't listen to him."

"We need to get her inside," Rob said. "And she needs some ice on her cheek. And maybe her arm. Melissa, could you look at her shoulder, too, before you leave?"

Melissa shuttled her inside. "Of course. Come on in, everyone. Yes, Rose, you too. Oh, Hannah! You poor thing."

When the door closed, Rob told Rose to go lie down. Then the three of them escorted Hannah into the living room.

After Melissa motioned her to the couch, York crouched down in front of Hannah. "Do you need to go home?"

She shook her head. "I'm fine. You need to work and I don't want to be any trouble—"

"Hannah, you're a part of our family! Caring about you isn't any trouble. Now, do you want to rest here for a few minutes, or can Melissa take you to our bedroom and look at your arm?"

Hannah glanced up at Rob. "Rob, you have gotten everyone spun up."

Ignoring her comment, he asked softly, "What do you want to do? Rest or get looked at?"

When she realized that none of them was going to back down, she sighed. "We can go look at my arm."

In no time, she was guided into the master bedroom. After Melissa closed the door, she said, "Where did that man grip you?"

"High on my left arm. Near my shoulder."

After helping Hannah take off her sweater, Melissa looked at the row of pins holding her dress together. "Do you want to slip your arm out, then call for me, or do you want help?"

Hannah knew she would forever wonder what had possessed her to say what she did, but instead of seeking privacy, she simply said, "You can help me, if you don't mind."

"Not at all." Looking intently at her dress, Melissa slipped out the first pin, then the second. After Hannah helped her with the third, Melissa said, "This might be enough." Then she helped Hannah ease the dress over her shoulder so only the cotton shift she wore underneath was visible.

Then she inhaled sharply. "Oh my goodness. You are quite bruised, Hannah. You've got several marks. They are going to be black and blue within an hour." Gazing at her face, she said, "I'm afraid your eye's going to look worse, too."

"I'll be okay." But still she walked to the mirror and examined herself. There she saw what Melissa had. A full set of angry bruises marked her skin.

"Thank goodness Rob came along."

"*Jah*."

"Is she okay?" York asked from outside the door. "We're going crazy out here."

"She's okay."

"How bad is it?"

Melissa glanced at Hannah. "You are covered up, but we can put a throw on you, too, so only your arm is visible. You can let my husband see or not, it's up to you. But if you wouldn't mind, it would make him feel better. He's worried about you."

"I don't mind. It's just my arm. Plus, he is a doctor."

Melissa smiled. "He is, indeed." But when she went to open the door, both Rob and York entered.

The moment Rob saw her state of undress, he stopped. "Sorry, Hannah. I'll wait outside."

She wasn't shy, and well, it was just her arm. It was actually kind of humorous the way everyone wanted to inspect her but not be offensive. Holding out her arm, she said, "I don't mind if you want to see, too."

He looked as if he was debating with himself, but eventually he stepped in behind York and glared at her bruises. "I'm so sorry, Hannah."

"There is nothing to be sorry about. You didn't do anything," she said as York passed Christopher to Melissa before carefully touching her bruises, then asked her to move her arm around.

Feeling self-conscious, she did as he asked. "See, I am going to be fine."

York stepped back toward the door. "I think you're going to be sore. We should probably put a cold compress on your arm and your cheek. And give you a couple of pain relievers. I'll go take care of that." He left down the hall, his footsteps sounding sure.

"We're going to take care of you," Melissa said, jiggling the baby against her hip. "Come along, Rob. Let's let Hannah get put back together. Take your time, dear."

When Hannah was alone, she closed her eyes. She felt anxious and exhausted. After giving into a bit of self-pity, she set her dress to rights, then went to the master bathroom and splashed water on her face.

Then, knowing the three of them were waiting for her, she opened the door.

Rob was leaning against the wall in the hallway. "You didn't have to wait."

"I wanted to." Dark concern was etched in his expression. "I can't stop wanting to simply stare at you. To make sure you are all right."

"He rattled me, but I'm fine, Rob," she said gently as they walked into the living room where York and Melissa were waiting on her. Christopher was lying on his favorite quilt in the middle of the room.

"I wish I would have gotten there earlier."

"This is as much my fault as anyone else's," York said from his position on the couch. "I knew we should have been driving you back and forth from your house. From now on, we'll do that."

Melissa nodded. "Hannah, why don't you take the rocking chair? I know how much you like to sit there."

Hannah did as Melissa bid. The moment she sat down, Melissa handed her a soft, cold fabric packet. "Put this on your arm."

Rob sat down across from her, his elbows braced on his knees. "Where can I find this guy?"

"Why?"

"I'm going to go talk to him."

She could only imagine the commotion that would cause! "*Nee*. You canna do that."

"I'm not going to hurt him, Hannah. But he needs to know that you are not alone."

As his words sank in, she blinked. She wasn't alone, was she? She had Mr. and Mrs. Ross and Rob and her family. Paul was gone but she had moved on, and she'd filled the hole he'd left with good, caring people.

Tears sprang to her eyes as she looked from Melissa to York and at last to Rob, who was so tense, it looked as if he was ready to spring into action to save her all over again. "I'm so blessed to have each of you," she said.

Then, to her distress and dismay, she promptly started crying. Again.

Immediately, Rob rushed to her side. He practically picked her up and carried her to the couch, then curled his arms around her, enveloping her in the best of hugs. As Melissa sat on her other side and patted her back, Rob murmured, "You cry all you want. We're here, Hannah. We're here and we're not going anywhere."

And so she did. Tears had never felt so cleansing.

Chapter 19

Aaron felt as if his body belonged to a different person. Every time he looked at his hands, he remembered them hurting Hannah Eicher. And with that vision came a shame like he'd never experienced, overwhelming him.

Yet again, his temper had overpowered what he knew to be right. Because of that, he'd hurt a woman, this time in front of half the town.

He could only imagine the rumors that would fly after his outburst today. People would no doubt avoid him. It was no less than he deserved. No, he deserved far more than that. He should be shunned.

With deep regret in his heart, he walked down the quiet street toward Hope's house. He remembered that today was her day off and he was thankful for that. Otherwise she might have witnessed his horrible behavior, too.

Now he only had to tell her about it.

Her mother answered the door with her usual smile. "Aaron, *gut matin*! What a nice surprise. Hope will be so happy to see you."

Taking off his hat, he glanced down the hall. "I need to speak with her, if I may."

"Of course you may talk with her," she said, concern clouding her eyes. "You know you never need to ask about that."

"*Danke.*"

"Well, come in. Would you like a slice of pie? I know it's still morning, but it's apple and it's warm. I just made it."

"I think it would be best if I talked with Hope out here, if she doesn't mind. I won't be staying long."

"Of course." She stepped back. "I'll go get her."

Aaron turned and took a seat in one of the white wicker chairs that decorated their wide front porch.

When Hope joined him, it was obvious that her mother had mentioned that he seemed agitated. Without a word, she closed the front door and sat in the love seat next to him. As usual, he couldn't get over how pretty she was. Today she had on a yellow dress. She was barefoot, too. She looked like a young girl. Actually, she looked like the girl he'd fallen in love with back when they were in school together.

For most of his life, he'd simply assumed that she would be his one day. His wife. The mother of his children. To his shame, he'd taken that for granted.

No longer, though, because now she was likely going to exist only in his dreams.

"Aaron, what's come over you?" she asked. "You're staring at me as if we were strangers."

"I, uh . . . I was just remembering what you looked like when you were eleven."

She wrinkled her nose. "I was gangly. All arms and legs. Please don't think of me like that."

He smiled. "I liked you then, too."

She smiled, but it didn't reach her eyes. "Why did you come over here?"

"I did something today that I need to tell you about." Knowing there was no good way to be gentle about what he was about to say, he blurted, "I . . . I hit Hannah Eicher. On Main."

She blinked. "What?" she whispered. "I'm . . . I'm afraid I don't understand."

Unable to see the confusion and disappointment in her eyes any longer, he looked down at his hands, which were folded between his knees. "Ever since my father died, I've been having a difficult time with my temper. I start out the day all right, but then, little by little, I feel an anger I've hidden deep inside me break free. Before long, it's taken ahold of me."

"I've never noticed that."

"I've kept it hidden from you." He forced himself to meet her gaze. She deserved to be spoken to directly and he deserved to observe her pain. "But, Hope, even though I've kept the worst of it from you, I haven't done the same with my family. I've lashed out at my sisters. At my brothers. Darla has gotten the worst of it. I've grabbed her too tightly. Bruised her. Said terrible things, hurtful things to her."

Hope shook her head. "Aaron, that ain't you. I bet you are making it worse than it is."

"*Nee*. I've been pretending I am better than I am." As he at last spied the dismay in her eyes, the sadness he had expected to see, he continued. "I've also been giving Hannah Eicher a difficult time."

"Why?"

"Because she was doing better, I guess. She loved Paul, but she got a new job. She seemed happy. She was coping, while I wasn't. Today, when I was badgering her yet again, she told me that she didn't want to be near me anymore." He took a calming breath. He didn't want to remember what had happened but he needed to be completely honest with someone. He knew it should be her. "When she pushed me away, when she rejected me, something snapped. I was so hurt. Frustrated. And then, before I quite knew what I was doing, I slapped her."

Hope released a ragged sigh. "Oh, Aaron."

Swallowing hard, he pushed on. "She has an English friend. He came to her rescue. He, well, I think if she hadn't been standing there, he probably would have slugged me. I would have deserved it, too."

Hope closed her eyes for a long moment before gazing at him in concern again.

He saw everything he'd ever wished to see in her eyes. Compassion, care. Love. But instead of making him feel better, that sweetness made him realize how undeserving he was. He needed to earn her love and compassion again.

"Hope, I need to break our engagement."

"Is that what you want?"

It wasn't what he wanted, but it was what needed to be done. There was no way he was going to risk hurting her. If he ever did that, he didn't know if he could live with himself. "I'm sorry. I'm sorry that I can't be the person you need me to be."

Aaron got to his feet. Now that he'd done what he had to do, he needed to get away from her. Needed to get away from everyone and figure out how to make things right.

As he turned away and started down her front steps, he didn't look back.

But he couldn't help but notice her silence.

He tried to find comfort in the fact that she wasn't calling him back. He knew he needed time and he wanted to be glad that she was giving that time to him. But right then, he had never felt more alone in his life.

LUKAS HAD JUST finished reviewing a new contract to install cherry flooring in a Columbus office building when his door blew open.

"Lukas, you'll never guess what happened," Rebecca announced as she rushed in.

Leaning back in his chair, he said, "How about I know that you entered my office yet again without knocking?"

It was a sure sign of how agitated she was that she didn't rise to the bait. "Aaron Kurtz grabbed Hannah Eicher on the street," she said in a rush of words. "And then guess what? He slapped her! Just as me and Anne Miller and Jody Yoder were about to step in, some Englisher came running up with his big dog and came to her aid."

Lukas blinked, sure he hadn't heard that correctly. "Say again?"

"You heard me. Aaron Kurtz hit Hannah Eicher."

He was torn between throwing his head back in a sigh and pounding his fist on his desk. He settled for attempting to keep his emotions in check. He needed to think clearly. "This is awful. Last time we talked, I thought he was going to attempt to change."

"Well, he didn't," she said as she plopped down on the couch.

"What happened?"

"I guess Aaron was yet again ranting about the fire and who knows what else and Hannah didn't want to hear it. Then, next thing she knew, he grabbed ahold of her arm, jerked her hard, and then slapped her cheek."

Lukas felt physically ill. Pushing back from his desk, he stumbled to his feet. He knew Hannah; they all did. There wasn't a sweeter girl in Charm. His buddy Paul had been smitten with her for the past two years. Now, though it didn't really make any sense, Lukas felt like she was partly his responsibility since Paul had passed away. He felt like everyone who was suffering the consequences of the accident was his responsibility.

Someone had to take ownership, and now that he ran the company, it might as well be him.

Oh, but he should have walked Aaron right over to the bishop. He'd been a fool to think that his threats had meant a single thing to Aaron.

"Is she okay?" he asked. "Where is she? Does she need me to call the doctor?"

Rebecca waved a hand, brushing off his concerns. "Don't worry, Lukas. If I was worried about her, I wouldn't be here in your office. I'd be at her side."

"So she's okay?"

"I think so. Like I said, this Englisher friend of hers seemed to take care of things." With a shake of her head, she continued. "You should have seen him, Luke. He was right in Aaron's face. I thought he was going to hit him." She sighed. "Anyway, once Aaron walked away, the man escorted her to Plum Street."

Englishers lived on Plum Street. It was full of fancy brick houses, each on two-acre lots.

"Why there? He should have brought her home to her mother."

"I thought the same thing, but Jody told me that Hannah works as a nanny for a doctor and a banker."

Yet again, he was amazed by Rebecca's detective skills. "I can't believe you know so much."

"It ain't anything, Lukas. Anyway, as soon as she went down Plum with that man, I had to come tell you." She shook her head. "Poor Hannah, right?"

"*Jah*. For sure." Crossing his arms across his chest, he thought about Aaron, thought about everything he'd tried that hadn't worked. "I wonder what I should do about Aaron now. If he's hitting poor Hannah, his violence has gone far enough."

"He has really become unpredictable."

He was just about to ask Rebecca to help him brainstorm some ideas when he saw Darla standing at the door. It was something of a shock. She hadn't been at the mill since the fire. Concerned, he took a step to greet her. "Hey."

"Hi." She looked from him to Rebecca, her eyes sad. "I guess you can imagine why I'm here."

"*Jah*."

"I'm sorry about Aaron," Rebecca said. "I don't know what's gotten into him."

"Where is he?" Lukas asked.

She shrugged. "I am not sure. Home, most likely."

"I don't want you seeing him right now." Lukas couldn't believe he was saying it, but he was truly afraid for what might happen if Darla got in her brother's way.

"I know you are busy, but that's why I came," Darla said. "I need someone to come with me when I go talk to him. He needs some help but I'm not sure how he's going to react to it."

Rebecca stared at her. "I'll go with you."

"Absolutely not," Lukas said. "I'll go."

After a moment's hesitation, Darla said, "You know, a year ago, I would have never imagined Aaron would act like this. We've always been different, but I never used to fear him. Now, I'm not only afraid of what he will do to me when he's angry, but who else he's going to hurt." Her last words had come out in a tremor. "This . . . this is so awful," she said as tears started to flow. "I feel like this is my fault even though I know it's not."

"It's not," Rebecca whispered. "This is Aaron's burden."

As if Rebecca's comforting words had unlocked a dam, Darla started crying harder. "I'm sorry. I didn't come over here to fall apart on your couch, but I don't know what to do."

Rebecca wrapped her arms around Darla, giving her a reassuring hug. When Darla pulled away, looking much resigned, Lukas crouched in front of her.

"I'll go over with you." After sharing a meaningful look with Rebecca, Lukas added, "I'll get a couple other men, too."

Darla's eyes widened in alarm. "Do you think that is necessary?"

"Maybe. I'm not afraid of being hurt but I don't want Aaron saying that I coerced him or threatened him in some way. We also need to meet with the bishop as soon as possible. If our church can't handle things, I fear the police are going to get involved."

Darla closed her eyes. "This is so awful. My father wouldn't recognize Aaron right now."

"I agree that he's not himself," Lukas said as he got to his feet. "But the time to worry about overreacting has passed." He was pretty certain he was going to do just about anything he could to put a stop to Aaron's behavior now.

Darla sighed. "I guess you are right." As she edged back to the doorway, she added, "I feel like I've inadvertently put you in the middle of this. I'm so sorry."

"I'm not. I don't want you facing anything by yourself ever again."

Rebecca hugged Darla once more. "Don't worry about Lukas. This is what friends do. We help each other, through thick and thin."

Steeling her shoulders, Darla nodded. "I hope we get to the thick part again real soon."

Lukas reached out and brushed a finger along her soft cheek. "We will, I promise," he said gently.

"Now, you sit tight with Rebecca. I'm going to go get some help."

"*Danke*, Lukas," she mumbled.

Unable to help himself, he bent down and pressed his lips to her temple. "Never thank me for helping you." Straightening, he winked, hoping to draw out a smile from her. "Don't forget, one of these days I'm counting on you to say yes when I ask you to marry me."

When she smiled, he felt like he'd just done something pretty special.

He kept his smile in place until he was out of the room, down the hall, and out of her sight. Only then did he clench his fists and lean his head against the wall in a mixture of frustration and anger. After allowing himself those few seconds, he forced himself to let it go. Anger would solve nothing.

Instead, he prayed to the one who could always be counted on. "Lord, I'm going to need You. Actually, I think a whole bunch of us are going to need Your help for the next couple of hours. Be with Darla and Hannah and Aaron and me, wouldja? We're going to need Your guidance in order to get through this day without making things worse."

Remembering to give thanks for his sister and for the fact that Darla now trusted him enough to seek him out, Lukas strode out the main door toward the warehouse where Simon Hochstetler was in charge.

Though they hadn't spent much time in each other's company lately, Lukas knew without a doubt that Simon would drop everything to help him and Darla. Lukas found him working next to a team of younger men, supervising inventory on a recent shipment that had arrived.

"Hey, boss," Simon said with a wink toward his team. "Coming to check on us?"

Though he was anxious to get back to Darla, Lukas knew his employees needed to hear some praise. "There's no need for that. I know each of you does a good job."

Simon looked at his crew with a fond expression. "We're doing our best. Ain't so?"

As the men on his team grinned and went back to work, Simon reached out and clasped his hand. "It's a shame that you've got to come out here just so we can catch up."

"I wish I was only dropping in for a visit. Unfortunately, I've got another reason."

"What happened? Please don't say we've had another accident."

"Oh, no. Nothing like that. I . . . well, I need you to leave work and come with me, if you would."

"Of course. Hold on a sec." Immediately, Simon stepped to Jake, an older man on his team, and spoke to him quietly. After Jake nodded, Simon led the way out of the warehouse.

When they were standing alone in the open air, he said, "How can I help you?"

"Darletta just came in seeking my help with Aaron."

Simon whistled low. "I heard about what happened this morning." A line formed in between his brows. "I canna even believe he dared to hit Hannah."

"I heard she's okay. Is that true?"

Simon shrugged. "I don't know. I heard some English friend of hers came to the rescue." He lowered his voice. "But how could she be all right? Aaron yelled and grabbed her in the middle of Main Street. Then he slapped her cheek. She's a gentle sort and her parents are, too. I can't imagine either of her parents ever laying a hand on her, and we know Paul never did such a thing."

"Of course not."

"John didn't raise him to be this way, either. He'd be so upset to learn about Aaron's behavior."

As they walked toward the main building, Lukas said, "Darla wants me to talk to him with her. I want you and me and someone else to go with her."

"You think he's that dangerous?"

"*Nee*, I fear he's that delusional. I'm afraid we

need more than the two of us there. I don't want Aaron to ever lie about our conversation or our actions. If three of us go, he can't later say we did something that we didn't."

Simon grunted. "Who else do you want to come? Levi?"

"I don't think Levi is the right choice."

"He's still blamin' John Kurtz for the fire?"

Lukas shrugged. "He would be on our side about Hannah, I don't doubt that. But I think his emotions are still too raw when it comes to Aaron and Darla."

"Who then?"

"Roman Schrock," Lukas replied after a moment's thought. "He's steady, well-respected by everyone, and a few years older than us. He might be the voice of reason Aaron needs."

Simon smiled slightly. "He's also as strong as an ox. If Aaron gets out of hand, we'll have no worries there. Roman will make sure he behaves himself."

Changing direction, Lukas headed toward the custom-woodworking warehouse. Roman was a master craftsman and was often called upon to work with some of their most demanding and wealthiest customers. No job was too difficult. He was calm in any situation.

He looked up from the board he was carving

when they entered. "Morning, Lukas. Simon. Can I help ya?"

"*Jah.* I'm afraid there's no easy way to say this except to come right out with it. I need you to come with Simon and me to talk to Aaron Kurtz."

Roman wiped down his station. "What's going on?"

"Aaron accosted Hannah Eicher on Main Street this morning. I know I might be overstepping my bounds, but I'd sure appreciate it if you could come with us now to try and convince Aaron to seek help."

"We're a community. A church community. One of our members needs help? Of course we need to help him. You're not overstepping anything, Lukas."

That was why Lukas had known Roman would be the right person to bring with him and Simon. Roman was devout. He also cared about everyone deeply. Just as important, he was known for being compassionate and level-headed.

"*Danke*," Lukas said.

As the three of them walked back to the main office, they stayed silent. Lukas had taken to praying for guidance again. He didn't know what was going through the other men's minds, but he imagined they were thinking many of the same things.

It seemed that another turning point had come in their lives, and this one could be just as devastating. Now, instead of fighting a fire, they were going to have to fight a man's bitterness and determination to ruin other people's lives. It was going to be up to Lukas, Simon, Roman, and Darla to make sure that didn't happen. And at the moment, the situation seemed as out of Lukas's control as the fire had been. Anything could happen.

And that meant it probably would.

Chapter 20

Darla had been biting her nails while she waited for Lukas to return to his office. Though he'd been gone for less than twenty minutes, it had felt like an eternity. She supposed that was what happened when a person was at a complete loss about what to do.

And that was how she felt about Aaron. Every time his anger snapped, she'd hoped it would be the very last time. She supposed there had been a part of her that had assumed he would simply wake up one day, apologize for the way he'd been acting, and return to his regular self.

But of course that hadn't happened.

Now he was hurting other people. Sweet Hannah Eicher, who had already lost Paul.

Darla felt partly responsible for the incident. She'd been so determined to not take her injuries seriously, so intent on protecting Aaron, that she hadn't done more to stop him.

And now it had come to this.

"Sorry you had to wait so long," Lukas said when he entered the room, Simon and Roman on his heels. Each was wearing a grim, determined expression. As a matter of fact, they looked like a trio not to be messed with. If she hadn't known they were on her side, she would've been anxious not to cross their path.

"It wasn't long." Darla deliberately folded her hands on her lap so she'd stop biting her nails. "Hi, Roman. Simon."

"Hey, Darla," Simon greeted her. Roman simply nodded.

Studying them, Darla couldn't help but approve of Lukas's choices for support. Both were good men whom she felt comfortable with.

After she got to her feet, Roman enfolded her in a gentle hug, much like she imagined he would have given his twin girls. "I'm so sorry, Darla."

She closed her eyes and let his comforting presence soothe her frayed nerves. He was a big man, and his hug made her think of a teddy bear. "*Danke*. I guess you're going to come help me talk to Aaron?"

"I wouldn't miss it." His usual pleasant expression turned hard. "Lukas shared that Hannah isn't the first woman he's treated roughly. I wish you would have reached out to me. I would have talked to your brother before now."

She tucked her head, hating the guilt that was consuming her. If she had spoken up more and hidden her pain and bruises less, could Hannah's pain have been prevented?

"Hey now," Lukas said as he lifted her chin with one finger and looked into her eyes. "No more guilt. For what it's worth, I don't think Aaron would have been any more receptive to interference from Roman or Simon than he was to me."

She took a shuddering breath. "You might be right."

He winked. "I know I am."

"Are you sure you don't want us to simply take care of things?" Simon asked. "You can go visit with Amelia Kinsinger. Lukas can come get you when we are back."

She glanced Lukas's way.

He nodded. "He's hurt you enough, Darla. He might lash out and say something to hurt your feelings if you are there. If you don't want to go to my farm, you're welcome to stay here. I'll make sure Rebecca sits with you."

It was tempting to simply put her needs into the hands of these three strong men. She knew they would not only have her best interests at heart, but they would also be pleased to help her. But if she let them take care of things, she would continue to be Aaron's victim. And, maybe, a victim of this whole tragedy. No, she needed to talk to Aaron once again. She also needed to be there for the rest of her family.

She couldn't hide from the truth any longer.

"I need to be there."

To her amazement, Lukas didn't argue. Instead, he smiled softly. "See? You are just as strong as you ever were. I'm proud of you. Let's go, then."

"I hope this doesn't go as badly as I fear it might," she said as they walked down the hall, their shoes and boots pattering softly against the wood floor that was shined to a deep polish.

"Something has to change. Aaron needs to remember who he is and what he believes in," Simon said quietly as they walked down the stairs toward the front reception area. "For some reason, he has forgotten."

"Let's go help him. It's time, I think."

She liked the way he phrased that. They weren't

going to simply put a stop to Aaron's poor choices and abuse, they were going to help him. If Aaron accepted their help, then he would no longer feel as if he was being ignored. He could begin to heal.

After checking in with Rebecca, they set off toward her farm, walking quietly two by two—Roman and Simon in front, Darla by Lukas's side right behind.

Their group of four drew many curious glances, and Darla supposed she couldn't blame anyone for staring at them. Moreover, she was thankful she was no longer alone. Walking into Kinsinger Mill by herself an hour ago had been one of the hardest things she'd ever done.

Now, at least, she was part of a group.

LUKAS HAD BEEN debating with himself the whole way to Darla's farm. He had mixed feelings about taking matters into his own hands, and even more mixed feelings about how to handle Darla.

He could tell that she was nervous for what was about to happen. He didn't blame her. She loved her brother and was still missing her father. In addition, she was part of a big family that no doubt had conflicting thoughts about both Aaron's behavior as well as the Kinsingers'. He didn't want to make the tension between her and her siblings worse than it already was.

By the time the four of them were halfway up the Kurtzes' driveway, Darla's twin brothers were standing on the front porch along with Patsy. All three were watching them approach with looks of concern on their faces.

Beside him, Darla inhaled sharply.

"You going to be able to handle this?" Lukas murmured under his breath.

She darted a glance his way. *"Jah."*

"If things get too tough, let me know, okay?"

"I'll be fine." Her blue eyes looked resolute, her posture stiff and sure.

But as they got closer, Lukas wasn't so sure. None of Darla's siblings looked all that pleased to see them. And so far none of them had said a word to Darla.

Just as he was about to ask them where Aaron was, Roman spoke.

"Hiya, Patsy. Hey, Samuel. Evan." He waved a hand, just like he'd stopped over for dessert after supper. "We stopped by to speak to Aaron. Is he around?"

Patsy crossed her arms over her chest. "What's going on?" she asked, her voice thick with worry. "It's the middle of the day. Did something happen at the mill?"

"I understand your concern, but we need to

speak to Aaron first," Roman said, his voice patient. "Where is he?"

"I'm not saying a thing until you tell me what's going on, Darla," Patsy replied.

After looking warily at Lukas, Darla stepped forward. "Patsy, Aaron caused some trouble in town this morning."

"What did he do?" Evan asked as he trotted down the steps.

Lukas released a breath he hadn't even realized he'd been holding. He was glad that Evan, at least, wasn't being standoffish toward his eldest sister. "Why don't you let us speak to Aaron first?" he said.

"I ain't a baby, Lukas. If something bad happened, we need to know." Lifting his chin, Evan continued. "You know I'm going to find out about it sooner or later."

Darla swallowed, then said, "He accosted Hannah Eicher on Main Street today."

All the salt and vinegar evaporated from Patsy's stance. After exchanging looks with Darla, she rushed down the stairs. "Is Hannah hurt?"

"We think so," Lukas replied. "Luckily, a friend of hers was nearby and took her to work."

Samuel ran down the stairs to stand beside his twin. "Lukas, are you sure that really happened?"

"It's true," Simon said, his expression quiet and stern. "A lot of people saw it."

Determined to get on with it, Lukas stared hard at Patsy. "Patsy, where's your *bruder*?"

"He's inside."

"Truly?" Roman raised his eyebrows. "He's hiding behind his sisters and brothers?"

For the first time, Patsy looked embarrassed. "He told me that Darla had probably made up another story about him."

Twin spots of color appeared on Darla's cheeks, making Lukas yearn to grab her brother and shake him until he promised to treat her with more respect.

"Do I need to go inside and get him, or will he come out?" Roman asked, his dark brown eyes staring at Patsy intensely.

After what felt like ten minutes, the door opened and Aaron walked out, pushing past Patsy. His eyes looked hooded but his voice was clear when he spoke. "It's the middle of the morning. I thought I was the only person not working at Kinsinger's anymore. Or are all of you paying a social call?"

"We wanted to talk to you about Hannah," Simon said. "Is there someplace we can speak?"

"What makes you think I'd welcome anything you had to say?"

"Because we've known each other a long time," Simon replied. "Because you must see that we want to help you."

Aaron crossed his arms and scowled at Darla. "Is this what your infatuation with Lukas has come to, sister? You are now making up tales about me and attempting to get the whole town to side against me?"

Darla's expression froze and pure pain entered her eyes. However, Lukas noticed that her voice didn't waver. "I'm not making up anything. I had nothing to do with this."

"No, you just brought them over here."

Lukas stepped forward, consciously blocking her from her brother's sight. "This isn't about Darla or your treatment of her, though I suspect I should have brought Roman and Simon with me the last time I came here to talk to you about your actions."

Roman coughed, gaining everyone's attention. "We need to talk, Aaron, and you need to listen. Where would you like to go?"

"Not in my home. Let's go to the back of the barn."

Lukas remembered there was an old picnic table behind the barn. "Let's go."

Aaron glared at his siblings. "All of you stay here. This ain't none of your business."

Samuel lifted his chin. After taking a visibly fortifying breath, he said, "It is if it's about you being mean and mad at all of us."

Beside him, Evan nodded. "We're tired of you yelling all the time. And you can't be mean to Darla anymore, neither."

Instead of looking at her siblings, Darla stared at Lukas, making him feel like he was ten feet tall. She was depending on him now, and he relished her belief in him.

Gently, he murmured, "I think it might be best if you stayed with Patsy and the boys."

To his relief, she nodded. "All right."

Though he was tempted to reach out and squeeze her hand in reassurance, he simply turned to Simon and Roman. "Let's go."

Neither man said a thing. Instead, they followed him and Aaron to the back of the barn.

It was time to take care of things. Lukas hoped God would give him the strength to do that in the right way.

Chapter 21

As Lukas perched on the top of an old picnic table behind the Kurtzes' barn, he couldn't help but remember the many times he'd spent lounging there, talking with Darla and her family. Though he loved his own home, he'd been here so often, and it brought back many fond memories of happier times—as well as more than a couple of less than happy ones.

Almost as if it had served as a cornerstone of his life.

He and Darla had carved their names in one of the picnic table legs and then spent days worrying about what would happen when her parents found out. It turned out they'd simply laughed when Darla had shamefully confessed their vandalism three days later. John had chuckled and said that he'd assumed it had been there for years.

Lukas had sat there with Darla when she'd had to help Gretel do homework. He'd kept Maisie company when she'd needed an escape from Patsy's nagging.

One hot day in July, Lukas had sat with Darla, Aaron, Rebecca, and the twins and gorged themselves on fresh vanilla ice cream. And John Kurtz had sat Lukas, Levi, and Aaron down when he'd gotten a report that the boys had been talking back to their teacher.

So, it was familiar. A place not much different from any other Amish family's backyard—filled with warm memories, private conversations, and a dozen benchmarks of childhood.

However, in all that time, he'd never felt as uncomfortable as he did at that moment. Here, he was sitting on top of the picnic table, as was Roman. Simon was sitting on one of the benches and Aaron was standing against the back wall of the barn, glaring at all of them.

"Say what's on your mind," Aaron said impatiently. "Unlike you three, I've got a lot planned. I'd like to get this over with as soon as possible."

Those words, said so dismissively, irked Lukas something fierce. Even before his father passed away, Lukas had been given a good amount of responsibility at the mill. He had been on the leadership team for years. Because of that, it was rare that any man in the community blatantly disregarded his presence. He had to remind himself that Aaron was feeling cornered, that the man needed compassion and patience instead of anger and accusations.

Thank goodness Roman didn't wait for Lukas to start things rolling. "Aaron, I'm afraid what I came to say can't be discussed quickly. Because I think we need to talk about your father."

Right then and there, the disdain that had filled Aaron's blue eyes evaporated. In its place was a new hesitancy highlighted by a fragile pain. After a second, he blinked, shuttering his expression. "I think not," Aaron said at last.

Lukas recognized that pain. He'd lived it. But he'd also witnessed the destruction it was causing. First with Darla, and now Hannah, and ultimately Aaron himself.

"I think differently," Lukas replied when he was sure he could keep his voice steady and calm. "Until you find a way to ease some of your pain, you are going to continue to carry it and hurt yourself and other people."

"I haven't hurt anyone."

Unable to stop himself, Lukas sprang to his

feet. "Don't lie. I've seen Darla's bruises. We've talked about it."

"Easy, Lukas," Roman said under his breath.

Aaron rubbed the back of his neck with one hand. "Stay out of my business. My sister ain't no concern of yours."

"What about Hannah Eicher?" Simon asked. "Whose business is she?"

Aaron stilled. "Is she okay?"

"You slapped her in the middle of Main Street," Simon replied. "How do you think she's doing?"

"What happened?" Roman asked. "How did you get so angry with her in the first place?"

Pure puzzlement filled Aaron's features. "I don't know. At first I just wanted to talk to her. I mean, I thought we'd become friends." His voice drifted off as he frowned. "But then she said she didn't want to talk to me. Not anymore." Staring at Roman, Aaron glared. "She was ignoring me. Ignoring Paul's death. She was ignoring everything I was telling her. I had to make her listen to me."

Lukas shook his head in disgust. "Hannah Eicher doesn't have a single reason to speak with you."

"Sure she did. Paul and I worked together."

"Aaron, we all worked together," Simon said.

"But that don't mean that Hannah's beholden to you."

"But she'd moved on. Like the fire didn't matter to her."

"Is that why you are so angry?" Lukas asked. "Is it because you don't want any of us to move on? Or is it that Mary Troyer blames your *daed*? Or is it because you think it was my fault? Do you really think that the fire could have been prevented?"

"It's everything," Aaron said at last. "I'm angry that it happened at all."

"It was no one's fault," Roman pointed out.

"*Nee*, it's the owners who are responsible. Lukas, your father should have known."

"How could he?" Simon pressed. "How would anyone have guessed that a rag could have started a spark in the middle of winter?"

"Well, my *daed* did not cause everyone's deaths."

"I know. We know," Lukas said. "I've never said differently."

"What about Levi?"

"Levi has his own opinion. He's working it out. Even though he's my brother, I don't agree with everything he says."

"Maybe you should be talking with him instead of me," Aaron said.

"Levi ain't attacking Hannah on the street,"

Simon said. "He's not hurting his sisters. You are. You need to get ahold of yourself, man."

Aaron deflated before their eyes. "I'm trying, but I can't seem to do that."

Roman leaned forward. "Why not? What purpose is it serving you?"

"If I move on, it means that our fathers' and friends' deaths didn't matter. I'm simply so frustrated. I feel like the Lord has forsaken all of us."

"The Lord did not forsake any of us," Roman said.

Aaron shook his head slowly. "But don't you see? He did. God wasn't with us the day of the fire. He wasn't there when the fire started. He looked the other way when the sirens went off. He ignored our prayers when so many people died. He stayed away when I was hurting and my *mamm* wouldn't get out of bed. He hasn't answered me when I've called for Him. He's left me alone."

Roman shook his head. "I hear you, Aaron, but I think you're wrong. God has been there all along. He hasn't left your side. Not once."

"Forgive me, but I don't feel his hands reaching out to me," Aaron said bitterly. "Especially not now."

Roman reached out and gripped Aaron's bicep. "What do you call this?" Aaron stilled. "The Lord gave us each other. He gave you plenty of people who have two good arms and two good hands. We're here right now reaching out to you. All you have to do is let us in."

"How can I?"

"Because to do otherwise would be the worst mistake," Simon answered. "We're here because we care. Because we want to help you."

After staring at them for a long moment, Aaron tilted his head back. "I've made so many mistakes. Do you think I can even be helped?" After a sigh, he stared at Lukas. "How am I going to be able to face Hannah ever again? How am I going to face her parents?"

Roman drew himself up to his impressive height. "Ask me to come with you."

Aaron stood up as well. "Why would any of you want to go with me?" His voice turned hard. Sarcastic. "So you can assure them that you gave me a talking-to?"

"If that's what it takes for them to believe you are sincere in your apology," Simon said, looking completely unfazed. "But more importantly, if we're by your side, maybe you'll finally remember that you aren't alone."

"I am alone."

"Not by a long shot," Roman said. "You might not think it, but there's a great many of us who want to help you."

For the first time, a glimpse of vulnerability shone in Aaron's eyes. "I'd like to think that is possible. But how are we all ever going to get past this? Those deaths are always going to be part of our lives."

"I'm not saying it's going to be easy, but it is possible. At least, I think it will be through prayer and patience," Roman said. "By reaching out to people instead of pushing them away. By waking up in the morning and hoping that each day will be easier than the day before."

"And if it's not?"

"Then remember you are in good company. All of us have trials that we're getting through, and if we don't, our turn will come soon enough."

Aaron opened his mouth, then to Lukas's surprise, he leaned his head back and sighed. "I don't know how my good intentions turned out so badly. I have hurt people." Glancing warily at Lukas, he added, "I told Hope that I'd like to end the engagement. I want to get better before we start a life together. She agreed. And Darla doesn't even trust me anymore."

"I don't blame Darla for not trusting you," Lukas said quietly.

"I don't blame her, either. I've hurt her in so many ways, I don't think I can ever make things right."

"You can start. Apologize. Ask for forgiveness. Then act differently. Be different."

"And if she's still upset?"

"Give her time," Lukas said. "And in the meantime, I'll help her, too. Because, you see, she's the best thing to ever happen to me. One day she is going to agree to marry me, too."

Roman laughed, breaking the tension between the four of them. "It's about time, Lukas. Honestly, only you would turn a conversation like this on its ear, Kinsinger."

Simon was grinning, too. "Any special reason why you chose to make your move in front of Roman and me?"

"Oh, for sure. I figured if you two were here Aaron wouldn't try to kill me. At least not until I said my piece."

Aaron shook his head. "You don't get it, do you?"

"Get what?"

"Even when I hated you, I knew that Darla was the girl for you. It can't be helped. You two have always been each other's best friend and sweethearts. No matter what someone else might try to do or say, nothing is ever going to change that." Sobering, he said, "Now I simply have to hope that I can repair the damage with my fiancée."

Simon said, "I don't have any experience in

engagements, but I have to believe that the right time for you and Hope will come when it really is the right time."

"Trust a man who has been married eight years," Roman said. "It's best to be sure of each other before vows are said."

That broke the ice. The four men looked at each other and grinned. Roman was known far and wide as being completely smitten with his bride.

Just as Lukas was about to offer his hand, Aaron beat him to it.

"*Danke*, Lukas," he said, reaching out. "I won't forget what you men did for me today."

Clasping his hand, Lukas said, "I won't, either."

Chapter 22

Two hours after Rob had escorted Hannah into the Rosses' house and everyone had inspected her bruises and stared at her like she might collapse into tears or faint, Hannah was alone with little Christopher again.

It had taken some doing to assure York and Melissa that she wanted to stay and work. And it took even more coaxing to get Rob to leave her side.

Now, as she sat across from Christopher in his high chair and attempted to get him to take a full bite of his rice cereal instead of spitting half of it onto his bib, Hannah couldn't help but reflect on how much things in her life had changed.

She no longer was relying on her parents to get through each day. Those days were far in the past. Now she sometimes wondered if she could ever go back to being the obedient, sheltered girl she'd been before the fire at the mill. She doubted it. Every week she took more things in the English world for granted.

She had also found a comfort and acceptance with Melissa, York, and Rob that had been missing in her Amish circle of friends. It wasn't as if they had changed; she had. She was different now. She no longer looked at her family as her foundation of support. Instead, it had become this group of people.

As a matter of fact, after Aaron had attacked her, it had never even occurred to her to ask to go home.

She wasn't sure what that meant. Had she taken a big step forward in her life, heading where the Lord had intended her to go? Or was she merely stumbling backward?

She wasn't sure.

Picking up the spoon again, she filled it halfway, then lifted it to the baby's lips. "Come now, Chris. Just another bite or two, if you please."

Christopher laughed, then popped open his lips, revealing two tiny bottom teeth. She quickly took advantage and slipped in the spoon—and sighed when he promptly spit the cereal out. Then, before she knew what he was about, he thrust his fist into the mess, grabbed ahold of her sleeve, and smeared it on her dress in record time. When he finished, he squealed.

"Ack," she said as she attempted to wipe it off. "Christopher, you are a messy babe."

When he giggled again, she smiled and set the bowl to one side. It was time to get him cleaned up and feed him a bottle. At least that activity was a clean one.

Just as she pulled off his bib, the back door opened and Melissa entered.

"Look at you two," she said. "I'm not sure who is going to need a bath more, him or you!"

"Probably me," Hannah said ruefully as she dampened a paper towel and began wiping the baby's cheeks and gooey hands. "Your son delights in spitting out cereal."

Instead of looking upset that Hannah wasn't keeping Christopher cleaner, Melissa laughed. "You might find this silly, but part of me is glad he is messy with you, too. Two nights ago he ruined a white blouse not five minutes after I had put it on. I'd actually begun to think I needed feeding lessons from you. You and Christopher always look as neat as pins when I come home from work every evening."

"That's because I do my best to clean us up—and the kitchen—during his afternoon nap."

"Now I feel better."

Hannah smiled. "My *mamm* always said that the Lord gave us babies so we wouldn't forget what it's like to cater to others without seeking anything in return. I guess that's what we're doing. Ain't so?"

Melissa nodded. "We certainly are. Please tell your mother that I think she's a wise woman."

"I will." After she wiped Christopher's tiny hands and mouth as best she could with the damp paper towel, Hannah detached the high chair tray and pulled him into her arms. "Did you decide to work from home again today?" she asked as she retrieved the bottle she'd warmed up earlier.

"Actually, no." She dragged out those two words, making Hannah stare at her in concern.

"Is something wrong?"

"No. Well, maybe. Hannah, when I got to work, I couldn't concentrate on anything. My mind kept drifting back to you and what happened to you this morning."

Hannah felt terrible. Melissa had an important job at the bank. Hannah was supposed to make her life easier, not cause more worry. "There was no need to disturb your day, Melissa."

"No need?" Looking a bit poleaxed, Melissa

walked to the living room. "I think we should have a talk, Hannah. Let's sit down."

Seeing that Melissa didn't mind her feeding Christopher his bottle, Hannah joined her in the living room. After sitting in her favorite rocking chair, she gave the baby his bottle and cuddled him close as he happily started drinking.

She knew from experience that his eyes would be closed before he quite finished it. He'd then take an hour nap. Usually, this was her favorite part of the morning, but now she knew she wasn't going to be able to relax.

Melissa was looking at her like she had a lot on her mind, and Hannah wasn't sure what to do next. She had no idea how to smooth things between them. Was Melissa so disturbed by what had happened with Aaron that she now feared for Christopher's safety? Though she knew Christopher was in no danger at all, Hannah couldn't think of any other reason for her boss to look so disturbed. Unless she suspected that Hannah had brought Aaron's anger on herself?

"I promise that I won't let what happened to me interfere with caring for your son," she said quietly. "I would never let any harm come to Christopher."

But instead of looking relieved, Melissa seemed even more agitated. After staring down at her hands for a moment, she spoke. "Hannah, I was concerned about *you*, not with you doing your job. I care about you, dear." She paused, letting Hannah dwell on that for a moment before continuing. "I came back because I felt guilty for leaving you like I did."

"Why would you feel that way?"

"Because York and I should have sat with you longer. Or made you some breakfast."

Now Hannah was really confused. "I ate breakfast at home."

Melissa smiled softly. "What I'm trying to say is that I shouldn't have put my job over your needs. We consider you part of the family now and family doesn't treat each other so callously." Looking agitated, she brushed back a strand of hair from her face. "I don't know what I was thinking. We should have driven you home so you could recover and rest. Instead, I left you to take care of my baby."

After glancing at Christopher and realizing he'd fallen fast asleep, Hannah shook her head. "I'm glad you did not."

"Are you sure? Because I would be happy to drive you home now."

"I don't want to go home." If she came home rattled, her parents would make her quit her job and stay home. It was going to be hard enough to face them when they discovered what Aaron Kurtz had done.

"May I ask why?"

Hannah wasn't sure if she could put into words how things had been for her for the last couple of months, but she supposed she would try, if for no other reason than to help Melissa understand why she liked being away from home as much as possible now.

To give herself some time, she put Christopher down on the cushioned floor of his playpen and tucked his blanket around him.

Then, after sitting back down in the rocking chair, Hannah was as honest as possible. "When Paul passed away, my parents were mighty concerned about me," she said slowly.

"I'm sure they were. What happened was a terrible tragedy."

Hannah nodded. "I love my parents and I am glad to be a daughter to two people who care about me so much." She sighed. "But they think I still need to talk about Paul and my loss and how much I miss him. All the time."

"But don't you want to do that? There's nothing wrong with grieving or missing your boyfriend."

"I did grieve. I did talk. I talked with my parents. I cried with my girlfriends. I prayed with the preacher, too. All of that helped. But after the first month, well, I wanted to move on. I knew Paul would have wanted that, too. He was never one for dwelling on the past." She pressed her lips together, deciding to continue to be blunt, even if it didn't put her in the best light. "Since you and York hired me, I have been much happier. I like my life here in your house. I love taking care of Christopher each day. I really do."

Melissa smiled. "We love having you here."

"This job has given me a reason to get up in the morning, a reason to go out and about. I feel like I am making some good friends, too. Friends like Rob."

A new shadow entered Melissa's eyes. "Yes. Well, um, I thought maybe we should talk about Rob, too."

Melissa looked so hesitant, Hannah grew concerned. "Why? When I first met him, you said he was your friend."

"He is."

"Rob has also been mighty nice to me." He'd been so kind and patient and easy to talk to. "Do you not like him?"

"I like him very much. He's a good man, Hannah. He's a successful writer. Really successful. He's caring, too. York and I talk to him quite a bit on the weekends."

"Oh. Well, good."

"Yes, but, um, Hannah, I think he also likes you a lot."

Hannah sighed in relief. "I like him, too." When Melissa didn't look all that pleased, she paused. "But that is good, right?"

Melissa shifted, tucking one of her legs beneath her. Somehow, even though she was in a gray suit, she managed to look completely comfortable and at ease. Far different from the concern shining in her light brown eyes. "Hannah, Rob was upset about that Amish man grabbing you. He was even more upset when he heard you being yelled at. And when he saw you get slapped? Well, I can pretty much promise you if that man wasn't Amish and if Rob wasn't so concerned about getting you inside our house, he would have hit him."

"Really?"

"Absolutely. After I took you into the bedroom, York had to physically stop Rob from going after that man."

"I'm glad he didn't do that."

"Hannah, what I'm trying to say is that York and I think that Rob doesn't just like you as a good friend. I think he really likes you. In a romantic way."

Hannah gaped. "Oh," she whispered. Then,

as the words continued to sink in, she uttered that same word again, only about a full octave higher. "Oh!"

Melissa chuckled. "Yes, oh. I'm glad I brought this up. You seem surprised."

"I suppose I am. I have been so focused on our differences I haven't allowed myself to imagine our relationship changing into something different."

"You don't look upset about this." Melissa's tone was a mixture of surprise and amusement.

Which, Hannah reflected, was a lot like how she felt. "I'm not. I'm not sure what to think about it, but his interest doesn't upset me." On the contrary, it made her feel energized, like she'd just become awake after a fitful sleep.

"He, um, well, he asked us some questions about you a couple of days ago. He wanted to know about being Amish and your family and your age."

"He should have simply asked me those things. I would have told him anything he wanted to know."

"He didn't want to scare you away. I thought that perhaps it was simply a passing infatuation, dear. That he would go out and about and meet some other women and realize that you and he should simply be friends. But today, based on what I saw in his eyes, I've realized that might not ever happen."

"Why not?" She was thoroughly confused now.

Melissa shifted again, this time perching on the edge of the couch. "Because I think he's falling in love with you, or is well on his way."

Love? "Are you sure?"

Biting her lip, Melissa nodded. "It was pretty apparent this morning. It made me realize that he's probably been attempting to hide his interest from both York and me as well as you."

Hannah knew she was blushing from her head to her toes.

"This morning, when we were all looking at your arm, his expression was unguarded," Melissa continued. "Every time you weren't looking his way, he was staring at you with such concern and tenderness . . . well, it sure looked like love to me."

As those words rang in her ears, Hannah gulped.

"That's the other reason why I came back early today. I wanted you to be aware of his feelings."

"*Danke.*" She felt shy and awkward. How was she supposed to respond to her boss about her neighbor's interest in her?

If Melissa was put off by her lack of response, she didn't show it. Instead, she said, "I wanted to talk to you about Rob's feelings, but even more than that, I wanted to see if you would like me to do anything about it."

What could Melissa do? This was between her and Rob and maybe her parents. Wasn't it? "I'm afraid I don't understand."

"I or York could speak to him," Melissa said quietly, resolve thick in her voice. "We could tell him that there's no way you would ever return his feelings. I could tell him that he's making you uncomfortable and that he needs to keep his distance from you."

Hannah felt as if all the air had just left her body. "Please—"

Melissa's expression was intense, giving Hannah a peek of what she must look like in her meetings at the bank. "I don't want to interfere in your life, but I would feel terrible if he was bothering you and you had no one to help you. Like I said, you're part of our family now. York and I want you happy when you come here, not worried about some neighbor of ours bothering you."

"Please don't tell Rob anything. He's not bothering me."

Melissa's eyes widened. "Hannah, are you sure?" she asked. "I feel like I should remind you that Rob is not a naïve young man. He's pretty worldly. I'm sure he's had several serious relationships before. He might expect you to be as experienced as he is. All I would do is remind him that you're a nice Amish girl. I won't embarrass you."

Though she had no doubt that Rob had many more experiences with the opposite sex than she did, Hannah also was positive that he didn't expect her to be like him. Besides, she'd had Paul. "I've been in a serious relationship before. I was almost engaged once, Melissa."

"Yes. Of course. I'm sorry. I guess I'm overstepping myself, aren't I?"

Hannah had little experience navigating conversations like this. Her mother had raised her to be a good Amish wife. Most of their conversations had revolved around household chores, raising *kinner*, and acting modestly.

Since Paul's death, her *mamm* had merely held Hannah and wanted to talk about her grief. Never had they talked about the future. Never had Hannah ever admitted that she wanted to have a life after Paul.

Stepping carefully, she said, "I know you care about me and I'm grateful that you do. I don't think you're overstepping things at all. But because I know what love feels like, I have to admit that I've started to have some romantic feelings for Rob, too." After taking a fortifying breath, she said, "Melissa, if he feels much the same way, I am pleased about this."

Melissa opened her mouth. Shut it. Blinked. Then leaned back in her chair. "I see," she said at last. "Are your parents going to be okay with this?"

Hannah shrugged. "I don't know. Actually, they most likely won't be. But they will respect my feelings. I had the life that was expected of me. I was looking forward to marrying Paul and I was more than happy to marry him and simply be his wife and raise our *kinner*. But the Lord had other plans."

"It seems He did."

"I know you don't want me to be hurt—and I don't want to be hurt, either—but I will not live my life with regrets or in fear of what might happen. Because of that, I intend to find out what will happen between me and this older, more experienced Englisher." And this time, when they stared at each other, it seemed neither could resist smiling. For the first time, they were smiling woman to woman.

It was as unexpected as Aaron's attack.

But instead of feeling scared and worried, Rob's attention and her developing feelings for him felt wonderful. Almost as if she had finally reached a decision about a problem she hadn't even known she had. Almost as if the Lord had given her a gift she hadn't ever expected to receive.

Life was too difficult to pass up the hope of something so wonderful.

AFTER AARON WENT into the barn, Lukas said good-bye to Simon and Roman. Then he searched for Darla. He found her sitting in the kitchen, absently flipping through an old magazine. To his surprise, no one else was around. He wondered if maybe Patsy had encouraged the rest of their siblings to give her some space.

"Hey. You're done," she said when he closed the door behind him.

"Yeah. I just said good-bye to Simon and Roman. They're going to head back to work. I'm going there, too, but I wanted to see you first."

"Is everything okay?" Every muscle in her body looked so tense, like she was in danger of breaking in two.

He took a seat next to her at the table. "I think so," he said with a reassuring smile. "Roman said a lot of good things. So did Aaron, actually. Simon and Roman are going to go with Aaron tonight to talk to Hannah and her parents."

Darla blinked. "*Gut*. That's wonderful."

"*Jah*," he said quietly. "I think he's finally ready

to move on. I'm sure he'll be making amends to you, too."

The tears that she was clearly trying so hard to hold at bay began to fall. "I just want him back."

"I know." Reaching out, he took her hand. "Just to let you know . . . tomorrow I'm going to pick you up from work. And then, we're going to spend the evening together."

"Lukas, now ain't the right time—"

"Sure it is," he interrupted. "It's the best time." More than ever, he wanted them both to have something to look forward to.

As he'd hoped, some of the sharpness eased in her expression. "I should probably tell you that you're gettin' awfully bossy."

He raised his brows in mock annoyance. "Getting? And here I thought I was bossy all the time."

Her lips twitched. "Some of those times are worse than others."

"This is one of those times, I'm afraid." Pushing forward, he said, "So, this is what you need to do. You need to decide if you want to be here or at my house or in the middle of the field. But we're going to spend time together and work things out."

She bit her lip.

"What time do you get off tomorrow?"

"Four," she said grudgingly.

"I'll be there at ten till, then." After a second, he added, "And Darla?"

"Jah?"

"I plan on asking you an important question tomorrow night."

"Again?" She pressed her palms on the top of the table, looking for all the world like she was annoyed.

But he knew she wasn't.

"Yep. So, you might want to start thinking about your answer to me."

"I'll do that."

When he left the room, he found Maisie and her brother Samuel standing in the hall, grinning like fools.

"Looks like you still like my sister," Maisie said.

He winked at her. "I do."

"You better watch out, 'cause she's stubborn," Samuel said.

"I know."

"If you try real hard, you might wear her down by Christmas, though," the boy added.

Lukas grunted. "Christmas? It's only April."

Maisie giggled. "Maybe she'll say yes by Thanksgiving, Lukas."

Patting her on the head, he said, "I'll keep my fingers crossed."

As Lukas walked out of their house and headed back to his office, where there was no doubt a stack of work waiting for him, he couldn't help but notice that he was smiling, genuinely smiling, for the first time in ages.

Things, at last, were finally getting better.

IT HAD BEEN a long day. A painful, scary day, too. But to Hannah's surprise, it had also been filled with some special moments, she decided as she folded up her lunch bag and slipped it into her tote.

After their heart-to-heart, Melissa had decided to stay home. But instead of taking Hannah right back to her house, she'd asked if Hannah would like to stay there for the rest of the day. Not as Christopher's paid nanny, but as her friend.

Hannah had instantly agreed.

They'd spent much of the day playing with Christopher, chatting about Melissa's job, York's practice, and Hannah's sister and brother. When Hannah offered to make them banana cupcakes with cream cheese frosting, Melissa asked if she could help. They'd put Christopher in his high chair and made twenty-four beautiful cupcakes— all while laughing. It had quickly become apparent that her boss's talents were in finance, not in flour and sugar.

Just as Melissa was changing Christopher's diaper before loading him and Hannah into her car, there was a knock at the door.

When Hannah realized the visitor was Rob, she let him in.

"Hi," she said shyly, Melissa's information extremely fresh in her mind.

Rob, on the other hand, seemed particularly quiet. "Hi, Hannah," he said. "How are you?"

"Fine," she said automatically. Then she shook her head and forced herself to be more honest. "Well, I'm kind of fine."

While he attempted to figure out that reply, Hannah noticed that he was sort of dressed up— well, for Rob. Instead of his usual shorts, he was wearing a faded pair of khakis. Instead of his usual T-shirt, he was wearing a black golf shirt. It was untucked, and he had on Converse tennis shoes. His hair was damp, as if he'd just gotten out of the shower. He smelled fresh and clean . . . and he was staring at her face.

"Your cheek is badly bruised," he blurted.

"I know." She would, indeed, have a black eye by morning. "It looks bad, but it will fade in time." Hoping to change the subject, she said, "You almost missed us. Melissa is about to take me home."

Rob turned to where Melissa and Christopher

had just appeared. Linking his hands behind his back, he said, "That's actually why I came over now. I'd like to take you home today, Hannah."

Hannah almost turned around to share a look with Melissa. Almost! Instead, she was simply grateful that Melissa had warned her about Rob's feelings. Otherwise she would have been constantly wondering if she was misunderstanding his words.

"*Danke*. I mean, thank you."

"So, that means you'll let me?"

He looked boyish and cute. She took a moment to remember how different Rob seemed to her now, compared to her first impression of him. She no longer felt compelled to only think of him as the Rosses' neighbor, or the English man she was becoming close to.

There was no need to label him or justify her feelings for him. Instead, he was simply Rob. And Rob was someone she wanted to be around as much as possible.

"Yes, I mean, as long as Melissa doesn't mind." At last she turned around and searched her boss's expression for a sign of what to do next.

Melissa simply set Christopher down on the floor. "Rob, that would be super. Now I don't have to load up the baby."

Reaching for Hannah's tote, he said, "Good. I mean, that's great. You ready?"

Looking back at Melissa, she exchanged a smile. Then she turned to him. "*Jah*, Rob, I am ready."

After saying good-bye and making plans to be back in two days—Melissa wanted Hannah to stay home and rest—Hannah walked out the door at Rob's side.

He kept looking at her, gazing at her as if she were the most precious thing in the world.

But instead of finding that awkward, Hannah liked it. And because of that, she realized that she really was ready. Ready to move forward and move on.

Ready for anything.

Chapter 23

April 13

Early the next morning, as Darla walked down Main Street, she couldn't help but smile. It seemed that Lukas was determined to get her to say yes to him. She wondered what she would say when he asked that evening.

If he finally told her those three words she'd been hoping to hear, she knew how she'd respond. She wanted to marry him more than anything, but it needed to be for the right reasons. Not to keep her safe or because they'd been friends for years and years.

No, she wanted them to get married for love. Well, rather, she wanted him to love her the way she loved him. She'd pretty much loved him all her life and the recent turn of events had only somehow strengthened those feelings.

If they had love, then she knew everything else would come together. Somehow, someway, they would work out their problems and one day marry. She wasn't sure if or when that would happen, but she didn't want to give up hope. More than ever, she needed hope.

"Hey, Darla?"

Looking up, she realized Aaron was standing outside the post office, hands in his pockets. Waiting for her.

"Hi," she said simply.

"I know you've got to work. But . . . can we talk?"

Immediately her muscles tensed. Looking at him warily, she noticed that Aaron wasn't radiating anger. Instead, he was staring at her with such honesty it took her breath away. Here was the brother she'd always known.

Swallowing, she nodded. "*Jah*. Amanda is in there now. I'm not actually supposed to go in today for another hour. I came to town early to run some errands."

The lines between his brows eased. "*Danke*." Pointing to the park a block away, he said, "Is over there all right?"

"Of course." She followed him down the sidewalk, taking care not to look anyone they passed in the eye. She needed to concentrate on her brother, not on what everyone around them thought.

When they got to the park, Aaron led the way to a bench that was apart from the others. "This will be *gut*. Ain't so?"

"*Jah*. It will be fine." No one was around and they'd have relative privacy there. They sat down, side by side. Only about six or seven inches separated them. Darla doubted they'd been so close, either literally or figuratively, in weeks. Not since the fire.

For a moment, they simply sat. The sun was bright and warm. Flowers were blooming in a bed nearby, their scent infusing the air. At last summer was near.

"I wanted to talk to you about yesterday," he said at last.

She nodded hesitantly. Though she didn't think he would snap at her or get mad, she didn't trust his reactions anymore.

He looked a little taken aback by her timid nod. Then, as if he was forcing himself to speak, he said, "Don't be scared of me."

"I can't help it," she said after debating the wisdom of being so honest. "I *am* scared of you now."

He squeezed his eyes tight. "I guess I deserve that."

"I'm not trying to make you upset or cause you pain. I am simply telling you how I feel."

"I know. And you have that right."

His responses were so different from what she was now used to, she hesitantly said, "You . . . you seem better."

"I think I might be. After I lost my temper with Hannah, those men, they made me listen to them. They had some good points."

"What did they say?"

"They talked about forgiveness and moving on." He ran a hand over his face before continuing. "At first I thought everything I was going to hear was no different from everything that had been shared a hundred times before."

"But?"

"But then Roman talked about open arms."

"I don't understand."

"Sometimes we humans like to think God has forsaken us when bad things happen. We fear that He has turned away because we ask for help and don't get it."

"Like when five people die in a fire."

"*Jah*. Like then." He sighed. "Roman's words reminded me of the scripture verse from Deuteronomy. About how the Lord doesn't need to be there to hold each of us."

"Why doesn't He?" she blurted.

"Because He has given us friends and family," he said quietly. Stretching out his arms, he said, "And many of us have two good arms to help support other people." He paused for a long moment.

When he spoke again, Darla heard the tension in his voice accompanied by a curious mixture of regret and hope. "Roman reminded me that I've been ignoring everyone who has had their arms out. And, worse, I've even been hurting the people who have tried so hard to be there for me. Like you." His voice cracked. "Oh, Darla, I'm so sorry. I know I've hurt you terribly. I canna believe I would ever sink so low."

Tears pricked her eyes. Never, never would she have imagined that Aaron would be so honest about his actions of late. And though a part of her wanted to immediately forgive him, the last few months' hardships had taken their toll.

She cleared her throat. "What else did Roman say?"

"He said maybe if I told you I'm sorry and begged for your forgiveness, one day you might be able to do that."

He wasn't looking at her. Instead, his elbows were resting on his knees. His shirtsleeves were rolled halfway up his arms, accentuating his muscles. But instead of looking strong he looked dejected.

Maybe she was weak . . . or maybe she was stronger than she thought she was. Whatever the reason, she started to speak. "Aaron—"

"Wait, Darla. Don't let me off."

"But . . ."

"*Nee*. I don't want your forgiveness yet."

She couldn't resist smiling. *"Bruder*, you have to stop telling me what to do. See, forgiveness doesn't work that way."

"It should, though." He sighed. "See, I forgot something when I was so eager to attach blame to someone for the fire."

"What was that?"

"I forgot my vow." After swallowing hard, he said, "When I graduated school, Daed took me for a long walk. He told me all about how my learning wasn't done even though my days of sitting behind a small wooden desk were."

"I think I got that same talk."

"If you did, then you might have made the same vow I did."

"What did you promise?"

"That I would be the best man I could be. That I would tend to our land and look after this family when the day came that he couldn't."

"What did you say?"

He straightened, kicking out his feet. "I promised him everything. I was cocky and full of myself and fourteen." He rolled his eyes. "Who really thinks they know everything at fourteen?"

"Pretty much everyone, I think."

"I suppose you're right. But see, it don't matter if I believed my promises or I simply said that I did. All that matters is that I made my vow and my *daed* believed it." At last he faced her directly. "He died believing that I would honor it, Darla."

"You shouldn't feel bad about that. I promised him much the same thing. I'm sure Patsy did, too."

He nodded. "I'm going to have to live with my failures for the rest of my life. But I want to make you another vow, right now." He reached out a hand.

She noticed it was shaking.

Though her brain was sending out warning messages about how she shouldn't trust him, about how it was too late to trust him, her heart was proclaiming a different story. Each beat seemed to bring with it a plea for her to believe him. Just like their father had believed in him.

Now it seemed, it was up to her to decide where their relationship could go next. Instinctively, she knew that if she rebuffed him Aaron would understand. But he might also walk away and never reach out to her again.

Her mouth went dry. Did she want that? Did

she want to look back at herself years from now and wish that she'd done things differently?

At last, she'd found her answer. She pressed her palm into his and couldn't help but notice that she was shaking like a leaf. Just like him.

Aaron shuddered in obvious relief.

After he visibly regained his composure, he looked her directly in the eye again. "Darla, from now on, I will do my best to honor Daed and my vow to him. I am sorry for the pain I caused you. I can't go back in time. All I can do is promise that I won't hurt you again."

His words sounded as if they'd been pulled from his soul. But perhaps they were being guided by his heart as well?

"I believe you, Aaron," she said quietly.

He blinked. "Already? Why?"

"Because you might be your father's son, but I am my father's daughter. I want to believe in the best of you, too."

Her words hung in the air, then at last, settling between them, becoming part of the fabric of their lives. Darla knew that no matter how old she lived to be, she would always remember this moment as one of her finest.

She knew because moments that were easy weren't memorable. They didn't last. It was the hard things, the challenges, the situations that took one's pain and suffering and wrought something beautiful, that were the moments worth savoring. Those were what changed lives. And because of that, perhaps they were the only moments that truly mattered.

Aaron blinked, showing her just how much her words had meant to him. "I love you, sister," he whispered, his voice hoarse with emotion.

Knowing she sounded much like him, she said the words that she needed to say just as much as he needed to hear. "I love you right back."

After a shared smile, they dropped their hands. Moments later, Aaron kicked his legs out and gazed out into the distance again. And so did she. But instead of moving apart, they stayed by each other's side. Not talking. Not arguing. There was nothing more to say and far too much to remember.

A DAY AFTER his life changed—this time for the better—Aaron returned to Hope Mast's house.

But before he was able to put one foot on Hope's front steps, she walked out the front door. His heart started beating quickly as hopefulness sprung forth. Maybe everything hadn't died between them. Or, rather, maybe he hadn't killed it.

As he took in her brown eyes and brown hair

that was so light it looked more like burnished gold, he knew he'd do anything he could to keep her.

If it wasn't too late.

He'd at last realized that he wanted—no, needed—her forgiveness more than anything. He wanted that even more than he wanted to forget his mistakes for the past few months.

She was his future, and he was going to be lost if she wasn't a part of it.

But it was now her turn. For too long he'd been the one saying all the words. He'd been making all the decisions. Now it was her turn. So he stood silently and watched her. Preparing himself for her decision. This was either going to be the beginning of the next chapter of their life together, or the end of it.

Either way, he figured that this moment was always going to stay with him.

"What are you doing here, Aaron?"

"I needed to see you."

"Why?"

"Because I wanted to listen to what you had to say."

She inhaled sharply. "Do you really want to hear me, or are you just saying that?"

Because he hated towering over her, he sat

down on the steps, allowing her to look down on him. "I really want to hear you. I'm listening."

Long seconds of silence seemed to drag as she stared at him again. Never had he seen her look so cautious or so disappointed. He missed the smile she used to have whenever he was near.

Finally, she sat down, too. She remained four steps above him, though. He was glad of it. He thought he was going to need the space to wrap his head around whatever she was going to say. He was now pretty sure that she was about to break up with him for good.

"Aaron, when I heard about Hannah, I realized that I've been living a lie with you."

"You weren't."

She fastened a hard glare on him. "Let me speak."

"Sorry."

"When I heard that you had jerked Hannah's arm right in the middle of the street, I was stunned. But what was more stunning was that I seemed to be the only person surprised by your actions." She shifted, resting her head in her hands and her elbows on her knees. "It seems that everyone else has known that you've had a terrible time with your temper and that you've been taking it out on your family most of all."

He couldn't deny it. Aaron nodded, hating how

miserable her words made him feel. Shame engulfed him.

"This bothers me, Aaron. Family counts for most everything, don't you think?"

He cleared his throat, or attempted to, because it was suddenly dry. *"Jah."*

"It pains me to imagine that Darla was actually afraid of you. And that Lukas Kinsinger needed to talk to you more than once about your treatment of her."

"I guess you've been hearing a lot of stories about me."

Hope sighed. "I've been hearing a lot of things that were a surprise." Looking at him intently, she said, "Aaron, did you ask people to keep secrets from me? Or did folks just decide to keep me in the dark all on their own?"

"I'm not sure what happened. I didn't ask anyone to lie to you, though."

"Are you sure about that?"

"Jah," he said quickly.

Her eyes narrowed. "I'm sorry, but I don't know if I can believe you."

"You can. Of course you can, Hope."

Looking crushed, she shook her head. "Are you ready to tell me the truth, even if it's something you know I'm not going to want to hear or agree with?"

"I want to." He yearned to say that he'd tell her the truth no matter what happened, but he wasn't sure he could make that promise. What if there came a time when he could shield her from pain? Would he keep something from her in order to save her from getting hurt?

"You *want* to?" she asked incredulously. "That's the best you can do?"

"I want to be completely honest with you. And that is why I'm afraid to tell you that I always will be, no matter what. But I will make you a promise, Hope. I will promise you that I will do my very best to be honest with you. I don't want to lose you."

"Do you think we still have a future?"

"I want one. I don't want to think of a future without you in it. I'd be lost without you," he admitted. There, he was as honest as he could possibly be. He'd laid his feelings and hopes out there.

"What are you going to do about the people you've hurt?"

"I'm going to continue to apologize. I've talked to Darla and asked for her forgiveness. I spoke to Hannah, and her family, too." Inwardly, he cringed, remembering the look of disgust her father had cast his way. It was no less than he deserved, though.

Because she was listening, he kept talking. "I'm

going to talk to the preachers some more, too. But mainly, I realized that I was hurting my father's memory by holding on to my anger. I was so filled with pain, sure the Lord had beseeched me, but I've come to realize that it isn't my duty to avenge a wrong. Especially when there wasn't a wrong. It was a terrible accident. That is all."

"I . . . I could go with you on your future visits, if you would like my company."

"I would love your company, but you don't need to do that. I don't want to burden you with my problems any more than I already have."

"It wouldn't be a burden. I want to."

"Why would you want to?"

"Because, I think your fiancée should be by your side to support you. For better or worse."

She still wanted to be his fiancée. He almost fell to his knees in relief. He'd come over, hoping she would still agree to talk to him. Never had he believed that Hope would believe in his future enough to honor their engagement. "Does that mean you've forgiven me?"

Slowly, she nodded. "I think it does." She exhaled. "I don't want to rush into marriage anymore, though. I want to make sure we are both ready for it."

"But you'll still be my girl?"

"*Jah.* I will still be yours." Slowly, she smiled.

And at last he saw the warmth that had always been in her gaze. There she was. His girl. His hope. His everything.

"*Danke*, Hope," he said around a sigh. "I know I don't deserve you, but I will one day. Somehow, someway, I'll make myself into the man you believe I can be. I promise you that."

The compassion he saw shining in her eyes was beautiful. "We already deserve each other, Aaron," she said softly. "I love you, you love me. And because of that, we'll make things work. I know that, without a doubt."

And because he knew she didn't lie, because he knew she was Hope, Aaron let himself believe her.

Epilogue

Six weeks later

School was out, the temperatures had risen, and the days were longer. As Darla walked along the main road from her house to the post office, she couldn't help but stop every few moments and appreciate her surroundings. The air was thick with chatter from birds, the ringing of machinery in fields, and the *clip-clop* of horses on the pavement.

Charm's rolling hills were either vibrant green or dark black dirt. Dotting the fields were plows and teams of Percherons. Closer to the road were several farmhouses and small cottages available for lease. Front yards were filled with snapdragons and daffodils and flowering pear trees as well as long lines of bright laundry fluttering in the breeze.

Summer had arrived in Charm and it was beautiful.

Or maybe it hadn't just arrived. Maybe it had been developing all along, little by little, washing the area in bright color, and it was only Darla who had just opened her eyes to it.

She supposed she'd had an excuse; things had been mighty busy.

Though their mother was still gone, she and her siblings had finally settled into a regular routine. Patsy helped out even more, Maisie looked after Gretel when she could, and Samuel and Evan now helped Aaron in the fields without complaint.

And Aaron? Well, Aaron had changed the most! He was still getting counseled by the bishop. Those talks, together with Hope's belief in him, had worked wonders. He was hardworking and at peace. He'd gone through their father's things, realized that their father had been something of a farm equipment hoarder, and held a tent auction. Everyone who had attended was very generous. The money collected had gone toward their bills, living expenses, and savings. In addition, he was helping out at a neighboring dairy farm. That extra money, along with Darla's income, kept the family firmly afloat.

Things were going to be all right. For all of them, it seemed.

When she turned the corner to head to the post office, she spotted Lukas standing outside the door, leaning against the brick wall, one of his feet braced up against it. Looking like he hadn't a care in the world.

"Lukas? What are you doing here?"

"Waiting for you."

"Why?" She pushed back the rush of happiness and tried to tamp it down with reality. "Is something wrong?"

"Nope." He grinned.

"Then?" Goodness, his lazy smile and short answers made this conversation like pulling teeth!

"Obviously, I wanted to talk to you. And since you are surrounded by too many people at your house, I figured this was the best place for us to speak privately."

"I am supposed to start working soon. We can't talk too long."

He shrugged. "If everyone has to wait, then they have to wait. Come on, Darla. Let me in."

She pulled out her keys and tried not to notice that her hands were shaking.

After she'd refused Lukas's proposal the night after he'd visited Aaron, Lukas had backed off a bit.

Oh, he hadn't been distant, but he hadn't flirted

with her, either. It was as if he'd pushed them firmly back into being just friends. Ironically, she hadn't liked that. She'd missed his touches, his teasing comments, even those heated glances he'd sent her from time to time.

But today, it seemed that had changed. He was staring at her intently. It seemed they were moving away from being just friends again. Glancing at him, she tried to guess what he was up to now.

But instead of giving her another sign, he merely held out a hand.

"Here. Let me." He took the keys from her, sorted through the ring, then finally inserted the proper key into the door. It unlocked easily.

"Um, this is a government office. Only I should be doing these things."

"I won't tell a soul if you don't," he said over his shoulder as he opened the door and guided her inside. The moment she walked through, he closed it behind her and locked it again.

"Lukas!"

"I meant it. I want to talk to you and I don't want to be interrupted."

After setting her tote and handbag on the counter, she folded her arms across her chest and attempted to look irritated. "Well, you have me now. Say what you need to say."

But instead of being cowed by her stance, he

laughed. "Oh, I will," he said as he stood directly in front of her.

She bit her lip and stared at him.

"Darla, you ready to listen?"

"I am."

He exhaled, looking pleased. "First off, I want you to know that I don't regret asking you to marry me so many times."

"If you don't, then why did you stop?"

"I realized you needed time. I wanted to give that to you."

"That was . . . that was mighty kind of you."

He shrugged. "It was nothing. I want to make you secure and happy, Darla. After all, that's what love is, right?"

Wait. Love? "Lukas, did you just say—"

"Darla, hold on a sec, wouldja? I practiced my speech and I'm sort of on a roll right now."

Still kind of stunned, she dropped her hands. "Is that right?"

Looking earnest, he nodded. "Yep. You see, you might not know it, but I figure I've been in love with you for some time. Years."

"Years?"

"*Jah*," he said, still looking as if he was intent on stating his piece. "However, I wasn't sure if you felt the same way, or if what I felt was merely friendship."

"I feel—"

"Darla, I know you like to talk, but let me finish this, okay?"

"All right," she said around a smile.

"*Danke*." His gaze turned tender as he lifted a hand and carefully brushed his palm against the curve of her jaw. "Um, as I was saying, I've loved you for a long time, but after the fire . . . well, everything went astray."

"I think I went astray for a while, too," she revealed. "I let all the pain in my heart cloud what I saw right before my eyes."

Lukas nodded. "We let so many people tell us what we should be feeling that we lost track of how important our feelings really were. That our feelings mattered, too." After taking a fortifying breath, he continued. "Darla, I'm just going to say this. I don't know what really happened that day of the fire. I don't know if I could have done a better job organizing everything in the warehouse. I don't know if Paul could have called for help sooner or if my *daed* should have acted more quickly or if your *daed* really did make a mistake. All I do know is that our fathers would not have wanted us to still be dwelling on it."

"I agree. Our fathers were the kind of men who appreciated each day. Who enjoyed living. Who enjoyed love and family and life."

"So, will you let me love you every day?"

"I will."

His expression warmed as his voice softened. "Will you let me court you, the way a lady like you deserves to be courted?"

"I think you've already been doing that. But yes, Lukas, I will let you."

He leaned closer. "Will you let me take you on more walks? If you want, I'll even break out my father's old courting buggy."

"You'd do that for me?"

"I'd do just about anything for you."

"I'd do just about anything for you, too," she said with a smile. "I'd even let you lock me inside the post office."

His grin was a beautiful thing to see.

At last, she could give him the answer he'd been looking for. "Lukas, ask me your question."

He went still. "Sure?"

"Very sure."

"All right." Taking a fortifying breath, he reached for her hand. "Darla, will you marry me?"

Staring up at him, she thought about everything she'd known him to be. When they were little, he'd been her swimming instructor and as they'd grown older, her confidant. Lately, he'd been her protector.

But through it all, more than anything, he'd

been her friend. She could laugh with him like no other. He could tease her and please her like no one else. They were both stubborn and steadfast. They were two people who were better together.

And it had always been that way.

Around a sigh, she at last said the words she'd always dreamed she'd say one day. "Yes, Lukas. I will marry you."

He grinned broadly again. At least, she thought he did. It was kind of hard to tell since he pulled her to him, hugged her close, then kissed her.

After a moment, she lifted her arms and pressed them against his chest, enjoying the feel of him.

"You make me happy, Darla," he breathed.

"You make me happy, too," she replied.

Just then someone started knocking at the door. "Hello?" a voice called. "It's nine A.M. Is anyone there? Darla?"

She broke away. "I must get that."

"You can. In a minute," he said as he kissed her cheek. "Just let me enjoy this moment."

More knocking erupted. Then voices and grumbling.

"But the mail . . ."

"Will wait."

As the pounding on the door got worse, she pulled away. "I need to open the door. I've got customers, you know."

"Fine." He turned, unlocked the door, and threw it open. "Hold on, everyone. Darla is busy with me."

A stream of seven faces gaped back at him. Finally, Mr. Carson called out, "Lukas Kinsinger, what are you doing in there?"

"Asking Darla to marry me."

While a couple of the ladies giggled, Mr. Carson tipped up his ball cap and glared. "Give him your answer, and be quick about it, Darla. I've got things to do."

As the crowd outside started laughing and calling out all kinds of comments, Lukas held up one finger. "Give us a sec, everyone," he said before closing the door once more.

"Lukas! You can't do that."

"Sure I can. It ain't every day that a couple gets engaged."

Smiling at him, Darla decided she couldn't fault his logic. Because right now, right that minute, she felt only happiness.

Happiness and joy.

Two things she'd never take for granted again.

Meet
Shelley Shepard Gray

People often ask how I started writing. Some believe I've been a writer all my life; others ask if I've always felt I had a story I needed to tell. I'm afraid my reasons couldn't be more different. See, I started writing one day because I didn't have anything to read.

I've always loved to read. I was the girl in the back of the classroom with her nose in a book, the mom who kept a couple of novels in her car to read during soccer practice, the person who made weekly visits to the bookstore and the library.

Back when I taught elementary school, I used to read during my lunch breaks. One day, when I realized I'd forgotten to bring something to read, I turned on my computer and took a leap of faith.

Feeling a little like I was doing something wrong, I typed those first words: *Chapter One.*

I didn't start writing with the intention of publishing a book. Actually, I just wrote for myself.

For the most part, I still write for myself, which is why, I think, I'm able to write so much. I write books that I'd like to read. Books that I would have liked to have in my old teacher tote bag. I'm always relieved and surprised and so happy when other people want to read my books, too!

Another question I'm often asked is why I choose to write inspirational fiction. Maybe at first glance, it does seem surprising. I'm not the type of person who usually talks about my faith in the line at the grocery store or when I'm out to lunch with friends. For me, my faith has always felt like more of a private thing. I feel that I'm still on my faith journey—still learning and studying God's word.

And that, I think, is why writing inspirational fiction is such a good fit for me. I enjoy writing about characters who happen to be in the middle of their faith journeys, too. They're not perfect, and they don't always make the right decisions. Sometimes they make mistakes, and sometimes they do something they're proud of. They're characters who are a lot like me.

Only God knows what else He has in store

for me. He's given me the will and the ability to write stories to glorify Him. He's put many people in my life who are supportive and caring. I feel blessed and thankful . . . and excited to see what will happen next!

Letter from the Author

Dear Reader,

Have you ever been to Charm, Ohio? My first experience in this little hamlet was when I drove home from Sugarcreek the first time by myself. Maybe I was singing along with the radio a bit too enthusiastically. Maybe I was too caught up with looking at all the haystacks dotting the fields. Or maybe my terrible sense of direction came into play. In any case, one moment I was where I was supposed to be and the next? Well, I was lost in Charm.

As you might imagine, my feeble attempts to get back on my way didn't end up with much success. After a good thirty minutes, I finally pulled to a stop in front of an Amish farm. There I was, attempting to make sense out of my written directions and wondering why my Garmin wasn't working, when a farmer wandered down to greet me.

I got out, told him where I'd come from and where I was trying to get to. He listened with a serious expression on his face, then pointed to the road I'd been driving on. "Just keep going. Before you know it, you'll be on your way in no time," he said.

Of course, that sounded a bit too easy. However, it also made a lot of sense. Because of that, I did as he suggested . . . and yes, before I knew it, I was back on my way home again. I've often thought about that advice the farmer gave me. Actually, in some ways, I think it might be some of the best advice I've ever been given! Don't we all need to just keep going, no matter what might be happening in our lives?

Because of that experience, I've always yearned to set a series of books in Charm. To me, Charm is more than just rolling hills and acres of farmland. It's more than farmers raising goats and sheep and cows. It's even more than cheese shops and lumber mills and quaint stores. It's a place where I got lost, met a kind man with good advice, and eventually found my way home again.

I hope you will enjoy this year's series, The Charmed Amish Life, as much as I am enjoying writing it.

And if by chance you ever find yourself lost in Charm? Simply keep on going! I promise that sooner or later you will eventually get where you need to be.

With blessings to you, and my thanks,
Shelley

P.S. I love to hear from readers, either on Facebook, through my website, or through the postal system! If you'd care to write and tell me what you thought of the book, please do!

Shelley Shepard Gray
10663 Loveland Madeira Rd. #167
Loveland, OH 45140

Questions for Discussion

1. When the book opens, Darla and Lukas are attempting to repair a broken friendship. As people grow and change, this no doubt often happens. Have you ever had a broken friendship that you've attempted to repair?

2. Each character in the novel is grieving in a different way. If you've lost an important family member, how did you cope?

3. What do you think about Lukas Kinsinger? What are his strengths? What are his weaknesses?

4. How did you like Hannah Eicher's story line? What do you think will happen to her with Rob and the Ross family?

5. The theme of family runs through the novel. Both Lukas's and Darla's families are struggling to rebuild themselves without parents. What do you think constitutes a family? How does one strengthen it?

6. Aaron Kurtz was a character filled with pain. What do you think he needs to do next in order to heal and find redemption? What do you think Hope should do?

7. The Amish proverb I used for the novel is the following:
   Reach up as far as you can. God will reach the rest of the way.

   How do you think it fits with this novel? Do you find it has meaning for you as well?

8. The scripture verse from Matthew 6:14 felt particularly meaningful to me while I wrote this book. "If you forgive those who sin against you, your heavenly Father will forgive you." How have you practiced forgiveness in your life?

9. I enjoyed exploring Charm when I researched the novel. Have you been to Charm before? What do you like about exploring Amish communities?

White Chocolate Cranberry Blondies

1 cup diced dried cranberries
2 cups hot water
¾ cup butter, softened
1½ cups brown sugar
4 teaspoons vanilla extract
2 eggs
1½ cups all-purpose flour
1 teaspoon baking powder
½ teaspoon salt
1 cup white chocolate chips

Preheat oven to 350°F. Grease a medium sheet pan and set aside.

In a small bowl, rehydrate the dried cranberries by combining with hot water. Allow to sit for one minute, then drain.

Cream together the butter and brown sugar until light and fluffy. Add vanilla and eggs, one at a time. Combine the flour, baking powder, and salt. Add to butter mixture and mix. Fold in the cranberries and white chocolate chips. Evenly press the batter into the prepared pan.

Bake 18 to 20 minutes until the top is a light golden brown. Allow to cool for 20 minutes, and then cut into squares.

Taken from *Country Blessings Cookbook* by Clara Coblentz. Used by permission of the Shrock's Homestead, 9943 Copperhead Rd. N.W., Sugar-creek, OH 44681.

A Few *Charming* Facts from Shelley Shepard Gray

1. Charm is located in the heart of Holmes County, home to the largest Amish and Mennonite population in the world.

2. The actual population of Charm is only 110 people.

3. One of the public schools in Charm is actually called "Charm School."

4. Charm was founded in 1886. It was once called Stevenson, in honor of a local Amish man, Stephan Yoder, and his son.

5. Charm also has a nickname that some locals still use. The name is "Putschtown," which is

derived from the word "putschka," meaning "small clump."

6. The annual "Charm Days" festival is held in the fall every year. The highlight of the festival is the "Wooly Worm Derby."

7. The largest business in Charm is Keim Lumber Company. Located on St. Route 557, it has a large retail showroom and website and is open to the public.

Read on for a sneak peek from

A DAUGHTER'S DREAM,

the second book in
The Charmed Amish Life Series.

Available now from Avon Inspire!

Keeping twenty-five schoolchildren reasonably happy and on task for a solid hour was harder than it looked.

As Rebecca Kinsinger stood at the front of the classroom and eyed the group of students staring right back at her, she realized she had seriously misjudged her ability to manage small children.

In the last hour, the twenty-five students, all ranging in ages from five to fourteen, had decidedly taken the upper hand. They'd talked to each other. They'd ignored her wishes. They didn't seem all that interested in the work their usual teacher had assigned them to do.

As the large clock above the door ticked on, Rebecca was coming to the conclusion that the only thing they did seem rather excited about was the approach of the end of the school day.

In fifteen minutes' time, to be exact.

She was starting to get excited about the end of the day, too.

As the low murmur of voices grew louder by

tiny degrees with each passing minute, Rebecca decided that she didn't blame Rachel Mast, the students' teacher, for taking her time to return to the building. Being alone with this bunch for eight hours at a time would make anyone yearn for a break.

As two sweet-looking girls sitting in the middle of the first row started giggling with each other, Rebecca knew that it was time to regain control. Otherwise, Rachel would never let her help out in her classroom again, and Rebecca really wanted to learn how to be a good teacher.

She clapped her hands lightly. "*Kinner*, please. All of you have assignments to complete. It is time to get busy and work on it."

After a pause, about half of them quieted and got to work. Two of the oldest boys, however, merely stared at her.

When it was apparent that neither of them was in any hurry to mind her, she wove her way through the line of desks until she stood directly in front of them. "I was talking to you boys as well."

The sandy-haired boy smirked. "Oh. I wasna sure, 'cause no one's called me a child for well on two years."

"You might not be a small child but you are certainly not a grown-up." She placed her hands on her hips and fastened her eyes on him. "Now, get busy."

The boy picked up his pencil, but his friend, who Rebecca knew to be Peter Beachy, folded his arms in front of his chest. "I'll do it later," Peter said. Then he lifted his chin, practically daring her to argue with his pronouncement.

Ack, but this was terrible! How come all the men at her family's lumber mill were always polite and amiable to her, but these . . . these *kinner* were not?

Attempting to look far more sure of herself than she felt, Rebecca said, "Peter, you'd best get to work. I know Mrs. Mast expects you to do it now."

"I'll talk to her when she gets back." With a shrug, he added, "I'm almost done with school, anyway. I'm fourteen. I'm already working part-time at the mill, you know."

Oh, she knew. Rebecca figured everyone in Charm knew of Peter Beachy. He'd been a handful when he was five and the last nine years hadn't changed him much . . . unless he was at the mill. There, he became a completely different person. He was respectful and hardworking. Polite and modest.

Lukas loved him. Lukas's best friend Simon did, too. They were constantly teasing Peter or giving him some kind of special errand to do because he was such a hard worker.

But here at school?

She had yet to see any of those qualities.

Perhaps it was time to try a little less patience and a little more steel. Straightening her backbone, she said, "Peter, you might be all of fourteen but you are still a student in this class. That means you need to be respectful and follow directions."

But instead of being cowed, Peter got to his feet. Even at fourteen, the boy was several inches taller than she was. "*Jah*, but you ain't my teacher, Miss Kinsinger. Only my boss's sister."

At a loss for words, Rebecca blinked. His harsh tone took her aback. Just as she was debating whether to remind him that she would not hesitate to tell on him to Luke, the door opened.

"That's enough, Peter," Rachel said sternly as she walked down the center aisle of the one-room schoolhouse's grouping of chairs. "Sit down and apologize to Miss Kinsinger."

Peter complied immediately. "I am sorry, Miss Kinsinger."

It was hard to come to terms with the immediate transformation that had taken place before her eyes. Peter's cocky bravado went into hiding. All at once, he looked exactly like he did at the mill. A strong boy who'd grown up doing chores and had a lifetime of hard work awaiting him at the lumber mill.

"No harm done," she said weakly.

"Hmph," Rachel said. Standing in front of her students, she placed her hands on her hips. The room went silent. "Scholars, I am most displeased by this behavior. I expect you all to behave much better when Miss Kinsinger is here."

All the students looked shamefaced.

Rebecca was so amazed by their reaction, she moved to stand against the wall and simply watched as Rachel competently walked up and down the rows, reviewing homework assignments. Every so often, she would touch a child's shoulder or point to the paper he or she was working on. She never raised her voice. She was gentle and kind, yet firm.

She was a marvel.

As she spoke, children wrote notes in their assignment booklets, gathered papers and textbooks, and generally acted like every word she said was the most important thing each had ever heard.

When she returned to the front of the classroom, Rachel smiled brightly. "*Kinner*, it's time to go home. Gather your lunch pails and backpacks, stack your chairs, and line up."

Again, each task was done immediately and

with care. Five minutes later, Rebecca watched Rachel walk to the door, open it wide, and dismiss the class.

She smiled at each one, gave a couple of the little girls hugs, and spoke softly to Peter.

When the last of the students were gone, Rachel turned to Rebecca and smiled. "*Danke* for helping me today, Rebecca. You were a lifesaver."

The praise was as embarrassing as it was unwarranted. "I don't think that was the case at all, Rachel. I tried my best, but chaos reigned. I don't know what happened—I was sure I would have been able to manage things easily for an hour."

She chuckled. "Don't fret. You did fine. It's simply children's natures to stretch their boundaries. They like to push a bit, just to see when someone will push right back."

"Well, they certainly pushed." They also won. Again, Rebecca wondered how it was possible for her to work so well with hundreds of grown men at the lumber mill but be putty in twenty-five children's hands? "I see I have a lot to learn about managing a classroom."

*G*ive in to your Impulses!

These unforgettable stories only take a second to buy and give you hours of reading pleasure!

Go to *www.AvonImpulse.com* and see what we have to offer.

Available wherever e-books are sold.

AVONIMPULSE